France
Orange ... ...
since written many television dramas, including
the award-winning BBC trilogy *A Divorce* and *A
Mother Like Him*, *Little Girls Don't* and *The Quiet
Days of Mrs Stafford* for ITV. She has also contributed episodes for such popular series as *Boon*.

She lives in London.

FRANCES GALLEYMORE

Dangerous Relations

WARNER BOOKS

A *Warner* Book

First published in Great Britain in 1994
by Little, Brown and Company

This edition published by Warner Books in 1995

A CIP catalogue record for this book
is available from the British Library.

ISBN 0 7515 0723 7

Printed in England by Clays Ltd, St Ives plc

Warner Books
A Division of
Little, Brown and Company (UK)
Brettenham House
Lancaster Place
London WC2E 7EN

*This novel is for the people
who helped it to happen,
especially Sophie Galleymore Bird, Jüri Gabriel,
Katherine Arnold, Chris Barlas,
David Grossman and Hilary Hale*

Dangerous Relations

Prologue

The man crouched hiding in the garden as evening came. Silent and still, waiting, almost invisible in that wilderness of bushes and trees. He watched as the house loomed dark and lights flicked on inside.

But the lights that should have appeared far below never did. The city had vanished. Mist was rising, thickening and creeping towards his hiding place. Coldly it fingered his bare arms and face, blotted him under its great shroud.

The waiting had gone on for so long. Where were they?

When it was late he crept towards the black mass of the house, pushing between dense fleshy stuff, ivy hanging ropes across him, sudden tearing nails of briar. His breath rasped as something loomed – a hunched creature with arms outstretched in the path – then sighed out. It was only the wheelbarrow, the tools.

Feeling not seeing, around the side. Feeble light rayed through the mist – candles or lamps, lit inside the dining room. He batted to the narrow arched window and caught its sill. Peered through the frame.

Those mirrored walls reflected the strange white night and his invisible self. The ornate black fireplace, the dining table. The four of them sat together in the glow of warmth but they were jerky as a puppet show, they were quarrelling.

He quickened, gazing at the scene. Until one of them gestured out at him – almost pointed straight to him, they'd seen him surely – his heart overturned with alarm. Hurled round inside, gliding back he sank like a stone into the undergrowth.

He knelt there, sat down on his ankles for long cold minutes in the raw night.

Someone came out. Almost silently. Looking for him? Searching, low cries muffled, a tall figure wispy in thick fog crashed unseeing through the bushes.

Slowly the man straightened, crept to his feet, taut.

Emerging then receding, the calls were strangled by the night growing nowhere near but searching everywhere – around the outhouse, towards the old orchard, the pergola and ponds. Then went back into the house.

He hissed, anger snapped after those invisible heels. In his hiding place he resumed the waiting. But a sense of chaos now, a danger with even the covering mist grown deceptive.

She had sent him here. He had to remember that.

Perhaps hours passed, the man had no way of knowing.

Later a light flipped on somewhere inside turning the mist to illuminated cotton wool. It was by the kitchen. The door thudded shut. A rustling from the porch down into the overgrown path.

A slight figure approached, seeming to glide silently through the fog. He drew in his breath, towed it to him on its thread. All of his thoughts, all his intentions directed it to his hiding place beside the path. And it wove straight to him. Insubstantial, looking at him briefly in a moon-faced question. Was he visible? She brushed past, a cold outbreath against his side that faded slowly away from him.

It wasn't his job to question the choice.

He was plugged into the life force now, a vital cog in the pattern humming with electric energy. Staying close, tracking her soft footfalls through the earthbound clouds.

If she'd turned she might have seen his darkness move in the pale midnight, or could have thought he was part of the garden, a trick of the shifting mist. She didn't turn or stop but took the path under high enclosing trees down to the ponds, the lake. The man kept his eyes fixed, afraid she might snap out of such blurred vision.

She'd stopped at the edge of the lake, was staring down into it though she wouldn't see a thing, not tonight. As he closed in, his mind and body synchronised into a brilliant machine, purpose-built and set in motion, running like a charm but something happened then – she turned round when he raised his hand.

He heard her gasp. And took her in his arms.

Part One

1

Looking again Jack saw a seed of light in the darkened screen. It swelled fast with a shining through taut skin, growing peaks and craters of shadow. For a moment he wondered what they were. The moon, or something germinating? Or contours of human bone. The features revolved, androgynous and sensual, somehow malevolent. Then they froze flickering in suspension and he made out what must've been there all along. Familiar hooded eyes, big crooked mouth, broken nose. The actor's head.

He laughed, zapping out the set as Paul stood up and whizzed back the blinds. Outside it was still daylight.

'Great close-up. It's looking good,' Jack commented, 'But – '

'We're getting the titles tomorrow. I know, it's a shame about the scheduling,' sighed Paul. 'They're doing it to protect the new medics drama, since that cost megabucks it gets our slot. And everyone trusts *Cragge* to do well – '

'Even if we compete with the BBC's top show? It's diabolical, Paul. What will happen to our ratings?'

Paul didn't answer but pounced on a ringing phone. His smooth face grew greedy under its youthful silver fringe, his voice lapping, 'When would you like to meet?'

Wandering to the walls of window Jack looked out from twenty floors up. London glittered like a handful of coins

7

hurled into the sun of late afternoon. He paced Paul's office. On the walls were location snaps of last summer's crew on a break, the cast clowning or in posed solidarity. Jack saw himself among them, between takes on a hot day at Brighton, talking to a trader in Camden market. *Cragge*'s star Richard stood arm in arm with him and they looked like twins.

'I've someone here so I'll call you back. What? Yes of course I will!' Paul flushed, replaced the phone tenderly then swivelled back to his scriptwriter. 'The vacation's over – let's go.'

'With those deadlines you gave me, what vacation?' Jack asked feelingly.

'Got the viewing figures for the Christmas Special. Fourteen million – that's not bad since satellite.' Paul drew a couple of scripts towards him. 'Bill's happy with how we're taking it into Europe but he thinks the character changes should go further. Oh and he's worried about the budget. Episode Thirteen, for example.'

'The fire? But that was Bill's suggestion.'

'Yes but fires get expensive, he's changed his mind. Maybe drown them instead?'

Feeling a sharp stab inside, Jack checked the bland expression of his producer. 'Cragge's wife and children? That wouldn't be big enough and besides – '

Paul interrupted, throwing him a quick glance, 'It's got to be big. But not expensive. A car crash?'

Jack insisted, 'You know I'm not happy about killing off Gemma and – '

'But it needs shaking up, Bill's right about that.'

'What about audience loyalty? And if we lose his family we lose all that dimension – '

'Try this: our man's on his own, through a crisis – an ordeal by fire. Or drowning. If the show comes back it'll be a new set-up.'

'Let me talk to Bill.'

'Sorry Jack, he's decided and he's the moneybags. Cheer up! It'll work.'

Jack grimaced, unhappy. 'If we do this, we've got to explore where else his character could go. Otherwise Bill's going to suggest a string of liaisons with photogenic woodentops. You know him.'

'And he knows the market,' Paul replied smoothly. 'Don't underestimate that. Right?'

After a moment's thought Jack answered, 'I'll sleep on it. Let's move on.' They discussed co-writers and Jack agreed to deliver new drafts in a week then begin the next two episodes. The production dates left them short of time.

'Got your invite for the Press Preview? Good luck.' Paul saw him out.

The afternoon had grown overcast as, pocketing a parking ticket, Jack drove the familiar backstreet route to Islington. His tall white house in Noel Terrace, bought when *Cragge* first hit the screen, symbolised success to him and boasted the shell of eighties affluence and gloss. Like his neighbours' on each side, the picture-book garden stretched down through pretty conservatories, rose trellises and wrought-iron furniture to the dank canal. There lurked the groundswell of nineties desperation. Murky water spawned abandoned factories, bust businesses, one of the roughest estates in town. The adventure playground stood empty because kids preferred real, rewarding adventures of theft and violence. Stinking bridges housed the tribes of homeless, they clung to existence there.

Troubled, that was what he felt. Some sense of fear or threat of loss, unaccountable really. His study soothed with its quiet space, huge desk, the waiting computer, fax and answerphone.

9

He flicked the switch on that. Justin Fairbrother's voice boomed, 'What happened to you? It's January the third and we've seen neither hide nor hair. Anna isn't going to forgive this.' Children shrieked in the background, Justin commanded, 'Quiet, animals!' and the phone crashed down.

Jack laughed wryly and dialled their number. It was engaged. He'd missed their New Year party, relentlessly finishing Episode Two then noticing with a shock that it was four in the morning.

Beyond black spiked railings the street was darkening, people jerked past under the lamps like shooting targets. A woman hurried by in heavy boots, a bearded old man clattered a pram and two lovers, impossibly young, stopped to clinch. They wound into a long, very long kiss. Dusk yawned into a blank evening and Jack was suddenly aware of himself from the outside, framed or suspended in the half-lit Georgian window. Deep in his nest walled with words. Solitary.

Restless, grabbing up his keys he went out as great drops of rain, visceral and black, began to fall.

The traffic crawled through a thickening downpour. At almost six he turned the VW up a cul-de-sac near Putney Heath and as he raised a hand to the bell the door opened. Justin's bulk dammed the light. 'Jack, where the hell did you get to? Come in.'

'Happy New Year,' he said, going in.

Justin shouted into the house, 'Anna, Jack's here!' There was no answer. 'Well, what's your excuse? And what's that?'

'A peace offering. I was writing, I forgot the time.'

'That's obscene.' Justin stared, eyes jealous over a ramshackle beard. 'Jack forgot our party because he was working!' he called up the stairs, then added, 'She's bathing the animals. They all got soaked.' The phone rang and Justin snatched it up. 'My agent,' he breathed urgently.

Hanging his coat, Jack rescued the champagne he'd brought and found three glasses, popped the cork. He went upstairs, past Justin booming to Gideon about a contract, and pushed open the first door on the landing.

The bathroom was hot, jungly with steam, white clouds like a thick fog drifting. Giant things grew in here, fronded palms and creepers trailing. Under the light a young girl stood. She was naked and beautiful, her skin luminous, and she was leaning over to coil her hair and wring out water.

Jack stood rooted. A draught tugged at swirls of mist and the girl turned, starting at the sight of him.

She was completely vulnerable.

'I'm sorry,' Jack said, stepping back.

She retorted as fast, 'That looks very much like champagne,' snatched up a towel but trailed it casually and with an odd confidence held out a hand that bore long scarlet fingernails.

His hand shook and champagne spilled from the glass. He was aware of her eyes that seemed black, of an intensity, a danger in them.

He stumbled the words, 'I thought you were the children,' and went out.

Anna's voice murmured sleep-persuasive behind a bedroom door, ' "It's a fabulous monster!" the Unicorn cried out, before Alice could reply. "Then hand round the plum-cake, Monster," the Lion said . . .'

Jack found he was trembling. He returned down the stairs and Justin stopped him. 'You won't believe what's happening on my film,' he groaned. 'Oh, the horrors of international co-production! The Americans want a complete rewrite making the American characters more heroic; the Australians want a complete rewrite setting all the action in their wonderful scenic country, and my poor old British producer – who invented the whole thing but didn't have any dosh – simply wants the film made before his next cardiac arrest.'

'We might have an episode of *Cragge* for you,' Jack joked. 'Did you know there's a strange woman in your bathroom?'

Justin took on a shifty look, as if he were about to lie. 'Oh, so you met Chloe. She isn't all that strange.'

'Jack, what a lovely surprise!' Anna came in looking frayed and damp, kissed him, melted on to the *chaise-longue*. 'We got caught in the rain on the Heath.' Accepting a glass of champagne she drained it rapidly.

'Is Chloe a friend, or what?'

Justin replied darkly, 'We've kept her hidden away specially, for years now.' Jack thought this might be true, you could see the strings as Justin played his friends. 'She's not for you.'

'Are you trying to protect me?' Jack laughed. He got no reply and glanced at Anna who just kicked off her shoes and smoothed her hair.

'How's the scripting?' she asked. 'Anything for me?' She'd been trying to get back into acting after four years. 'The kids are at nursery now. I don't care how small the part is.'

'It's early days,' he answered. There were a couple of roles she'd play well but the stories might be changed, the characters cut. He didn't want Anna getting hopeful. 'We're still fighting over basics.' He stretched his legs comfortably towards the fire.

When she walked in he wouldn't have recognised her. Maybe it was the clothes, the emphatic blackness of the bodysuit she wore and the too-big leather flying jacket thrown round her shoulders. Bright scarlet lipstick clashed with a feyness in her eyes.

Anna refilled their glasses. 'You don't know Jack.'

Chloe smiled. 'He knows me better than I know him.'

'Jack Maine,' Justin emphasised in a warning way.

She hesitated, seeming to recognise his name. The moment passed and he offered his hand.

'I'm Chloe Rushe.' It was a direct plugging into the life force, a chymical change. Sex, he thought. Plus curiosity. But what does she think of me?

He said, 'I've known these two for years. Why haven't we met before?'

Chloe shook her head, glanced at Justin. 'I suppose I'm mostly Anna's friend.' Kneeling by the fire she bent to dry her hair. A coal tumbled and ash fell, a flare rising made her like a catastrophe.

He frowned, 'Are you an actress?'

'Oh no, I can't act.' It was edgy with self-mockery.

Anna countered, 'Chloe's a photographer. She's brilliant.'

'These two always hype their friends,' Chloe said briskly.

'And she also transcribes my illegible hieroglyphics into word-processed perfection,' Justin added self-importantly, left out.

'A photographer?' She looked too young, more like a student. She didn't respond so Jack went on, 'Justin must be the last writer in the world, still scratching on cave walls with a quill pen.'

'A quill pen?' Chloe laughed. 'Is that what he does. It explains a lot!' Curling cat-like, she moved a basket to the hearth and took out sweet chestnuts, put them on the fire to roast.

Justin was opening a bottle of wine. 'Did you know I've joined the board of Centaur Theatre? Stanislaw is chairman – I'm showing him my new idea, it's a fantastic

13

story I've just thought up! Listen to this...' And he droned along like a person snoring.

There was something about the way she moved, her attitudes. Blowing on her fingers scorched by the tongs, then leaning forward as if to offer him a personal gift – blackened and crumbling into charcoal as it was. The bitter shell plucked at his fingers then fell away into dust and biting its insides he tasted tenderness, honeyed and astonishing. Looking at the girl he found her watching and entered into something with her gaze, her eyes, that turned into – he thought – an intent compact.

Justin intercepted it. Loud. 'So we're being treated to another three months of *Cragge*! The mixture as before?'

'Taste it and see,' Jack suggested.

Chloe unfolded her limbs and said, 'You're the writer.'

He nodded, was about to say more when Justin cut in, 'Who's producing? Is it still Paul Mann?'

'Yes, I'm working with Paul. We're scripting now.'

'Quite a slippery fish, isn't he. What d'you think of *Cragge*, Chloe?'

'I've never watched it.' She sounded angry.

'Not at all, in the last four years?' Justin began to smile. 'That's quite hard to achieve – missing the whole thing! Don't you like detective series?'

'I don't especially dislike them.' Chloe was glaring, furious and Jack felt a loss because Justin had shattered something. He was using a secret that belonged between the two of them and delighted him, upset her.

He was goading with mock sympathy, 'You can't stand television then?'

Chloe ran a hand through her long pale hair; it had dried. 'I must be getting home.' She was putting her arms into the sleeves of the jacket, Justin helped her. It was as if he'd decided she should go. Quickly she was leaving, crossing towards the hall. 'Bye.'

14

Jack went out as she opened the front door. 'It's still raining. I'll give you a lift.'

'My home's very close by.' She added, 'And I've got a car. Thanks.'

It was completely unexpected: she stepped close to him and kissed his mouth with lips that were open in a shocking, killingly sensual assault. He put out a hand – to hold her, to steady himself – but she slipped away instantly into the night and closed the front door, decisive.

Jack stood for a minute hearing a car's powerful engine start with a roar. It drove off.

Slowly he turned and went back into the Fairbrothers' living room. Anna lay fast asleep on the *chaise-longue*. Justin was putting on his raincoat. 'Come along, my friend. We both need a drunken evening.'

'What was all that about?' Jack demanded. 'Why did you do that?'

'Ask no questions, hear no lies. There's a new wine bar opened by the Heath. The only question is, which restaurant to book for later ... And by the way, you've got lipstick on your mouth.'

It was a bad night and a worse morning. His head felt like a set of tracks at Clapham Junction. He gave up trying to sleep, swallowed black coffee and aspirins then took a shower. On his way to the wardrobe, passing the mirror he paused.

Was he ageing like Richard, when the actor was in Rick Cragge's character? His body, mature and strong at thirty-five, appeared heavier and older than he remembered, more ruined by booze than he'd noticed. The black towel-dried hair was wild, stubble scratched his chin. There was even some grey in the stubble. I look villainous, he thought: a villainous wreck. What could a twenty-year-old see in that?

Sitting at his desk he groaned. Procrastination, that was the thing. VAT accounts then a cheque to Customs and Excise, another cheque to the Writers' Guild. The craving for martyrdom lightened and he lunched in the pub, walked through Bloomsbury. OK, Cragge would lose his family. They'd drown in a boating accident, but not till the conflict between his own fanatical war on crime and the needs of Gemma and their kids had built up to the crisis of a trial separation. If *Cragge* returned in future years the character would be altered – by guilt.

It was twenty to seven and had long been dark outside. Jack thought of the evening before. The girl, Chloe, had been on his mind all day and he remembered how she'd looked and laughed. That kiss . . . With an effort he shut her out of his mind.

A monk-like existence for a few days produced a new story development. The rest was routine cut-and-paste on the Amstrad, made bearable by evenings out and the Press screenings. Series Five was not news to the country's TV critics, only seven turned up. Saturday morning brought a crop of notices that were mixed and his mood of insecurity returned. Anxiously re-reading everything, Jack set up the printer.

Its alarm brought him hurrying back from the kitchen. The machine needed a new ribbon but he stood looking at it for several moments.

Jack smiled to himself, picked up the phone and called the Fairbrothers.

Seeing her house he realised at once that Chloe Rushe wouldn't live alone. It explained everything: her ambiguity and early departure, Justin and Anna's discouragement. Field Mews was cobbled and cosmetic, her home the kind of *bijou* town base that actors invest in after television stardom. The white Maserati outside would

16

belong to the husband or boyfriend who'd answer the door.

Will it stop me? he wondered, and still had no answer as he got out of the car.

Piano music spilled from an upstairs window. Recognising a Brahms concerto, he thought it was the radio till it stopped at the sound of the bell. When the door swung back on a shadowy hall and the girl looked out she was like a rabbit hunted, little and timid, rather comical.

'This is kind of you, hello,' he greeted her too heartily.

She dissolved into a great smile. Looked suddenly happy then, 'Come in.'

Up the wooden steps lay a long room awash with light, crammed with plants and photos. Surely hers, nobody else's. The piano was by the window with music open and behind a Chinese screen stood her computer.

He watched as she fetched a bottle of wine and two glasses. She was wearing narrow black jeans and a big shirt, her bare feet were long and pale. Seeming older, confident, Chloe set up the system and he explained the files and formats on the disks. The printer printed, they went through to the kitchen. 'Thanks for helping me out,' he said again.

Her smile held a certain mischief then. She'd guessed it was an excuse, he thought uncomfortably. Justin would've talked to her about him – and whatever his motive, would've wanted to put her off. If they'd met differently, in a neutral place with no one around ... Her eyes were a deep blue. They'd grown warm and concerned and no longer held any amusement.

'I'm glad you rang,' she said. 'Really.'

'Yes.'

Then a silence. Jack felt an intensity of awareness that was exquisitely pleasurable, an animating vibrance to every colour and form, sound and particle of space in the

17

room between himself and this woman who was still a stranger to him. She had to be feeling it too, surely? With a questioning look she got up, went to re-set the printer.

He told himself to listen to his own confusion and to something that was saying: stay away from her.

Chloe was twenty-four – older than he'd thought – and was working in a photographers' gallery in Soho. She told him this house belonged to friends and she was looking after it while they were in the States. That was fine until he noticed that her clothes and jewellery were very class stuff, really expensive, and this puzzled him.

Chloe was saying, 'I've heard a lot about *Cragge* – everyone has.'

'A new series begins tomorrow.'

'I won't be able to watch. But I will soon, now that I've met you.'

A silence fell again as they looked at each other. Jack sensed a high tension singing in her. It was desire, echoing his own. Or was it fear?

Reaching out a hand he touched her. Her arm felt very warm, startling under chill white silk. She became still, poised in hesitation or surprise and he waited, searching her face. Then she seemed to soften, he drew her towards him with the idea that she knew it was inevitable. His heart was banging, his body drumming but as they started to kiss he became aware, as if from a long distance, of a telephone somewhere. And Chloe was pulling away.

'Let it ring.'

'No, no I can't.' And she spun off into another room, shutting the door.

Jack breathed out, long and slow. He began to pace the confines of the kitchen, circling between its cluttered walls where every inch was covered in monochrome photographs. They were cityscapes but *rus in urbe* with a violence by which natural force consumed anything

18

man-made. Concrete lay cracked in crazed patterns by drought, the shoots of new trees stabbing through. Walls of buildings hung deconstructed in neglect, as if suspended for a second from awesomely solid storm clouds. The pictures showed no human life, were stamped with a dislocated reality.

When Chloe came back she seemed completely different, abstracted and distant, almost surprised at seeing him still there.

Looking for contact again he asked, 'Are the pictures yours?'

She nodded, diffident. 'They go back a few years.'

There was one in a frame and he stopped in front of it. An old house, extraordinary, Victorian gothic with spindly tower and spiky gables laced in ornament, arched windows that should have belonged to a church. It was buried in ivy, guarded and half swallowed by two black cedar trees.

He made out a title: *Whitting House*.

'Looks more like a film set than a house. Where is it?'

Chloe looked away. 'Oh, I forget. It's just somewhere I saw.' The printer stopped and she began to gather pages. 'Actually, I've got to go out in ten minutes.'

Jack felt dismissed, then annoyed. She was behaving as if nothing at all had happened between them. Two could play at that. Taking the printout he thanked her and started down the stairs. Then he sensed her eyes on him – she was willing him to stop and turn back. And he half wanted to stay, half wanted to walk straight out.

'Jack.' It was soft, sort of apologetic and his steps slowed down. 'I just had – that call – sort of bad news. Please don't rush away.'

Much later, remembering that moment he wondered if it was all decided then, in that instant of his choice, before he drove away to work again on those storylines and character changes.

2

Art stood jangling a pocketful of coins and cast a glance round at the emptying street market. He was a tall man, broad in the chest. His long coat was black hide, his face lay bleached by weather like stone carved under angelic curls. At twenty-seven he counted himself a survivor.

The girl prompted him, 'Let's go, it's perishing tonight.'

Dusk was driving the punters home. They were mostly kids like her and, loosely in couples, heading home for Sunday tea. So the traders were starting to pack up: the scruffy and exotic, the ethnic and the cheaply glittering were being stowed away.

His stall was good old British bric-à-brac, Victorian china, pots and ornaments, anything that caught his fancy. Jodie packed it swiftly into suitcases and when she'd finished Art rolled up the carpet from underneath, dismantled the assembly of wood crates and loaded up the transit van.

While they'd worked the street had suddenly grown black, gusting like a tunnel, chaotic with leavings. There were hoots and shouts, tribal calls. Litter blew in the icy wake of wheels and feet and the tarmac thinned to desolation, scavengers rustled waiting.

Round the van Jodie slapped her hands together, getting the circulation going. Layers of jumpers were stuffed inside her red cord jacket, then purple trousers, two pairs of socks and boots with silver chains. Her breath puffed like a dragon's. From the passenger-seat she scooped up the sleeping baby, tiny and heavily wrapped in blankets, to kiss his cheek. 'He's warm and soft as a kitten,' she smiled.

Art tooted, clearing a path through the exodus of stragglers, steering the battered van between pothole valleys and hills of rubbish. 'Might try that pitch up Hampstead way. What d'you reckon, next weekend?'

'We didn't do badly at Camden. January's a low time.'

In the side roads lights flicked on as families gathered in houses brightly done up. Turning a corner into Junction Road, Art passed the mean shops all closed with steel barriers, and drew up outside *A'Laddinscave*. Its window was shadowed with dim shapes of old furniture, crowded with unknown past lives.

Jodie was pointing. 'Look. He's seen us.'

Someone was coming out of the flats and crossing to the van. It was Cooper.

Art jumped out with a small grimace. 'Evening.'

The landlord nodded, his eyes flicked across the baby and Jodie. 'We need a word, Mr Adams.'

Opening the passenger-door, gentlemanly, Art asked, 'Hope you got the rent all right, I posted it Thursday in your letter-box.'

Jodie put in quickly, 'You know we can't use that back room at all – you need to do something about the damp.'

'The fact is, it's a single-person flat.' Cooper's well-fed, ruddy face adopted a sorrowful expression that clashed. 'And I've had complaints about the noise, the child crying.'

Art's voice rose, 'I've always seen you right – nine, ten years now. Or doesn't that count?'

'I have to consider my other tenants.'

'I paid very dear for that key.'

'Key money isn't legal now. And you've broken the terms of the tenancy. You're living here on a quite untenable basis.'

'What d'you mean to do about it then?' Art's pale eyes had turned icy.

'You're not going to turn us out?' Jodie asked. 'You can't – not with a baby.'

Cooper avoided looking at her now. 'I gave you warning, plenty of time to find somewhere. You've always known there was a "no children" – '

'You're talking about my home.' Art took a step forward, and Jodie grabbed his sleeve.

The landlord unlocked his dark green Jaguar. He slid inside, started the engine as Art's fist thudded on a sleek rear wing. The car growled softly down the street.

They watched it out of sight. 'Could've kept him sweet,' Jodie protested. 'Could've kept him talking. Now what'll happen?'

Art snapped towards her tight as a wire so she shut up. He let them in through the narrow passageway, up stairs that smelled of stale cooking and old dogs.

'Get the fires on,' Jodie said. Then to the wailing baby, 'Poor Raphael . . .' Sitting down on the bed she pulled up her layers of clothes and put him to her breast.

The front room was cold, sharp with damp. Art switched on the electric fan and the Calor-gas stove. He looked across at the girl and said, 'There's more to it than you know, but I can't tell.'

'What d'you mean? D'you want to stay here without us, is that it?'

'I'll look after you,' he said as if it was a fact.

'If you got a proper job we could move.'

'I'm not going on their records and registers and questionnaires,' he retorted. 'They'd never leave me alone.'

'What, then? I can't go back to the Bridge, not now with the baby. And we can't go for help – they might take him away from me . . .'

'Don't cry. I'll think of something.'

Jodie put out a hand to touch him, seemed not to notice he shrank away. 'You've been so good to me, Art. I trust you.'

In the early hours the traffic was eerily absent: without its judder and thud he felt like a ghost. He lay listening to the breathing of the girl and baby beside him, watching the clock's green eyes pulse through the dark: 05:55.

Sliding from the mattress, Art drew a rug around him and stepped to the window. Shut his eyes before looking down through the sodium chill.

A black car sighed past below.

It was what he'd hoped to see.

A surge of purpose, a certainty so strong it must be visible – but it was all right, on the bed the girl was still asleep.

Going out later something told him not to use the van today. He wove between the seething webs of cars that hooted and stuck, started and stopped. On the long climb to Highgate the cold tugged bitter at his lungs and his coat flapped out behind him like dark wings. A church bell tolled, he crossed to the left then at the village turned from West Hill to Hill Grove.

The road narrowed and few cars passed. Trees touched, arching overhead, a black lace veiling the dead season; silence stalked Art's footsteps on the icy surface of the lane. Passing wrought-iron gates he entered the shadow of a wall. Its crumbling bricks were crowned with broken glass, stitched and swollen by dark ivy. Only a glimpse of Whitting House was visible: a steep corner of purple slated roof, a red front heavy with rotted ornament and

24

the tiny blind window of the tower shuttered from the road. In secrecy the house brooded over the city.

Art came to the side gate, stepping urgently with his slightly stilted, long-legged walk. He unfastened a rusty latch. The path ahead was deep with weeds, creepers caught at his face and hair. He looked down on the gardens beyond, a wilderness of bramble thickets where spindly trees fought giant shrubs. Pavings had erupted, split by thrusting weeds, the ponds had greened to grass and roses become thistles high as a ten-year-old child.

Fate had decided it would be like this.

When he was a boy Rose would bring him here and he remembered how she'd stood on the far boundary, staring in silence at the house. 'I'm hungry, Mum, I'm tired!' he'd cried, growing frightened and grasping at her. Years later he'd returned alone, scaling a corner of the wall and jumping down. It became his secret, magic place and he learned to be invisible by following a certain path. He'd scurry between tall statues then past a waterfall and ponds. In the orchard there was fruit left rotting on the ground. Art would watch the house, imagine huge rooms like in a palace and sometimes he glimpsed the man and the child who lived there then.

He was being watched. Art turned sharply. Rachel Rushe stood in the side porch peering from strands of long grey hair. She was draped in an old dressing-gown and the burgundy cardigan round her shoulders was full of holes. Blinking at the weak daylight she called, 'Good morning, Adams.'

Art made his way through the undergrowth. 'All right then?' He ought to be used to it by now, the way she always made him jump. She was like a spook. 'Leg feeling better?'

'I can,' Mrs Rushe said over-carefully, 'hobble about like a very ancient crone.'

25

She's pissed already, Art thought. 'You? Still young, for all the pretending.'

'Flattery!' she snorted. 'I haven't forgotten it's pay day.'

Picking up a box of groceries from the top step, he followed her through the tiled passage into the kitchen. The box held bottles of whisky and tins for the cats festooning the place. He thumped it down close to an outsize ginger creature. The cats hated him and this one vanished fast.

Rachel Rushe said, 'Look, that window's gone.'

It was a large pane above the sink. Among unwashed crockery and spikes of glass Art found a piece of brick and he held it up for her, frowning, 'Kids! Vandals, Mrs R. It's because they know you're here alone . . . You ought to ask someone to look after things properly. To live here maybe.' He waited but she wasn't listening, was standing gazing into space. 'Ought to let me put bars on, like everyone has. Or people will break in.'

She looked at him vaguely, pulled the tattered cardigan close and called imperiously to a black and white cat on the draining board, 'Isolde! Isolde, mind the glass!' The thing jumped down and she turned remote eyes back to Art. 'Put something over the window, Adams. Seal it up for now.'

Art glared at her for ignoring him. She muttered, 'The house and I will go together. This was my husband's pride, it will be my tower of silence.'

Self-pity left him loathing her. This place had so much of his boyhood self. There was a seed of magic, of lost power, long buried somewhere inside.

He watched her go out through the hall. She went suddenly as if she sensed something.

He shovelled ashes out of the Aga, spilling some and trampling them underfoot. The place was filthy, Jodie would have a fit if she saw it. No one ever came to the house and no wonder – the old bat made you feel like nothing. Over the years there'd been times he felt they were thick as thieves, with her relying on him like family, and there'd been other times when he couldn't stand her.

Busily Art took out rubbish and empties, dumped them. Then to the outhouse ... This was his place. Big, and private, liveable in really. It might've been stables at one time with room for carriages, it had plenty of history – and what a history, for him! Unlocking the door he stepped inside, breathed deep until his sense of self flooded back. She never came in here. Not since her old man died, he guessed.

She'd had it done out afterwards but the same things were still here and in real terms they were his. Most of the tools were ancient, big ungainly old-fashioned things but he kept them oiled and sharpened, hanging from hooks. Good craftsmanship had gone into those and he wouldn't throw them out.

Taking up the axe he tested the blade, chopped kindling and swept the bits. Firewood went into the kitchen. He smashed the broken glass through and boarded up the window for her. In the garden paths had to be hacked back so she could walk around. It was five to two when he finished; he was hungry and tired. At least he could get his dosh.

'Mrs R – I'll be off now!' He went through the big hallway looking for her. There was music from the drawing room.

'So you're going to leave me all alone.'

Her hair was pinned up now and he stared at the long rope-like neck as she counted out coins from her purse. The black holes of those hooded eyes were like suicide jumps and his own eyes felt drawn tight by the cords that worked her head.

*

Returning up the lane he remembered Jodie crying last night. When she cried she sounded like a young boy, with a reedy wail that went through him. It was vital that she didn't leave.

The city lay spread far below. Offices dwarfed the dome of St Paul's, beyond lay a faint smudge of hills. Art looked at the clean lines of London and thought how in exchange for guidance received he'd become the servant, her working hands. His interference helped make space for clear life patterns. He walked on and the little building blocks of the city passed out of sight before he came to St Pius's.

The church was empty, magnifying tiny scuffles as he genuflected, made the sign of the cross with holy water like stale perfume. Stillness, silence. Like coming home. There was Jesus with the Sacred Heart: the Son of God had been guided through the world by his Father sending signs. Skirting the altar with its tall bouquets of scarlet, Art came to the Virgin's chapel and sat on a bench.

It was his great secret, something he'd never tell anybody, not even Jodie. She'd never understand – how could she? He himself only knew how it had worked out since he was a boy and left alone. In the weeks following Rose's death he'd been overwhelmed by the simplicity: she'd gone because her time had come, and there'd been clues enough if he'd only noticed them. Art knew he'd reached a good agreement with the randomness of life, he'd formed a co-operative bond instead of struggling like others did. The relationship had flourished from that point of surrender, it had given him his strength.

Art stared intently at the Madonna holding her boy child. He closed his eyes, remembering.

When he'd first been tested, he hadn't even known what was happening. He'd done what he was told to do, with blind trust. And he'd been rewarded, embraced by her new benevolence. Shaken and humbled, he'd no thought after that but to obey, whatever kind of sense it made.

Someone was entering the church. Soft footfalls approached and passed by. So this was it. He waited a few seconds then, receptive to whatever came, opened his eyes.

A woman was kneeling, praying to the Madonna and child. The hooded cape she wore was of deep burgundy. The exact same colour as Rachel Rushe's cardigan.

Mother and child . . .

He drew in a sharp breath as the future spanned out unknown to him but in his hands. All he had to do was act, obey with faith.

3

Slipping back into *Cragge's* world was like putting on a winter coat, as each November to August Jack wrote for the detective. He'd tramp cold streets for hours, thinking, then back at his desk labour through the night. Seeing each dawn he felt like a farmer sowing a landscape that would ripen later, in its own time if conditions were right.

But there was nothing natural about it. By Thursday he had thirteen characters and their stories with subplots mapped out on pages above his desk – with locations for each sequence, minutes or seconds of probable screen time and even the emotions they might generate. Days of thought had gone into plotting the stories' reversals, changing act structures, moving and re-moving commercial breaks.

He'd arranged to see Chloe in the evening. They were going to have dinner with time to talk and he'd chosen a restaurant overlooking the Regent's Canal. The food was good, and no friends were likely to go there. It was near enough to his home – he half hoped she might come back with him – but not too obviously close.

That half-hope meant a day of clearing up. His creative self was like a child about the age of three and his house had spawned a thick patina of displaced things; it looked burgled. He'd changed the sheets and was about to tackle crusts of kitchen grease when Paul rang.

'I've been trying to get hold of you,' Jack said.

'There's been every kind of catastrophe here – nothing to do with the show ... You've heard about the viewing figures?'

'Down two and a half million. Why? Is it just the scheduling or is it sinister? And what's Bill making of it?'

Paul sounded tired, or despondent. 'I've been on to Publicity – we didn't get enough hype. It'll soon pick up. The audience reactions were good.'

'Are they committed to making Series Six?'

'Absolutely! I'll look at your rewrites this evening. Push on, Jack. Don't worry.'

He hung up slowly, worrying. There was nothing he could do except trust Paul.

Freshly showered and shaved he dithered over what to wear and soon half the contents of his wardrobe lay draped around the bedroom again. Nothing seemed right. In the end he chose black Italian trousers and a loose jacket of fine dark tweed. 'A mixed metaphor,' he muttered, stuffing everything back into cupboards and realising he was about to be late. 'You're behaving like a teenager, Maine.'

He shot across the bridge then crawled impatiently through crowded Putney. The evening had grown raw. Blustery rain gusted the glass and on the Heath black trees danced in tribal clumps. Missing a turning he got lost, arrived in the mews ten minutes late. Chloe's house was in darkness. Jack knocked, waited, went back to wait in the car. Rain fell relentless and harsh, thrusting waves over flooded cobblestones, battering at tubs and window-boxes. A million drops spiked out, all light-shot like shattering glass, around the Victorian carriage lamps.

Fragmented images of Chloe had slipped into his

31

moments of waking up and falling asleep but he'd pushed them away. Stray memories drifted to him now of women he'd known in the past. Of relationships. Of something wrong.

Twenty minutes passed. Had she forgotten or had they got the day mixed up? Was ten minutes late too late? Then he began to wonder if she might've had some accident. That seemed ridiculous: it was clear he was being stood up. With a strong impulse to leave he reached out and turned on the ignition.

The white Maserati sluiced into the mews and its powerful lights caught him in their beam.

She ran through the torrents, bare-headed and laughing to let them in, and collapsed in apology, shedding jacket and bag then shoes across her living room. 'Sorry Jack – I'm so late!'

His relief at her turning up was mixed with anger now: she seemed too certain that he'd wait. 'I was about to give up on you and go. What happened?'

Chloe's attention sobered. 'There was a vast traffic jam coming back into town – I was visiting friends in Berkshire. But now here we are – hello,' she said softly.

Kissing her hello, ignoring the flood of senses he asked, 'Did you take the day off work?'

'Oh, that job's only part time. Look, I'm absolutely soaked through. I'll have to shower and change and dry my hair.'

He sat and waited, thinking: she's twenty-four years old, works part time and drives a Maserati, wears a gold Bulova watch – and that's for everyday. And she doesn't give a damn . . . He phoned to change their booking for nine o'clock.

And then she said it was an odd choice, so far to go and somewhere local would've been all right. Sipping

32

neat vodka, perusing the canal view, devouring the menu lengthily as if tasting everything on it. His confusion of feelings was toppling with criticism, unwanted and prickly. She was acting a spoilt brat but he glimpsed something else, blade-sharp inside the coating of indulgence. There was a hunger in it.

Chloe gazed across at him. 'I think you're making character notes. Come on, tell me.'

'You might not want to hear them.' He returned that quizzical stare, challenging.

'Try me.'

After a moment Jack began, 'If you were a character of mine I'd say you'd been an only child, much adored and raised in plenty. Home Counties? Somewhere cosy. You're not independent but like to think you are. There's a lot of beginning things and not following through.' She looked annoyed, but she'd asked for it. 'All that security – you're under-motivated. And haven't a clue where you belong.' He thought but didn't quite say: you're the kind of girl who'd have an affair with a married, older man. A Daddy's girl on a practice run.

The waiter brought plates of artistry: basil leaves and prosciutto wrapped the largest prawns he'd ever seen, crisp pastry boats lay plump with he knew not what.

Chloe smiled at Jack in a pitying way. 'And here was I, thinking your perceptions might be interesting. Or even accurate. Because underneath that repetitive, boring, stock format, Cragge's quite a quirky and sensitive character – '

He interrupted her, 'You've never watched it.'

'I saw a video last night,' she retorted too fast, so he had the feeling she was lying and might've watched the show for years. 'You've got nothing right about me at all.' And she turned her attention to eating with an interest that excluded him. The strappy red dress she'd chosen to wear made her look ten years older. He didn't like it.

Chloe said, 'My father is Charles Arthur Rushe, the concert pianist. You haven't heard of my father? Hm, so this man is ignorant of music! We were not cosy and never secure. I travelled with him, before boarding school. He's retired now.'

Remembering the beguiling Brahms, Jack said, 'You play the piano well.'

'I studied at the Royal College,' she replied carelessly. 'But then other things seemed more interesting. It's such a help financially, Giles and Tessa lending me their house – now I've decided to be a photographer.'

'I was pretty accurate,' Jack pointed out. He saw her flush of annoyance, the hesitation before she smiled acknowledgement. There was grace and humour in that smile.

'*Touché*,' murmured Chloe, then, 'And what about you? I think you think that you like women.'

'What does that mean?'

She asked smoothly, 'How many of your women characters have been likeable, or morally admirable? Strong or successful in life and love? You haven't even noticed your own attitudes.'

He felt condemned. Managed a counterattack, 'If that's what you think, then I wonder what you're doing here with me.'

'A good question.' She rested her hand across the warm, flat length and breadth of his hand. Light, unmoving yet somehow it felt like a caress. And she shrugged and smiled at him.

He felt a wish to crush and silence her. To possess. Uneasily he wondered if she could be right.

Chloe was taking away her hand, asking in a friendly

34

way, 'Now – what else shall we argue about, Jack? Tell me what you've written.'

'Before *Cragge*? A first novel.'

'Was it a success?'

'That depends on what you mean by success. It had good reviews, OK sales. I adapted it for film, but it hasn't been made yet. Then *Cragge* happened. And now any new ideas get swallowed up in his enormous annual meal.'

She frowned. 'Time to do another book then, don't you think?'

'I needed time to catch up with what I was trying to do. Or perhaps I lack neuroses? It was my parents' fault for loving me.'

Chloe laughed, she sparkled, 'Tell me all about it, sweetheart.'

Looking at her laughing mouth he saw how it curved at the corners in an irresistible way. He ached to kiss her, and thought: I'm infatuated, I don't know her at all, she's just a kid anyway. He began to tell her about his brother, how Michael had quit Britain, studied business then set up a greetings card company. He'd married a Spanish woman, adopted her faith and her country and fathered five children all in twelve years. 'Michael's the achiever and I'm the black sheep. A wastrel, no less.'

It brought an echo of a smile. 'Sibling rivalry – I never had that.'

'We're not rivals,' Jack denied quickly.

She was devouring, with new concentration, an extraordinary looking concoction: a long lean limb of meat, feline yet very black in sauce so mysteriously rich it looked a hundred years old. The dish was hare in chocolate with kernels of pine but the way she was tearing at that leg – ripping it apart, feral – made her seem oddly like a cannibal.

'How is your very dull grilled steak?' Finding the right

size morsel of hare, Chloe speared and popped it into his mouth. Sweetness, sourness, a gamey wildness and smooth confection mingled. Too much.

He sawed at steak and said, 'Now tell me how you know Justin and Anna.'

A look of carefulness came over her, an evasion. Then he sensed her searching for what she would tell him. 'I was friends with Anna's younger sister at school. I sort of – stayed with her and so on.'

'Does that make Anna some kind of a surrogate mother to you?'

Chloe unpeeled with delicious laughter. 'She wouldn't thank you for that description! But we do go back a long way. And you?'

'Justin and I met trying to work together. Then he tried to script *Cragge* but it was a disaster. That man's ego could sink the planet.'

'Would Justin say the same of you?'

'Oh, I'm just dull, boring and repetitive – as you keep kindly pointing out.'

'I never said that at all,' she argued. 'I don't know anything much about you but I'd like to. I hope we'll both learn more . . .'

Then he knew for certain they'd soon be lovers and, in that warm flood of knowing, began to ignore all the confusion and all his doubts.

They were the last to leave, the restaurant had closed. She didn't want to go back to Islington. He would drive her home. She took his hand as they stepped out into the near-dark, walked a little way through the stormy night then paused to look along the canal. A small boat was approaching. Unknowable, with a soft throb it glided by. Lights glittered in black water, broken by turbulence. Jack kissed Chloe, glorying in her instant response. For a long time they stood rooted together. Rain started to fall heavily.

In the calm and quiet of the car he stroked the wet hair from her eyes and kissed her again. Chloe looked pale in the gleam of white from a neon sign. She was silent.

Some accident on Putney Hill had left three cars spewed sideways at a junction pavement like dead animals. A little chorus of dark figures stood around, the lights of the wrecks were dim and rheumy. Driving past, avoiding bits of glass, he crossed the Heath to her home.

She'd forgotten her key and dug around in the left-hand window-box to find a spare kept hidden there. 'You should never do that,' Jack told her off. 'It's the first place a thief would look.' The house was vulnerable with its moneyed exterior and quiet approach; along its side was an unlit passageway. She was careless. Didn't it worry her?

Then going in with her, he forgot all the flashes of anger and resentment that had punctuated their evening. They faded – or he suppressed them – because he couldn't imagine going home alone or being apart from her tonight.

In the kitchen he watched while she made coffee and put it on a tray, taking hours over this before she turned round and they looked at each other, words about something or nothing stuttering out. He held her and they kissed, warm and intimate in her home, available to each other. He felt turbulent in a blissful way.

Then she drew back. 'Jack, listen. I'm not sure this is a good idea – or not so quickly. Or if I can cope with it.'

'Why not?' He kissed her again. What on earth was she talking about?

'It's complicated.' She was anxious and he studied her face, completely puzzled. 'I mean, having the same friends.'

37

Jack laughed aloud, relieved at such a simple doubt. 'How could that be complicated? We want each other – nothing else really matters.'

Sliding the heavy jacket from her shoulders, Jack let it fall. He stroked his hands over her face, her bare shoulders and arms. She seemed delicate to him, and vulnerable. Tracing outlines with each finger he touched her breasts through the fabric. Felt sharp longing, felt the echoing wave in her of hunger. He unfastened the dress, it fell to her waist and he bent to kiss her throat, those softly swelling, naked breasts.

Chloe drew a shuddery breath, like someone drowning suddenly. 'I do want you so much,' she whispered.

She pulled him close urgently, seeking his mouth and tongue with her tongue, wrapping her legs around him completely and fiercely and achingly desirous, taking him off balance in a storm of response. He seemed to have waited so long, caught up in too many conflicting needs now to slow down, wanting to take her right there. Peeling away that dress he somehow lurched back straight into the table and dislodged things – fragile china things – that fell crashing with a terrible resoundingness all around them.

It broke the spell. Jack cursed himself for impossible clumsiness then began to laugh. 'Damn it – what was that?' because she was laughing now.

'Come with me.' Chloe had both his hands, she was towing him along to stumble willingly, blindly up more stairs. She was mischievous, full of a gleaming viscous effervescence as he caught up with her and they clung together again in a breathless, hurrying, laughing tangle in the middle of the stairs before she stood and tugged him after her. 'Come on, my love, and don't break up the place like a bull in a china shop.'

4

Now it would take all Jack's emotional energy to step out of Chloe's front door or to let her go from his bed. Once alone he felt in a dream where no ideas could penetrate. Words on the screen were a meaningless scramble, he was a puzzled amnesiac. And he couldn't work if she stayed: in his study with the door firmly shut, he'd find every atom of consciousness had fled to wherever she was.

Eventually he gave up trying to function normally. It wasn't a normal time. Reason told him this vivid sphere would fade, become familiar one day. He had no firm deadlines, the contracts hadn't arrived and Paul was out of touch. Leaping into the hiatus he felt it widen at his fall; he was empowered so long as he didn't try to stop.

He knew she really wanted him now. She'd stopped going in to work at the gallery and he felt satisfied, selfish, not wanting to ask her about it. Days and nights merged. They saw no one, lived in a space capsule delicious with sensuality, touch and sound and smell, and talked of nothing but themselves. He felt hungry to know her passions and pleasures, history and hopes. While the outside world floated off in a little cloud, inconsequentially.

Perhaps they should've heeded it more.

It was the last day of January when everything changed. They'd woken late, breakfasted in bed, spun out the morning with a bath that began as hers then turned into theirs. Lying in the scented water, his thighs entangled with her thighs, idly soaping an ankle that lodged near his ear, he noticed fresh snow pressed against the window-sill. The day was white, a blank. 'We should go out,' he said.

So they walked to Camden, shopped at a deli, stopped for coffee and cakes at a brasserie. Some of the traders were starting to pack up when they reached the market and wandered among stalls. He bought a piece of Victoriana that Chloe admired among the bric-à-brac – an over-ornate black vase, something at home in a conservatory as a centrepiece – although it was heavy to carry.

Heading back down the tow-path to Islington they stepped through a skin of snow and somewhere, distant, a church bell tolled.

Chloe said, quiet and thoughtful, 'We've been together for fourteen days.'

It sounded like nothing. Surely it had been months? Sometimes they were giggly and infantile: hurling snow-balls with gleeful accuracy, plastering too much jam on hot buttered crumpets. He felt like a kid. At other times the familiarity was so strong, when they wandered arm in arm or paused to feed the frozen ducks he felt they'd had a lifetime together.

He stopped and, holding her gloved hand, gazed into the skim of thin ice. Among weeds and murk something stirred. Splitting reflected factory chimneys, it made the shadows erupt.

Chloe shivered. 'A water snake. It must devour everything from here to King's Cross.'

'There are no water snakes in Britain,' Jack pointed out. 'A grass snake would be hibernating, and an eel – '

'So literal-minded,' she mocked. 'Over-educated –

you'd factualise everything out of existence. To me it was a water snake.'

'All right,' he agreed readily. 'That's what we'll think it was.' Knowing she'd left school at sixteen and was sensitive about it.

'Huh,' Chloe snorted as if in disgust. 'Thanks very much.'

They watched for a while but the creature had gone. Running home along the tow-path, their boots thudded silent in the snow and their breath steamed. He'd left the gate unlocked and they turned at the narrow-boats' moorings, went up six steps into the garden. Overgrown branches splattered flakes like soggy petals. Chloe said, 'We'll do your garden when the snow's cleared. Such a wilderness!'

'There are things trying to grow under that lot,' he agreed, 'you'd never dream of.'

She was picking wild rosehips on long stems. 'Don't you like gardening?'

'There's never time for it.' Jack unlocked the back door, stepped into the warm kitchen.

She kissed him with tenderness. 'We will have time,' she said.

Jack felt the heat between them spark and sharpen. Taking her hand he tugged her into the warmer bedroom where he unwrapped them both like peeling husks from buds, part full and ready, part numb with frost. With her fingers and toes tucked into armpits and under knees he began to recite bits of her he specially liked: the egg-shell hollow of her throat, the long middle phalange of each finger, the miraculous bone structure of those knees.

She grew restless, frustrated by the litany and she wriggled free. Began to kiss, to lick with her flicking tongue from fingers to toes and over every bit of him, in a seriously volcanic ritual of her own. They'd reached a time

41

that mixed new discoveries with knowingness but of that evening he was to remember – later – her familiar sounds that were soft and guttural, deepening as if with an odd despair he hadn't heard before, until she came. He felt powerful watching her abandonment, owning it.

Lying curled together they grew a nest of caresses, murmurings. Their woven limbs were melted and heavy with the scent of sex sharp in her skin. He wanted to hold her like that and fall asleep.

'I'm hungry,' Chloe complained. 'I'm going to start supper.'

His protests wouldn't keep her. She seemed uncomfortable now. He got out of the very empty bed and put on a dressing-gown.

There were two messages on the answerphone. His father: 'We weren't sure about the schools' corruption story. Not convincing! Your mother's been given a goose – come and eat Sunday lunch.' Then Sarah, her voice uncharacteristically anxious,

'Jack – call me back. Are you OK?'

Still nothing from Paul, he thought with mixed relief and foreboding. Dialling Sarah's number he got her machine and began, 'Sarah, it's me. Sorry I've been out of touch – ' then sensed Chloe and looked round. Something in her face made him put down the phone.

'Anything interesting?' she asked, handing him a glass of wine.

Sitting her down on his lap he shared the wine with her. 'My father. Roast goose on Sunday? I don't have to.'

'Life goes on. Who's Sarah?'

'One of my oldest friends. Justin and Anna know Sarah, she works at the BBC. You'll meet her.'

Chloe seemed oddly quiet. 'Thirty-five years of you I've never known. I don't know anything about you, really. You don't know me.'

'We will have time. As you said.' But she had withdrawn and left him in some indefinable way, so quickly. He felt desperately lonely suddenly. He sounded calm, 'We could both go on Sunday. Would you like to?'

'No. That's your world, not mine.' It was definitely said and inexplicably wounding. She stood up and they went to cook supper but the togetherness, that they'd kept as celebratory, had now turned hollow.

'What is it?' he asked.

'Nothing.' Chloe looked unhappy. 'We're just two people who've been around for a while, that's all.' She poured more wine and changed the subject. 'Why d'you write a detective series, why that? What's interesting about the detection of a crime?'

He went along with it. She'd entered a strange and hurtful mood but it would change again. 'The detective story,' he told her, 'is everyman's search for the truth, nothing more and nothing less. It's formal, rooted in the mundane and familiar. Rick Cragge happened, while other things didn't.'

'That isn't a proper reason.'

'No, but it's the truth. Come with me on Sunday to Clapham. Make the mundane familiar.'

She shook her head. 'I'll probably spend the day with my father.'

They were talking like children; it was a game that would end in laughter or tears, a swearing of lifelong blood-loyalty or enmity and feud. She was frowning and he laughed. She looked annoyed.

'In Aldeburgh,' Chloe elaborated. 'I haven't seen Charles for a couple of weeks. He misses my mother. She died soon after I left home and he's been on his own ever since.'

Jack asked, 'Will you go for a seaside walk? Then play a little duet together? And listen while Charles reminisces

43

about his years of glory?' She was glaring at him now. He went on, 'I don't believe you're quite who you say you are, Chloe Rushe. Or that you went to those correct boarding schools, somehow.'

It was only as he said the words that he realised they were true. There was something baroque in her history and something animal breathing in her. If she knew the rules she hadn't learned to play by them. There was no social insulation, and no genuine confidence. She was raw inside.

She pushed back her chair from the kitchen table, and a strange closed look came over her face. 'D'you think I've lied to you?' she asked, quiet and strained and dangerous.

'I don't know.' He felt confused, alarmed. 'Would it really matter if you had, or if I do? Long term...' He wanted to add: remember today and how great it's been, how can it matter what we say?

'Long term? What're you talking about?' She was walking back and forth agitatedly across the kitchen, throwing out troubled glances. She looked ill, drawn in her expression. Jack got up and went to stop her. He held out his arms but she ignored the gesture.

'Let's stop talking,' he said. 'Come here.'

'You don't believe me. Don't trust me, Jack! Why should you, after all? We don't even really know each other. What am I doing here?'

They'd left her car in Putney. She wanted to call a cab. Persuading her to stay the night, he was sure closeness and sleep would banish whatever had hurled itself in their path. Morning would dawn innocent, healing; by late tomorrow they'd laugh together at this first, stupid quarrel.

But he couldn't sleep and eventually got up and dressed, went out and later found himself driving in bright moonlight. To Suffolk where he walked by the sea quite alone and sea grass stretched for miles bruising coarse beneath his soles. And when he got back his house was empty: barren of Chloe, of furnishings or his possessions; of doors and windows too. With a start he saw the ground had fallen away and left the shell clinging to a precipice and very far below the tide had drained out completely. Weed wreathed stones of shining black and a bright canary crane above swung a wreckers' ball of steel to him. He shouted a warning but no sound came and the giant bullet bulldozed him, light as feathers and like a feather he lightly fell and into wakefulness.

The bed was empty. Chloe knelt on the kitchen floor, her left hand running blood from a cut. Around her lay a scrambled rope of thorns, jagged edges of black china vase. It had fallen, she said, and she'd been trying to collect the bits. She seemed distraught at the accident.

Why didn't he believe her?

Taking her back to bed he held her close, but neither of them slept again. In the morning he realised: nothing he could do or say would bring her back from wherever she'd gone. Driving her to Putney he said goodbye. Chloe had the thinned and whitened look of someone in a state of shock but he told himself it was tiredness. 'Take a couple of your valium, and get some sleep. I'll call you later.'

'Jack, I can't go on like this. I've got to be free.'

Exhausted, he felt full of foreboding now. 'You are free, in what way aren't you free?' Should he call on Justin and Anna, confide in them? It seemed too disloyal.

The next few days they talked only on the phone. Chloe told him she couldn't cope with the relationship. He mustn't phone, he should forget her.

What was she playing at? He lost his temper, 'You've

never stuck at anything in your life – isn't it time you grew up?'

She shouted back, 'You're smug and judgmental and you understand nothing . . . Just leave me alone!'

Slamming down the phone he hurled it across the room. Later he retrieved the thing and found it was still working. He dialled her number. She didn't answer. Driving to her house he knocked on the door till a neighbour opened a window and looked out. He knew Chloe was there. He couldn't believe she could go on ignoring him.

Jack felt like murdering someone. He spent the day walking the dead, blackened, roaring streets of the city berating himself. Long ago he'd recognised that pit of obsession, the part of his nature which caused and defined his writing. Never before had it ruled any of his relationships. It wasn't going to start now. He thought all the negative thoughts he could until he felt some relief. He hated Chloe Rushe.

'I've just finished Episode Three. I think you'll like it.'

Paul looked worried, sat down in Jack's favourite armchair. 'That's wonderful, Jack. That's just as well.'

It had been two unbroken days and nights of lunatic writing and rewriting. Paul's words took time to sink in. 'What d'you mean, just as well? Here.' Jack placed fresh printed copies on the table between them. The script was good and he wanted Paul to read it immediately, reach into his briefcase and say, 'Here's your contract for the next episodes.'

But Paul, gazing out of the window said, 'You may as well hear it from me, Jack. It looks as if I'll have to leave the show.'

He realised something like this had hung in the air for weeks. It still came as a shock. Reeling he asked, 'What's happened?'

46

'It's Bill. We can't see eye to eye on this one, I'm afraid. God knows, I've fought like a tiger. Sorry – after six years . . . Look, I can't stay long. I wanted to let you know, personally.'

'To let me know . . . What happens now, Paul? We're ten scripts short, no producer and production starts in three months – or doesn't it? And what will you do?'

'Oh, something will turn up.'

He's had another offer, Jack knew suddenly. And he's accepted it. 'I thought you were under contract to XLTV?'

'They're very slow in that department, as you know.' So Paul hadn't signed, and he was off the show. Would the series be ditched? And why hadn't he been told before? He stayed dead calm. 'What happens to *Cragge*?'

Paul looked out of the window again. 'They're not happy about the drop in viewing figures. I'm not sure what Bill will decide. Take it up with the boss.'

'I will. They've spent enough on options, retainers . . . Does Richard know? Or the others?'

'Nobody. Keep this under your hat till you've talked with the chief. Look, sorry. I've got another meeting and I'm running late.'

'Of course.'

'Good luck, Jack.' They shook hands. 'I'm in the market as a freelance. When there's anything I can do.'

'Yes. Well, good luck.'

'You must come to dinner, I'll talk to Grace.'

'Goodbye, Paul.'

Jack closed the front door. The second post had come. Absently picking up envelopes he took them into the kitchen and stood staring out at the barren snow, gathering resolve to phone the head of Drama.

'Bill, please. This is Jack Maine.'

'Hello, Jack. I'm afraid Bill's in New York.'

Had Paul known? Or was this paranoia? 'Until when?'

'Next Thursday.'

'I need him, Susan. It's urgent.'

Getting the Manhattan number, he worked out it was ten in the morning there and phoned. Bill Bishop wasn't at the hotel. Jack left another message.

There was nothing to work on, no consolation. Days lay permeated with a leaden, primitive dread. Of redundancy, rejection by the pack. The hunt with no kill. He'd never write again, he wouldn't want to live. The bank would take his house, he'd join the city derelicts . . .

Snap out of it, Maine, he thought. But day and night, images of loss and despair haunted him. He thought: what if it does end now, everything has to end sometime. He ordered himself to look to . . . what future?

Chloe had been right to leave. Curled inside him slept some shadow that knew only its own survival. She'd cast a bright light and this had stirred.

After a lot of hesitation he called Sarah.

Familiar and reassuring, she was putting on the coffee filter and pouring two generous brandies. In the months since their affair broke up he'd forgotten Sarah's laughter and the cheerful way she moved around. Her attic flat over a gift shop on Fulham Road had a faint hum of city busyness and it set off memories for him of conversations – long and impassioned, about writing – carried on till four in the morning between the tangled sheets of lovers.

Sitting down in the collapsed sofa she took his hand. He felt a rush of affection: she was still here, and a friend – no hurtfulness about it.

'Look, Jack,' she was saying emphatically, 'think about it clearly – a change of producer does not mean the end of the show.'

'But Bill Bishop's keeping well out of touch and – '

'He's away in the States.'

'How do you know that?' She worked as a script editor but for the BBC, surviving on a low salary and juggling the needs of two producers on several series at once.

'I know most of what happens,' Sarah shrugged. 'You must stop hurting yourself,' she went on quickly. 'This could be a new beginning. You could get someone fresh, more enthusiastic for the series.'

'It'll just be axed now,' he growled.

Sarah looked very troubled. 'It won't be!' she insisted. She hesitated then went on, 'If by any chance it was, that just might be the right thing for you. I've always said you should be doing other stuff, not only *Cragge*.'

'Sounds easy!' Jack retorted. 'I don't know whether I can write without *Cragge*, now ... Television looks so simple – drafting a map for a hundred other professionals to go hiking all over.'

'Write more films,' she commanded stoutly. 'You've got to get new projects started – whatever happens. Maybe I could help?'

'You're a good friend,' he said miserably.

Sarah winced as if that hurt. She was studying him. 'You look awfully rough, I'm sorry.'

'It's hardly your fault ... And it isn't only work.'

'You've been seeing someone,' she said after a moment. 'Who is she?'

'No one you know. Anyway, it's over before it really began.'

'I'm sorry,' Sarah said again, with a kind of intensity. She paused then added, 'Have you seen Justin recently?'

'Not since New Year. Have you?'

'Oh, I don't see them much. There isn't time, I've been frantically busy.'

'You need a holiday, Sarah. A month in the country, at least.' It was a joke between them and she smiled slightly. She hated the country, silence and space and animals all

49

alarmed her. She craved the adrenalin of city life, terminal insecurity and the media. After the coffee and brandies she'd swallow several sleeping pills, wake as late as she dared and start on coffee and deadlines again.

'It's been really good to see you.' Jack squeezed her hand and stood up to go. It was pretty late.

Sarah stood up too, she put her arms round him in a hug. 'You could stay the night, love. Why don't you?'

They were kissing, he found, and first felt the old warmth and comfort of that familiarity, her large soft breasts against him. He wanted so much to love her again. Shutting his eyes he held her close, caressing, and imagined making love to her now. Then he realised she'd become alien to him, physically a stranger. And almost repulsive. Her fullness, and her mouth: he couldn't kiss her but, avoiding kissing, grasped her tighter and more desperately, trying to remember them and how it had been, running his hands all over her to remind them both.

'For old times' sake,' Sarah murmured in his ear. 'It would cheer you up, to forget whoever she is.'

It was no good. He felt drained by despair, heavy and cold. Chloe had got deep into him.

'I'd better go,' he said, drawing back a little. 'Too much booze – sorry, love.'

Sarah released him then. 'Look at you. That's no state to drive home in, at all. Stay and sleep here, Jack.'

'I must be very drunk,' he agreed, lying.

5

Jodie laughed as the water splashed and the baby clasping up his fingers chortled, kicking out. Then a waterfall from a bright red cup: Raphael's eyes grew huge, intent with wonder so that she felt like a magician. 'I'd do anything for you, babe.' And she kissed his downy head that smelled of soap, patted him dry with a dust of talc, felt his breathing soft on her skin as they cuddled.

Once he was dressed and warm she could let the bath water out of the sink, carry the fires from the back room to the front again. It was damp and cold, the baby so frail and new that she lay awake at nights worrying. But then compared to the streets, Art's flat was paradise.

Six weeks she'd lived rough. That was after migrating to London last year. October, November days and nights shot through with trains, baggage and people's legs. Home was her pitch among the dossers under the South Bank's concrete arches. She'd found herself an older protector and learned to be hard, among their sort of tribe. Often she wondered what had become of the others. But she'd never go back.

Her cardboard sign had said *Homeless & Hungry.* Drawn deep into herself, hunched awkward over an open palm she'd mutter hour on hour, 'Spare any loose change'. Most of them made her invisible. 'Spare any loose change.' Some offered advice or gave the coins she lived on. Was it really her doing that, getting so low? Winter grew closer, sharper and she felt a change in her with an angry edge of violence: she wanted to take, to disturb and to cost.

Then someone had stopped and just stared for long minutes. It was Art. Later he'd come back and offered her somewhere to stay. She was grateful and loved him for it.

Jodie smudged on lipstick, pulled a comb through her curly black hair. The patch of sky was yellow behind the factory roof and she wrapped the baby warm in a blanket. 'Better buy your dad's tea. We're a proper family and we'll stay where we belong, all together.' Locking the door, clattering down flights of stairs, she thought about the social workers and health visitors who'd started in on them before. How Art had hated it! She'd lied through her teeth about everything – his earnings, her age and name and old address: she'd had to.

The street was sullen under bruised cloud, waiting. Cars glided through tracks of black slush with an electric throbbing hum and sharp bites of wind tore the bent-down, dragged-down passers-by. She tottered to the corner shop, a small thin figure swamped by clothes and clasping the baby like a doll.

Art would get his favourite tea.

She'd filled up again with those anxieties – no money, no home – even living with Art was turning out the same. And she had responsibility now, the baby to think of.

It was only mid afternoon but the lights were on, ghostly in the gloom. Coming back she stopped at *A'Laddins-cave* then went in.

A fractured tunnel wound through stacks of dead men's stuff. Massive oak chests and craning standard lamps, ornate carved writing-desks and armchairs fat with buttons, crowded and dark like a forest.

There he was in the back with the accounts. Tony hadn't heard the door. Jodie stepped near soundlessly, took a black opera hat from a hook then swept it down on to his bent head.

'Gotcha,' she sang, giggling at his shock. 'You need a louder bell on the door!'

'Mary and the Archangel,' he laughed, and switched off the droning radio.

'Keep the hat on,' she said because he looked good in it, having a somehow old-fashioned face. Maybe it was that long chin, and a fullness round the eyes that seemed of another century. They were smiley eyes. He was putting on the kettle for tea, then holding out his arms to take Raphael.

'Weighs megatons. They do spread like grass at this age.'

'Go on – you say the nicest things.'

'Got any teeth yet?' He tugged gently at the shawl and Raffy's face appeared, a flower in soft folds with a great blue gaze.

Jodie looked round critically at the stock. 'You've not sold a thing since I left. Hardly anything at all.'

'Trade won't pick up much till spring, I reckon.'

It had been fun working days in the shop. The cash was the first she'd earned in London and that feeling was fantastic, not having to ask Art for money. She'd got to find a job now, but who'd want her with a small baby? 'I could soon shift some of this,' she told Tony with a made-up confidence.

'What about Art?'

'I could talk him into letting me. We need the money. We've had an eviction notice, you see.'

Tony frowned, said nothing while she made the tea.

'There's some biscuits in the tin . . . Why not go to the Citizens' Advice?'

'You know why. I just need a job again.'

'I'm not sure how Art would take it, love. He's not exactly friendly – '

'Only because you don't like him. Art's a good person, he's been so generous. I wish you'd make it up with him.'

'He wants nothing to do with me – '

Jodie cut in, 'Art only takes against people if he thinks you've got it in for him. He'll come round.' She wandered towards the rail of clothes: old dance gowns, sequinned stoles, top hats and penguin suits. A black lace mantilla went over her head like a veil.

'Gipsy lady,' Tony smiled. 'Tell my fortune?'

'A tramp lady.' She was putting on a long, narrow black coat with little buttons all the way up the front. Striking a pose, looking across to the mirror opposite, 'Well?'

'Fall Of The House Of Usher,' he replied.

'What's that?'

'A horror story.'

'Oh, you . . .!' She took off the coat, put it back on the rail and suddenly saw the time. 'Hey – gotta go.'

Tony returned the baby to her. 'Why not mention the job, see what Art says?'

'OK! You're a good mate, Tony. Thanks.'

'Chin up. And you, little fella.'

She sped back, up the stairs and into the flat. Art was already there and waiting. Straight off she could feel he was in one of his moods; her heart flipped downwards. 'Hello,' she tried with a forced cheerfulness.

'Where were you?' he asked.

Jodie hesitated for an instant. 'Went to buy your favourite tea. We've got sausages and beans. You hungry?'

Art gripped her arm tightly. He was intent, so strange. 'Listen, there's something you've got to do . . . For me.'

Climbing the long expanse of Highgate Hill he strode ahead then paused and waited. A car passed, tyres hissing and splattering the dirty snow. Jodie looked at his back, the leather coat rippling as he climbed. She'd do what he wanted, whatever would make him pleased with her again. The baby weighed heavy, her head and eyes ached from worry, from lack of sleep. Cooper wouldn't let them stay at the flat: she and the baby were homeless.

They reached the village. She followed him into South Grove then down a turning, a twisted lane dark with snow-laden trees. There was a great hush as if nothing lived for miles. Art stopped by tall iron gates and pointed out the tradesman's door that stood unlocked. He'd told her about the big house and about Rachel Rushe, adrift alone somewhere inside. Speaking softly, moving away to leave her, his face was vital with eyes that glittered. What was it he wanted from her coming here, asking for help? His independence – it had to be.

'I can't beg again, Art.' She was very close to tears. 'Don't you love me?'

'Knock it off . . . I'll wait an hour down the square. And remember – no mention of me. Right?'

'I don't understand.'

'Go on.'

There were so many things Art never explained. The baby was starting to wail again, his face red from the cold. Jodie pulled the tatty blanket close round him and set off through the side gate without another word.

From wintry dead undergrowth she climbed the crumbling steps and knocked. The house was tomb-like and silent, killed by nature. Shivering, she stared at the closed door as the baby's crying got louder. Somewhere inside was Rachel Rushe. Suddenly she thought: what if the woman's died somehow, maybe yesterday, and nobody knows?

Frightened, Jodie opened the door and peered into a dark passageway. Something hanging startled her: a gust of wind animated the stiff, creaking folds of an old raincoat. She went in, stepping through the tiled passage into the warmth of a huge kitchen. Deeper in the house a high clear voice was singing, ebbing and flowing on a great swell of harmony. She thought: Rachel Rushe is listening to the radio – and I'm trespassing. Drawing up a rocking-chair to the stove, she sat down with the baby and put him to the breast.

'Who are you? What are you doing in my house!'

The voice was shrill and Jodie jumped. Then turned, careful not to disturb Raphael's feed. The woman wore a long grey dress that clung to her bony frame. Wisps of pale hair stood round her outraged face.

The baby stopped suckling. Jodie nestled the weight of his head in her hand until, comforted, he began to drink again.

Mrs Rushe stepped closer, gazing at the baby for a long moment. 'How did you get in?' she interrogated as if the house had been locked. 'Who are you?'

'You never heard me knocking and the door was open. My baby was cold and hungry, I couldn't feed him out in the street.'

'Wherever have you come from?' asked Rachel Rushe faintly. She sat down in one of the chairs at the long wooden table. 'And is he warmer now?'

Jodie nodded. 'I'm sorry we startled you – '

'Who sent you?'

'What?'

'Who told you to come?' The voice was a knife.

Jodie reasoned quickly: she can't know . . . But the woman got up, stiff and abrupt, tapping her way along the tiles to the click of an opened door; a long pause. She's looking for him, Jodie thought and shivered. When

Mrs Rushe came back, had seen nobody, was looking down at her with a puzzled, wondering expression, Jodie said, 'It's just me and the baby, no one else. I was passing by.'

'You thought the house was empty and you'd be a squatter. I live here, young lady! And I don't believe a word of it.'

'We've nowhere to go and that's the truth.' Mrs Rushe was a suspicious old thing who'd begrudge shelter to any living creature. 'I'll be off directly, and leave you to yourself.' Raffy was starting to doze comfortably. She thought of Art waiting by the square, and how they'd walk down to Junction Road together.

Rachel Rushe took a kettle and filled it. 'If you're really destitute, why not go to the welfare office? Live off my back like all young people seem to.'

'It isn't my fault. And you've got to have a home first, see.' Mrs Rushe was very out of touch. Watching her fetch a caddy and teapot Jodie thought: she's lonely, that's what it is.

'I'm sure there must be Homes for unmarried mothers, if they're as young as you.'

'Maybe,' Jodie retorted. 'But who'd want to live in one! Would you?'

A gleam came into the woman's eye; it was almost a smile. 'Of course these days you're all dignified with the title of single parents – or almost virgin mothers – which naturally makes every bit of difference.'

She'd ignore the sarcasm. 'My baby, my little Raphael, he deserves the very best in life.'

Mrs Rushe did smile at that: widely and unexpectedly. 'Raphael? Is that what you call him. Here – a dirt-strong brew of artisan's muck. Drink it hot before I turn you out into the Dickensian blizzard. Now tell me how you propose to give Raphael the best in life – on the streets in winter. If what you say is true?'

Jodie thought about the landlord's threats. About sleeping rough and begging on the Bridge. She rocked the drowsy baby in the comforting warmth of the fire.

'I don't know,' she said.

'Look!' Jodie scattered cash triumphantly across their bed. 'A week's wages in advance. Mrs Rushe wants me to go every morning and clean her house. This was for a bed and breakfast.'

Art looked at the money, then slowly up at her. 'You're going to be her cleaner? I see. Said it would be all right, didn't I, girl?'

'She's not a dragon either, not really. And she trusts me to go back and work. It's warm there. But half that house must be empty, all those big rooms shut up.' Raphael woke as she started putting him to bed. 'Hush . . . Hey, d'you think Cooper would take a double rent? Or if he calls round when I'm not here you could say I left . . . It'll be funny pretending to Mrs Rushe . . . Art? Could we tell her about you and me?'

He looked up, edgy, 'Don't do that! It would sound all wrong now.'

'But she thinks Raffy's dad did a runner.'

Art explained firmly, 'She'd send you away, say I must cut it. We've got to look after the baby's future.'

'It's him she's interested in. Says she never had a child. Poor old thing, is she lonely, d'you think?'

'Rachel Rushe,' said Art thoughtfully, 'hasn't got family or friends. Nobody ever goes to see her.'

Now she understood him. Art had grown to care about the old woman, though he didn't like to say so. Suddenly Jodie saw the real reason for deceiving Mrs Rushe – Art must feel bad because they couldn't marry, she was seventeen and didn't have consent. She looked across at him. He'd turned on the TV to watch a detective show.

Sitting down beside him Jodie cuddled up and started laughing quietly. 'You,' she murmured. 'You're really a great big softie. Just don't want anyone to know, do you?'

He smiled a bit at her. She stroked his arm wistfully. It was months since they'd had sex, anything more than the slightest cuddles. The baby seemed to have put him right off. And Art was looking away from her now, concentrating on the TV.

DI Rick Cragge filled the screen. They often watched the series and she liked the big gruff detective. He was solid and mature, knew about law and guns, men's minds and more unusual things – old landscape paintings, Egyptian history. And it was easy to tell that he really loved his family, Gemma his wife, and the two children.

She settled down close with Art to watch *Cragge*.

6

Last night a girl came and sat on your steps for hours.
I asked what she was doing but she wouldn't give her
name and went away. Is the family silver intact?

W. Hughes.

Jack put down his neighbour's note, heart jumping.

Chloe! It must be. But why do that, after days of
silence? And on the one night he'd stayed with Sarah.
Why hadn't she phoned or written?

From the edge of his memory a picture emerged of
Chloe's handwriting. Backward slanting, looped and
disconnected ... and, half seen, his own name written
by her recently. Hurrying into the kitchen Jack shuffled
through a heap of unopened mail. There it was. Her
writing on the small blue envelope, the postmark – SW15
– dated 5 February. Three days ago. He tore it open.

Can you ever forgive me for the way you've been
treated? Jack, I miss you terribly. I must explain everything, then perhaps you'll understand. Please let me
know you forgive me for leaving – I love you. Chloe.

Reading and re-reading he could scarcely breathe, felt

60

like shouting. She wanted him back. A kind of shell, tight and brittle, dissolved as he realised how dead he'd been, how locked in misery. Memories of her flooded hotly through him.

He dialled her number but she wasn't home. At the gallery they said she'd left the job two weeks ago.

It was lunchtime, she'd be meeting friends or shopping. Vibrant with energy Jack called his agent, heard the reassurances he'd been needing. A lost producer? Others would give their eye teeth for *Cragge* – even one or two on the agency's books. He gave Bishop's New York number to Gideon.

He kept on phoning her until a slight uneasiness began. He was due at BAFTA for an awards evening; it ended late and he couldn't get out of it.

Anxiety woke him around dawn. Chloe's note had made her very vulnerable. It was pleading, unanswered; she'd come to his home and waited overnight while he stayed at Sarah's . . . What might Chloe be thinking?

He got dressed, started the Golf and drove through silent streets.

The mews was empty except for a milkman and his boy helper. Chloe's car was gone, the shutters fastened. She didn't ever do that . . . Jack knocked on the door.

'No one living there,' said the boy.

'Is she away or what?' he asked.

The milkman snapped, 'I suppose you'll be handing out keys next!' and their van whirred off. What had the boy meant? What had happened to Chloe?

She kept all those sleeping pills, of course.

Something icy crept into his bones.

Scrabbling in the window-box he felt the hard metal key. It was a single lock: the door slid open. Inside the house was chill and dark. He stumbled, waited to quiet the deafening rush of his breathing.

The rooms were both familiar and strange, subtly altered because she wasn't there. Adjusting to that, and to his criminality, he searched for clues. She still lived here – but half her clothes were missing and the electricity was off. Nothing suggested where she might've gone.

Then he was staring at the wall of photos, at the gables and tower of that gothic fantasy house. It must mean a lot to her, it had been framed with great style. A label said in neat copperplate *Whitting House* and on the back: *Dobson of Bond Street*.

Loud as a shot, a key turned in the door downstairs. She was home.

But the footsteps climbing were a man's tread. The big bulk of Justin Fairbrother walked into the room and seeing him, stopped abruptly.

They looked at each other with equal astonishment. Then Jack knew: this great fat bearded bullying friend of his was Chloe's lover.

Justin said, 'Jack. What're you doing? How'd you get in?'

'I was taught breaking and entering by an Inspector in the CID,' Jack replied. 'What're you doing with a key?'

'Watering the damn plants, picking up the post, what else?'

'Where's Chloe? What's happened?'

'Come and have breakfast. You look dreadful.'

Driving past the Heath, Jack asked, 'The mews cottage – does it belong to her?'

Justin looked oddly at him. 'Of course it's her house, who else could it belong to?'

In the Fairbrothers' kitchen Anna was trying to wipe breakfast off the faces of Sasha and Benjamin as they escaped from the table. Justin shooed them out of the room. 'Upstairs, animals! Go and scrub the jam from your chops.' Then to Anna, 'I found him skulking in Chloe's house, would you believe it.'

'Ah. Coffee, Jack?'

'Thank you. Is it true,' he asked warily, 'that her father's a famous concert pianist, retired and living in Aldeburgh?'

There was a brief pause. Then Justin roared with laughter. Anna looked reproachful but he was beyond noticing. 'Is that what she told you?'

'Yes. I gather that wasn't true either.'

Anna said quietly, 'Chloe's father died in a terrible accident at home when she was young. She found him – and that's what caused all her problems.'

'What kind of problems?'

'We've got to tell him,' Justin told Anna, then to Jack, 'Chloe's more than a bit loopy. Couldn't you tell? She's been in and out of the loony-bin for donkey's years.'

'She had a couple of breakdowns,' Anna qualified, 'and needs a quiet life. Not being pressured, like you've done.'

'What pressure?' Suddenly Jack felt furious. 'I've done nothing but respond! She behaved appallingly to me – '

'And now you know why. Leave it, Jack,' Justin said firmly. 'The girl's poison.'

Anna argued, 'But none of it's her fault.' She turned to Jack. 'You've done her no good at all. There's something about the way you grab hold of things and – pursue them to death. This is real life – '

'Where is she? Where are you sending her post?'

'We can't tell you.'

'Chloe wants to be left alone from now on,' Justin elaborated with relish. 'And if you've any sense at all, you'll keep away. Now tell me, you old fraud – what're all these interesting rumours about your series?'

Bullying didn't extract anything more from Anna or Justin.

How would Rick Cragge tackle this?

Driving uphill he knew the house was somewhere near. It was the key to her, she'd turned away at its name and seemed to lie about knowing it. She'd lied a lot and he needed answers.

A house was real, bricks and mortar. Maybe some retreat she'd vanished to? Crazy she might be – though Justin was famed for exaggeration, and jealous of the affair – but he'd got to find her again. He'd combed through London and Suffolk phone books: no one knew her. At Dobson's Gallery he drew another blank, the framing was done years ago. Then somebody said, 'It must be North London. Around Highgate Hill where Dick Whittington heard Bow bells. Lots of buildings there use the name.'

Jack inched the Volkswagen into a double yellow space in the village. The newsagent had no account for the house and didn't know where it was. Why not try the Highgate Society or Institution? Through Pond Square he reached a quiet grove and set behind railings a row of old houses, the name on a plaque.

A woman said, 'Whitting House? That's very near.'

He came to the silence of Hill Grove and entered its descending slope; behind a garden wall he glimpsed the steep roof, that narrow tower. The heads of cedars moved slowly in the wind, black mouths murmured in a watchful sky. He stopped at the gate and looked through its iron circles.

Whitting House loomed tall, crumbling into the past, held there like a myth through generations. He was transfixed by recognition, stretching back across time beyond his own life. That silence under the whispering, those details of the architect's mad fantasy: he felt lives, events, relationships – and the truth in its neglect. All effort and all vanity swallowed by ravenous plant life.

Was he about to find her here? The house looked unoccupied but in the present day it should be a warren of new apartments or some commercial centre.

The gate creaked stiffly when he raised the latch. Between bramble thickets the path was freshly cleared. He stepped into the house's shadow and knew he was being watched: glancing up at narrow windows he glimpsed a pale face, and caught his breath. It could've been her but drew back too fast for him to be certain. A desecrator, he banged on the door.

Greened gargoyles leered, mocking from above. From the bushes gleamed several pairs of eyes. Cats began to emerge, various coloured and hungry-looking. He knocked again, heard a bolt drawn inside and a key in the lock. The front door was pulled open with difficulty.

A girl stood with a baby in her arms. About sixteen, he thought, black-haired and skinny, oddly dressed in a cut-down tweed skirt and too big sweater. She seemed suspicious at having a visitor, braced like a little guardian.

'There now, they'll be after the cheese!' she cried crossly as the cats all shot into a semi-visible dark hall.

Jack smiled, she seemed suddenly comical. 'I'm sorry to disturb you.'

She smiled back sunnily. 'That's all right. If they get the cheese they won't get anything else for supper. Are you from the conservationists?'

Jack shook his head. 'I'm looking for someone called Chloe Rushe. Is she staying here?'

It startled the girl, her friendliness vanished. 'There's no one called Chloe here,' she said sharply.

'Or Rushe,' he persisted. 'She knows this house.'

The girl looked frightened. 'We can't help you. I'm sorry. Goodbye.'

She swung the door shut before he could answer. The bolt and key clattered. He wanted to know who else lived here; surely she wasn't all alone. Returning to the gate Jack held it wide and looked back. The girl was watching from a downstairs window. She didn't draw away this time but waited for him to go.

He found the woman who'd directed him. 'Did you see Whitting House? Remarkable – the last creation of Arkhurst before he died.'

'It is extraordinary,' he agreed. 'Who owns it?'

'That site was a hermitage once. Then an asylum which burned down, it's in our archives. And now? A private house – I believe Mrs Rushe still lives there.'

He touched the answerphone, it whirred then delivered: 'Jack – Bill Bishop here. Of course we hope to go ahead with *Cragge*! I've an excellent producer in mind and we're having talks. I'll catch you later in the week.'

A little hope filtered into his heart. Quickly, cynically squashed. The message was meant to keep him quiet and it would succeed. Mentally he was burying *Cragge*.

Whitting House... Chloe's mother must live there. Why was he reluctant to go back and try again? He had such a strong feeling that Chloe wasn't at the house after all. But she couldn't have disappeared from the face of the earth. She was somewhere.

It was that darkest, ebb-tide hour of the night, in the lowest month of February. He flicked the pages of a TV guide – soaps and game shows, documentaries, sport and news, films and 999 series. He'd tapped the life pulse of a nation and through his corny folk invention had woven tales round thorns of concern: the drugs problem, protection racketeering, property scandals, political corruption,

violent crime, the youth problem, the age problem . . .
Revolving in the wheels of deadlines, of being relied on.

Gaudy pages offered golden beaches and blue skies.
Spain and Portugal. Humbler monochrome dreams of
Pembrokeshire, Welsh cottages. A drawing caught his eye
of a stone cottage among mountains – its roof steep to
the ground with a tall chimney – because the Fairbrothers
owned something similar, he'd been there.

Jack threw down the magazine. Most of the time their
second home stood empty. It was in a remote moorland
area, at Llanydd among the Black Mountains.

He dialled. The phone rang for a long time before
Justin answered.

'Listen to me, Justin – Chloe's staying at Llanydd, isn't
she?'

'D'you know what time it is? It's four in the morning!'

'I'm going there,' Jack replied. 'Remind me of the
address.'

'Now you've woken Anna. Listen, don't do anything
stupid. Chloe's finished with you, she doesn't want any
involvement.'

'I've had a letter from her, to the contrary.' He listened
carefully to the silence that followed.

'Recently? When?'

Jack asked, 'Are you having an affair with her?'

Justin laughed. 'Give me credit for some intelligence.
Anna, d'you know what Jack suggested?' Now he heard
them both laughing. His anger grew.

Anna came to the phone. 'Don't start it up again,' she
began. 'You're all wrong for each other.'

'She's living in your cottage – at Llanydd? And alone
there in midwinter?' He was boiling with fury. 'Anything
could happen – there isn't even a telephone!'

'It's what she needs,' Anna retorted indignantly then
started to repeat her fatuous warnings. Jack slammed the

phone down. He was tingling with hope. He knew where Chloe was and had some idea how to get there. Her note to him was more than a week old but he re-read it to give himself faith. Throwing a few clothes into a bag, he left.

Dawn broke as he crossed into Wiltshire. The motorway was icy, snow fell and settled. Near Swindon he stopped for coffee with bacon and eggs. He was filled with more happiness than he'd felt since January. Buying an Ordnance Survey map he studied the moorland contours, found the tiny village of Llanydd. The cottage, he remembered, lay at the end of a track: it wasn't marked at all. If he could find the way and if the roads were open, he might get there by noon.

Filling the Volkswagen's tank he set off west again. Snow flurried over the road ahead, blurring out the sparse traffic. He sped past Bristol, crossed the Severn. Silver sea faded into white mud, the horizon was black and the world had turned upside down.

The snow decided his route. At Newport he turned for Abergavenny. On a quiet stretch of road, cars had skidded into a lorry that lay wedged across both lanes. Jack sat in a queue of traffic and remembered the accident he'd passed with Chloe on their first night together.

By afternoon he'd reached a narrow pass up to the moors. Snow had fallen all day. He drove slowly as the road twisted along the vanished landscape. A truck and abandoned car were stuck in drifts and a farmer, waiting for help, shouted at him not to go on since the upper moors had been snowbound this past week.

Jack called his thanks but drove on uphill. The cottage must be cut off. Did Chloe have food and dry fuel? How could she cope with such isolation? The tiny building would feel dark, closed like a tomb.

Two miles outside the village he inched round a precipice. The gorge fell sheer below to his left. Sighing into a drift the car stuck fast and he dug with his hands, clearing snow from its wheels. He revved the engine and it strained. Then the car skidded on black ice towards the unfenced ravine.

It stopped very close. Jack climbed out, shaking.

Abandoning the car he set off on foot. The cold was desperate, tearing into his body; the afternoon was quickly darkening, all life seemed frozen out of it. He felt like a man walking on a strange planet, stumbling through unmarked aching space.

Then he recognised the lane, because a phone-box roof jutted from the sea of white. He'd used it, walked along this lane in summer five years ago. It was bordered then with purple heathers, yellow gorse and bees busy in hot silence. He'd wandered here with Anna, slowly because she was eight months pregnant with her first child.

The track led across the moors from a ruined chapel. Jack tore off a dead hawthorn branch and sank it into the snow, trying to find solid ground. Peering through the gloom he frowned with astonishment, like a man who'd thought his race extinct: footprints led round the ruin. He remembered Chloe's feet, narrow and long-toed. He'd kissed them and it wasn't long ago but felt like years.

He cursed himself for having no torch, followed the prints and stumbled headlong into a drift. He couldn't see in the dusk and was hurrying towards a horizon grown invisible. The alien moonscape of moors stretched around in huge, still phosphorescent curves.

Then he exclaimed aloud because through the half-dark the light of a torch was bobbing gradually nearer. He thought it must be her and called. Silent in the snow the light and its bearer drew close, came by and stopped. It was an old bent mountain man.

Disappointment mingled with relief as Jack greeted him. The man looked out from layers of clothing, cautious as a moorland creature. 'Are you walking to the cottage, is it?' he asked.

'I'm a friend of the owner's, visiting. Is the woman still staying there?'

The old man seemed to pause for a long time. 'You need to be careful,' he replied slowly. 'Turn back if you don't know the path. This moor, she kills men easy in the winter.'

'But it isn't much further?'

'We get corpses, bury them.'

'I know the path,' Jack said and set off again.

But he didn't remember and soon fell into drifts in the dark. His clothes were saturated, heavy with ice. His body was numb and wouldn't obey him. Snow clung frozen to the mask of his face, his lungs burned as he climbed.

He saw the cottage far ahead, squatting low-roofed in its hollow. He gave a croaking cheer. No lights were on but the building seemed to glow with something, candles or lamps that she'd lit. Then it was lost round a whited-out slagtip from the old mines.

From the crest of a hill he saw it again much nearer, and began to stumble down the slope battering at the bright light snow like a moth bedraggled, flying between the mountains and the sky.

On the path he saw a deep drift had been dug from the door. He knocked and heard a voice, muffled, something he couldn't make out but it was her.

'Chloe!'

She couldn't get the door to open, and he leant forward shoving it with all his weight until suddenly it gave.

In the lamp's shadows he saw the extraordinary leaping in her face, as she opened her arms to him.

7

While she slept he'd entered her. Watched her wake to him inside, hot and hard, urgently spilling into her. Seeing her break: from realisation into a passive, chosen surrender, almost instantaneous.

Their skins were the same skin. The warmth of their bodies dissolved his mind and their limbs, tangled and heavy, fused into delicious drowsiness. Under low beams the black stove squatted, a red eye breathing scented woodsmoke. More snow wrapped the cottage in the dawn, silent and secret as a chrysalis. Chloe's face lay pressed into his cheek on the pillow.

Then he felt some small tension start, in her or in him, of separateness.

'You came all this way – for me?' she whispered. Then shifted away to look at him. 'My letter ... Why didn't you answer, Jack?'

'I never got it. When I did, you'd vanished.' He stretched, turned on to his side. 'And there was a crisis – *Cragge*'s producer left, my show is probably finished.'

'Paul Mann? He let you down like that?' Chloe seemed furious, biting back more words. He wondered at it because she didn't know what was involved. 'It mustn't be finished,' she said then sat up, hesitating. There was pain on her face. 'I waited for you all that night. Where were you?'

71

'Staying at a friend's. OK, at Sarah's.' A jolt went through her body and he hurried on. 'On her sofa. Nothing happened. I'd just drunk too much to drive home.'

Chloe was looking carefully at him. Did she believe him? He hadn't slept on Sarah's sofa. Quickly Jack asked, 'Why did you lie about your father? And the mews cottage, saying it wasn't yours?'

'You would've despised me for being loaded, you'd have run away. But then, it was me who ran.'

'Why, Chloe?'

'Something happened . . .'

'When I called Sarah back. What happened?'

But she looked puzzled, shook her head as if she didn't understand either. Jack said, 'I went to Whitting.'

He felt her sense of invasion. 'No . . . why?'

'Because of the photo. I thought it must be important.' Chloe said nothing and he went on, 'A girl came to the door and – '

'What girl? There isn't any girl at Whitting.'

'I don't know who she was. She had a young baby . . . Your mother lives there, doesn't she?'

Chloe answered, 'My mother died when I was born. But Charles and I were very close, and we were happy there together. He bought a publicity outfit and built it up – they had international orchestras, opera companies. My father was a remarkable man . . . Then he travelled across India and met this schoolteacher – Rachel – and suddenly married her.'

'It's her living at Whitting?'

Chloe nodded. 'And she loathes me. I was ten and he was all I'd known till she came between us. I ran so wild! They sent me away to school and I hated them more. Then I found him dead.'

He put an arm around her. 'Why didn't you tell me before?'

'I made up stories, even to myself, to try and forget. I had to. When you didn't believe me, it all started to close in again. I was ill before.' And she stopped.

'It's all right.'

'Anna told you? And you still came to find me?' Chloe seemed surprised. Then took a deep breath. 'I wonder how much you know. After my father died I was living on the edge, irrational for months. Then again later, a bit.' She went silent, waiting for his reaction.

So he said calmly, 'It's all right, you're well now.'

'The last few years, yes. But – you seemed to bring things back again, Jack. I felt – hunted.'

'Maybe,' he suggested, 'everything has to come back.' She was afraid, and he regretted saying it. He started reciting his angst of the past two weeks, confected into high comedy with a climactic flounder in snow-drifts. He got her laughing, just for a minute.

'No more separations.' She kissed him tenderly. 'We wouldn't survive, darling. We're meant to be together.'

Yes, Jack thought, we are meant to be. There was inevitability to it: fear, edgy with anger, shifted through him. While Chloe went downstairs to start breakfast, he lay thinking about what he'd learned.

People's lives and minds were his job. He had a little knowledge and realised that in psychological terms Chloe Rushe was the murderer of her parents. What might this mean? How might it manifest in the future? Skeletons in the mind must rattle and walk sometime, but he couldn't guess how.

Making his way down the narrow stone stairs he paused, surprised. On a shelf set into the rock stood a small torch shaped like a pen. He picked it up: it was the torch he'd given Sarah a couple of years ago . . . But it couldn't be, because Sarah wouldn't come to a place like this in a million years. And she wouldn't give his present to the Fairbrothers. It must be a similar one, which Justin or Anna had bought in London.

Now Chloe was bubbling with high spirits. It was the relief of self-revelation, the confession principle. And she was, he realised, very much in love with him. His own feelings had quietened into acceptance. He'd regained her. Now her dark secrets were out, he felt shadowed.

The fourth morning, they made a sledge of a tin-top table to carry drums of ashes from the stoves. Reaching the car they laid ash trails to the snow-ploughed road, later setting off for London.

Chloe was going to stay in Islington. They'd always got on best alone together but real life must include everything. She wanted to meet his friends. Jack felt critical of her dilettante existence – if she'd left the job at the gallery she should find another.

'People earn money when they grow up,' he insisted. 'Even mixed-up little rich girls.'

'You're just envious,' she retaliated.

They carried their bags into the house and immediately the phone rang. The voice was chilly and peremptory, 'My name is Ross Cammell. I'm the producer of *Cragge*.'

It had to be a joke – Justin, or Richard with his gift for mimicry – and he stayed silent thinking of a response. The voice queried sharply, 'Is that Jack Maine?'

'It is, yes.'

'Bill Bishop has put me in charge. We have a show but no scripts. When can we meet?'

'When would you like to?' Jack countered faintly.

'Say half an hour?'

'Give me an hour.'

'I look forward to meeting with you.'

Jack took a shower, shaved and changed, threw stories

and scripts into his documents case. He found a cab and was only five minutes late.

Ross Cammell was perhaps twenty-four, fresh out of college with a head full of seen productions and the brashness of ignorance. He'd been handed an opportunity and was going to push it for all he was worth. He was not friendly and seemed to see *Cragge*'s inventor as his adversary. A map of Europe had been pinned to one wall of Paul's former office, the separated pages of a large calendar to another. Each month was marked with different coloured pins as if by a campaigning general.

'I won't beat about the bush, Jack. What you've done so far is – uh, interesting. But we can't use it.'

'You can't?' Could he say goodbye so easily to working with Paul? Sitting opposite his new boss, Jack felt the burden of his own twelve years' experience.

'No. Frankly what we need is something newer and – well, younger.' Ross got up, he loped over the flesh-soft carpet. 'There is the ghost of a good idea in one of your stories,' he conceded. 'Where you bring in the young French-born detective. What I propose is that Pierre turns out to be Rick Cragge's long-lost son. And we redevelop the show between the two of them.' He paused for effect, so Jack smiled broadly. Ross went on, 'Pierre was born to Rick's first love, a singer in Paris, during his university days. Rick didn't know, of course. It gives us the Euro and youth factors all in one. What d'you think?'

The silence grew too long. Jack began laughing. '*Son Of Cragge! Cragge Et Fils* . . .? What're you planning to do with the old devil?'

He'd assumed the notion was a test, or a joke. Suddenly he realised that the man staring icily at him was deadly serious. Jack straightened his face.

Ross Cammell explained, 'We have serious budget problems, if we want *Cragge* to look like a contender.

And I do. We need co-production money. We're going to script it for Alain Duval.'

'You've talked to him?' asked Jack in surprise. Duval was a new film luminary with European appeal. Of course, the TV show would bring him a larger English-speaking audience. It would sell him to America.

'We've got him. If he approves the story outlines next week.'

'I see. What about Richard?'

'He drinks too much and he's going bald,' said Ross with finality. 'Oh, don't worry, we'll keep him on. But he must've found the main action rather a strain at his age.'

Jack started, 'Bollocks! Thanks to him, the show – '

'And another thing – the writing team,' Ross interrupted crisply. 'Writers in Britain have had far too much say. Action series in the States move faster and they're de-personalised. I'm going to hire a team of young professionals who'll rewrite each other's writing. With none of Ye Olde English crap cult about sanctity of the text.'

. . . Cragge takes the buck at French HQ for the red-light Mafiosi's catastrophic revenge raid. Simmering hatred between himself and Lecamp explodes in a violent row.

A message arrives from the crippled Tiefel: Cragge takes a helicopter with Hank to Fontainebleau and desperately tries to warn Lisette of the trap. But he finds Pierre has taken her place.

Trying to escape, the three men are caught in the crossfire of a running gang battle through the forest. Hank is killed. Cragge is driving his son to safety when Pierre is shot.

End of Episode Thirteen

Chloe glanced up at him from the printout.

'You hate it.' Flinging himself out of the chair Jack stood waiting to hear.

'No, darling. The stories work – XLTV ought to be pleased with them ... I just wondered why you're doing it.'

He thought: because I don't want to be left behind. He said, 'Because Cragge's my man. They mustn't kill him off. And as you know I'm an obstinate creature.'

Smiling at this she turned back to the story outlines. Jack realised he was so obstinate – or tunnel visioned, as Sarah had once described him – that this first week home together had turned out to be all meetings, all writing to deadlines again. He'd scarcely had any time for Chloe.

While she sorted the pages he concocted a tactful letter to Ross Cammell then sent off the lot by motorbike courier. He breathed a sigh of relief. 'Come here,' he said, enclosing Chloe in a long needy hug.

They lay together on the sofa. Her hand moved over his body, friendly and soothing. Then more insistent, becoming predatory. Until she got her way – he wanted her – but he wasn't in any mood for it.

'What're you doing?' he complained. 'I'm completely exhausted – knackered.'

'You poor old man,' she whispered, syrupy with false sympathy. 'What a terribly sad case he's become.' Breathing heavily into his ear she began to nibble the lobes, to lick then penetrate with her tongue. He caught her quick kindling, her hand stroked up his thigh to squeeze his cock. It had a life of its own. 'Is he really too worn out,' she went on, 'too utterly past it for me?'

Stopping her mockery with his mouth he kissed her searchingly, his tongue exploring, his mouth contained by hers. Rolled over on top of her, trapped that hand against his hardness. Now he wanted to explode – but no, not yet.

'Is that what you think?' Jack demanded, biting at her neck, nipping down past the collar-bone to her breast, nuzzling and grazing there at a taut nipple. Clothing tugged away so he could take her over, playing her. Finding the petals and bud of her, she was juicy and swollen, soft with longing and he delayed a while, idling with her to hear her cries, taking her very close to the edge. Then slowing and almost stopping, leaving her right there wanting him. Because he had to be deep inside her.

'On the rug,' she groaned and they slid from the sofa. 'Oh, please, you bastard . . .'

Her hands pulled at his zip but she was shaking, he had to help her and tore off his jeans, got free and rolled her over, stroked the curve of her buttocks from under the tee-shirt, pushing her legs apart as she guided his hand back under her.

He felt huge, as if he might break that soft body with his great hard eager cock, as if he might damage her. Went gently in and stayed motionless, poised there with her hair in his mouth, salt of her scalp under his lips, warmth and smell, animal and loving. Soft moans of some strange creature rising from her. He moved so slightly, fitting them together, all his weight on his elbows and knees so she was free, writhing and circling with impatience under him. Then thrust deep with a singing current that built flowing strong, throbbing all the way from his soles to his palms and the top of his skull, felt her contracting, a sweet contracting, that was exploding from her into him all the way through, lighting waves that rolled into every millimetre of his delicious body.

Then he must've fallen asleep.

Chloe woke him a bit later. He was thirsty and cold, half-undressed on the floor. She was pouring tea – and grinning all over her face. He felt like that too. It was the best they'd ever timed it, the first time they'd come

78

together. Jack felt elated now. They cuddled and kissed. As she went about that evening he couldn't leave her alone, stayed hungry for her. He said, 'Not so old. Not so worn out?'

Chloe laughed at him. 'Well – not completely, darling.'

'You're a terrible tease.'

'Oh, while you were busy earlier, Richard rang again. Why don't we ask him round – maybe tomorrow evening?'

'We're having lunch with my parents tomorrow.'

'We'll tell him – eight o'clock.'

'All that lot in one day?'

She laughed again. 'It'll be fun.' Her happiness was catching, an irresistible high. He found himself thinking it couldn't last.

Watching his mother's secret bewilderment he saw the four of them as random escapees: the lunch table, laden with niceties, became a liferaft drifting as each caught at anything solid, each hoped for common ground to appear.

Disembarking into the muggy conservatory they talked of his brother, visits to grandchildren. He thought: I've always disappointed them by being me.

'How is *Cragge*?' his father asked out of loyal habit.

'They're planning to face-lift the series,' Jack answered briefly, 'and stitch it new.'

'Oh, why?' Mary asked. 'Everyone we know likes *Cragge* the way it is. Now, Chloe, would you like to see the garden?'

Through the glass Jack saw Mary with Chloe, armoured in coats, step carefully together up the path. They made a strangely assorted couple. George quickly lit the pipe that his wife hated. 'Your mother's desperately curious,' he observed with some slyness. 'The girl's staying with you now, is she?'

'Yes.'

'Bit young – that'll be the verdict. She'd be a pretty thing in a different kind of get-up.'

Jack raised sardonic eyebrows, kept mute. George talked about plans for his department, Mary's pending retirement from the classroom. Mary and Chloe loomed re-emergent under the green glass waves.

On the way home Chloe was quiet. 'What're you thinking?' he asked as they went in.

'Your parents. They're so normal,' she marvelled. 'And naturally kind. You're lucky.'

'You've got to be joking,' he replied in amazement. 'They're OK, I suppose, but can't you see how she controls people? Manipulates and smothers – she weakens him.'

'Are you sure? They seemed – '

'Don't be fooled,' he told her. 'You don't know them like I do.'

Chloe said nothing. She was filling a vase with water, arranging the long gold stems of winter jasmine that his mother had cut for her. Then, 'Mary said you'd been unlucky with love. D'you think that's true?'

'Perhaps love has been unlucky with me, and never stood too much of a chance.'

'What d'you mean?' she asked.

He shrugged, thinking better of it. 'Nothing.'

'Well of course,' she retorted severely, 'you are an obsessive introverted fantasist, towing a terrible track record. Don't know why I'm with such a crusty old bachelor.' Then she grinned, flicking water at him from the sink.

They started cooking dinner together, Richard was due in half an hour. Jack washed the steamer, Chloe chopped vegetables. He tried out, 'You have a family, or part of one.'

Chloe turned hot blue eyes on him. 'Do you mean Rachel? Forget it. You've no idea what you're talking about there.'

After a moment he persisted, 'It's easy to see why you and Rachel did that wicked stepmother thing. Don't you think it must've been hard for her as well?'

'Of course it was.' Chloe frowned, intense. 'Contending with me, then bereavement. She got cheated by the fates too. But there was no love lost between us – ever.'

He didn't believe it and said so, strongly. 'But you loved the same person, that gives you everything in common. And if she's all the family you've got – '

'We're not family! You don't understand. That woman couldn't stand me. I grew up burdened by her hatred.'

'And you still are burdened, Chloe. By your feelings about her. I can sense them in you – cold and unforgiving.'

She was upset now. 'That's a horrible thing to say. I've had to put her into the past, to survive. What're you suggesting?'

'That it would be different now, because nothing stays the same. You need to get in touch – to lay the ghost. She's old, and you're all she's got left, too.'

'I can't do it, Jack. I lost contact with Rachel six years ago – deliberately. And I've never been back to Whitting. Why d'you want this? We're all right.'

An image came into his head of Whitting. Magnetic and haunting. He craved to see it again, to see more of it. 'We are now, more or less,' he agreed. 'But I think you'll need to sort it out – '

'With her? You're joking.'

Why was she so reluctant? He couldn't see any reason. 'With yourself, by meeting her again. Why not try – just once?'

Suddenly she was spitting aggression, and Jack stepped back involuntarily as she yelled, 'Stop mixing it, stop

81

getting at me!' She was shaking with rage. He felt electric, hyper-alert because if she threw anything, the nearest things were the boiling water or the knife and he could sense she was out of control. 'Leave me alone and stop meddling, Mr Amateur Shrink! If I did what you're stupidly trying to get me to do – you'd be sorry.'

They stood staring at each other. He felt a chaos inside him, it was coming from her. He began, 'Chloe, calm down – ' when the doorbell rang. She turned and disappeared up the stairs.

Jack took a deep breath and let in Richard. He poured drinks, put on vegetables to cook, peppered the steak and sat trying to talk normally.

Ten minutes passed before Chloe came down. She was pale but calm, deliberately friendly – and the actor wasn't to know how subdued she'd become. His tough-guy features lit up as they were introduced, his performance sparkled. Chloe relaxed in that wine-soaked, self-obsessed company until it was almost as if there'd been no quarrel.

Richard had met Ross Cammell and was gearing up for the battle ahead. 'I've been doing a bit of checking up on Wonder Boy,' he started with satisfaction as they ate dinner. 'It seems the lad's never produced a thing in his life before.'

'Doesn't surprise me,' Jack agreed. 'But apart from gross incompetence you've nothing to worry about.'

'They're not planning to kill me off?'

Jack reassured him. 'How could they – you are Rick Cragge. OK, Paul used to show you the storylines, so now I will. You're on every page.' He gave Richard a copy. And noticed that he had indeed started going bald.

Guiding the drunken actor into a cab, he went back to find Chloe. She was standing under the fire escape and staring out at the dark red city sky. Jack stood behind her, put his arms round her waist. She felt insubstantial, a chill wispy creature of the night. Somewhere far across the canal a dog barked aimlessly.

'We're a good team,' he said. 'Are you all right?'

She answered, 'I don't know what to do, what's best. I can't just leave it now.' Then she turned and looked into his eyes. 'Jack, I feel afraid. Hold me?'

8

Art lay thinking.

Sounds of traffic passing played faint chords in his memory. Day was light, night was sodium, each took turns at replacing the other. He'd stopped living but time crept on. Since the trinity was stolen away, the solidity of things and their everyday meanings had been stripped of clarity.

The street below was out of bounds while Goldman could wander there. Outside were dangers he could keenly sense. Letting slip the weekend market and odd jobs, even Whitting because his connection to the old woman felt so hostile. But cash for food was running scarce.

Now and then he'd go to the altar chest, draw the cloth of white damask and unpack from it the dice and cards, incense, two candles in tall silver stands. He'd set it up. Kneel on his heels, stay unmoving staring at twin flames until his vision changed, then close his eyes to see inside. He'd lose all sense of time passing but afterwards, when he looked again, he and the dice or cards were ready for their exchange.

Their answers kept returning him to waiting. Several black eyes of dice revealed no major change: six and one continued to escape him. The cards confirmed – he turned over the blindfold maiden, Two of Swords, the mysterious figure of the High Priestess, the stone tomb and its warrior – Four of Swords. Mutely, patient and passive like these symbols, he had to wait.

Art was in the kitchen and hungry. It was night. White fluorescence glowed over scrambles of the used and discarded and mould grew linking them into one. Checking empty cupboard shelves he filled the kettle then started back, nauseous as the gas flame jumped and crockery shifted. Something fell, cracked. It was an empty cup that broke clean into halves and he knelt down wondering. Above him gas hissed, the kettle waited cold.

When it grew lighter the traffic shrouded any secret intelligence. He crept, heart juddering, down the stairs and to the shop, took a loaf of bread with a plastic bag and hurried back. The electric shop held a dozen TVs zapping signals with babbling lights in a medley of messages and behind were music boxes, metal gadgets and his own reflection not belonging. Frowning fierce at squared screen circles, seeing someone he shot round, raking pedestrians that dodged him. No one met his eyes.

But the man was approaching. Art darted into a doorway, stood there with his spine curled like a shell. Too late.

Tony Ladd. Blocking his way. 'Morning.'

Art faced him. 'Off to work?' He grinned defiantly. 'Early to catch a few?'

'Ten o'clock? Some would call that downright indolent. How's things, Art? How's Jodie? Haven't seen her or the baby for a while.'

He'd ignore that. Let Cooper find a new informant if he could. 'I've things to do,' Art snapped and danced forward lowering his head.

The man retreated, Art got free and headed for his door as Tony said, 'You've dropped your shopping,' but

Art kept going. 'Want to come in and see my new stock?' the other persisted.

It was so transparent – pathetic really. 'Too busy right now.' Art darted inside. He held his breath, checking for sounds. A dark tunnel led up through smells of frying oil, the undertow of mildewed walls. He was home, locking the door. Breathing deep, gasping for air. No bread to eat but he was safe, and wiser. He wouldn't be lured out again in a hurry.

He'd turned up the Knight of Cups: arrival, approach, a messenger.

There wasn't long to wait. Art was aware of a change between him and the street, his breathing grew shallow as he concentrated. Then a key fitted into the lock.

It wouldn't turn. Someone knocked and called, 'Hey, Art!'

Jodie's voice. He noticed it was daylight and a long time since she'd visited. Cautious, he crept to the door and listened. 'The key won't turn,' she called. 'Take the catch off – let us in.'

Then disconnected gurgling sounds like someone snuffing it. The baby. Sliding up the catch he opened the door.

'Who'd you think it was?' Jodie stood with the baby fatter than ever. 'Had to wait hours for that stupid bus.' She wrinkled her nose. 'What a pong.'

Sulphur, or the melted wax. Art said, 'The gas, they put the dead inside.' That isn't right, he thought, adding, 'I didn't know it was Wednesday.'

She gave him a funny look. He must concentrate. 'I can see we're missed all right.' She set the baby down, looked around then back to him. 'Are you OK?'

Art nodded and switched on the TV, it spouted voices. 'I wasn't expecting you, Jodie.'

Getting up she stepped round his collection of electric

fires. 'All this stuff . . . You know, people throw these out because no one'd ever buy them.'

Concentrate. She was clattering round making tea, that's what she did when she visited. The baby played with its mittens: they were hanging on strings from wrists all stretched and bulbous with fat, glistening.

Jodie came through with the tray. 'You might give Raphael a cuddle, or play with him – your son. Isn't he lovely. Hasn't he grown up a lot?'

'He's bigger,' Art agreed. 'You're doing a good job there.' And he poured for them, steadying his hands with concentration.

Fixing a bib round Raffy's neck, 'He loves this banana yoghurt. Want to feed him, Art?'

'You'd do it better,' he said quickly, pleasing her, ''cause you know how.' Stirring sugar into tea he put the mug beside her while she spooned gluey substances into the baby's mouth. Soon its face was covered in yoghurt like a fruit.

He dragged his attention away from this. Needed to know what was going on. 'Well,' he asked, 'how's your posh life, up there?'

'Sort of paradise, to be honest . . . You ought to look after things, take care of yourself.'

'Can't manage without you,' he joked.

'Art.' She put out a hand, he winced. 'I've missed you. Were you ill? You look ever so pale.'

'Ah. I had the flu,' Art replied.

'Poor thing. Why didn't you let me know? Never mind, you'll get well and spring's coming so there'll be plenty of jobs. Your dad's clever,' she told Raffy. 'He can do so many things . . . I hope Cooper's leaving you alone now. He'll let you stay but – '

Stupid ignorant bitch! In rage he cut her prattle, turning up the TV and shouting, 'This is my home!'

She looked frightened so he smiled. 'It cost me, see. I could only pay with a gold Rolex I found, sold it down-stairs for the key.'

'About ten years ago, before Tony bought the shop –?'

'He's got to leave me alone,' Art spat in a harsh whis-per. 'Cooper's moved in others – you ought to know.'

Jodie was staring. Art glared back, argued with himself. Well, she couldn't understand. He tried, 'They're out for me – ' then changed tack fast, 'How's old Mrs R then?'

'Rachel and I are quite like friends – yeah, I call her that now. I wouldn't have it if she treated me like some servant.'

Jodie appeared so innocent but he could, of course, be wrong . . . 'Friends. What d'you talk about?' And a little laugh. 'Yours truly, I suppose. Nice one.'

'Funny old Art. Why would we? You're the odd-job man, to Rachel.' And she chattered on about life at the house, at his place. He marvelled at her lack of knowledge or awareness. Eventually she looked at the clock and got ready to go. 'Any chance of a lift up the hill, if you got those brakes fixed?'

'Ignition's gone,' he muttered. Then angrily at her look, 'It's dangerous, could blow up – I'll not get fried to a cinder.' Her disbelief could cover a knot of trickery. She needn't think he'd risk his life.

Steeling himself Art walked with them up Junction Road. At the bus stop she turned to him. 'What're we doing, Art? I like old Rachel, but she isn't easy and I can't stay there for ever. The baby needs – '

'It's not up to me, not what I want.'

She looked puzzled, 'Then who is it up to?'

'I can't tell you any more – just leave it!' The bus whooshed up on the sudden flood-tide of his red anger.

'Well. Take care,' she said, going to get on.

Art looked at the baby looking back at him over Jodie's

shoulder: it was succulent, like a piglet. A sucking pig, a plump tender little morsel that would be juicy and slightly salt with a light pork taste and those limbs would tear off easily, like jointing a skinned chicken.

The bus rose up the hill. The pale blur of baby was lost under Jodie's waving arm.

9

Warm, the kitchen. Earthen tiles with rugs scattered. Solid, grainy wooden table. Gleam of copper pans, newly shined; heat of the Aga, comforting. She'd put a lot of work into this place. She lived here.

The baby sat watching, propped among cushions in the rocking-chair. His eyes were big and anxious, they stayed on Jodie as she peeled the potatoes, braised the lamb. It upsets him, she thought. He gets unsettled going back.

Down by Archway there was a woman who begged near the supermarket with her little girl. That kid would grow up a beggar believing she must depend on handouts, on chance. It was clear Art saw himself as the victim of something more powerful outside. He'd told her to go to Whitting House, Rachel had asked her to move in – now Art was getting creepy, more peculiar. And did he care at all about them?

Picking up the rattle from where it had fallen, she shook it so the silver bells all rang in silvery sounds and Raphael's face broke into laughter. She kissed him. Her heart ached. Somehow he'd got to grow up knowing he was fine and the world a good place, a place to belong. He needed security and all that stuff – and she was beginning to wonder, should she stop seeing Art?

'So you came back.' Rachel Rushe's sudden, quavering voice made Jodie jump guiltily.

'Thought you'd got rid of us? No such luck.' It was lightly said but she noticed Rachel's unsteadiness – she'd been boozing already – as she pottered about putting things on the trolley.

'What's for dinner? You seem very busy playing at house, little girl.'

'It's a surprise, a special feast if I can cope with these funny recipes. You'd better be hungry.'

'As this appears to be some occasion,' Rachel mused, 'let us be properly festive.'

It was the first time they'd eaten in the mirrored dining room. A blaze in the big fireplace lit the carved surrounds, candles threw shadows with long tongues. They dressed up, Rachel in a black dress and diamonds. She looked quite something. The lamb goulash, she said, was celestial, as were the duchesse potatoes. And she chuckled over Raphael who'd refused to go to bed. 'Let him stay, why should he miss the fun?'

The benevolence was over-oiled. While Jodie heated the butterscotch pie Rachel insisted on looking after Raphael. Soon the baby grew unhappy, and the woman's temper darkened with a wine flush on her cheeks. Then it started – aggression and accusations, misery and self-pity. 'I'm not a complete fool, little girl. I know that one of these Wednesdays – wherever it is you really go, you'll not come back.'

'We go to the clinic,' Jodie lied doggedly. 'So they can check the baby and I can talk with other mums.'

'Since I never had a child, I'm not good enough for you? Except to be exploited.'

'Come off it. I earn my keep. It's not as if you're paying me anything now.'

'I'm just a poor old woman. Nobody cares. I might as well be dead.'

Sometimes she'd joke her out of it. 'You're so terrible,' Jodie agreed, 'people are scared to come near the place.'

Slopping more brandy into her glass, Rachel sulked for a while. She wore loneliness like a huge black cloak to frighten people away. 'You'll leave too,' she moaned. 'Nobody cares for the elderly. In this culture an emotional genocide is practised. But age was revered in India. In Bombay where I met Charles . . .'

She'd go on for hours about her wonderful husband, her perfect marriage. Only tonight she didn't. The baby was beginning to cry and his head felt hot. 'He's teething, poor love.' Jodie cuddled him; she'd already put some stuff on his gums.

'He's always bad when you've been to your mythical clinic. Then I have to suffer. Is it some sleazy rendezvous and you're ashamed to tell me?'

'Look at him – he's hurting! You might have a bit of sympathy for him.'

'You only go there to upset me,' Rachel ploughed on. 'I suppose it is some boy? I can see why your parents decided you're beyond help. They chucked you out, didn't they?'

Jodie felt sore and jagged from the baby's pain. She looked at the old woman's sharp, malevolent features hovering in the candles' flicker. The words burst out from her, 'You keep us like prisoners here, not even letting me go out once. We're trapped and don't you know it. You're a spiteful old thing – and now you can throw us out!'

Triumph twisted Rachel's voice, clear now, less slurred, 'You don't deserve to have a baby. I'll get him taken away from you first.'

Her heart stopped. But it was only the booze, wasn't it? 'If you did . . . then I'd kill you. I would, Rachel.'

'You are a piece of cheap rubbish. A failure who couldn't even keep her man.'

The booze, she reminded herself. Counted to ten, swallowed hard. 'When you're at the bottle all day – when you're like this – it just isn't worth me staying here.'

Rachel Rushe stared for long minutes, her eyes were ragged punctures. Then she got up and went out. The distant bang of a door. She'd gone to bed.

Jodie nursed the baby through the night. Now they'd be on the streets. Rachel was a lush and must've been this way for many years. Drink had turned her mind so she didn't belong with people. She was poisonous, and Raphael sensed it.

He slept now in her arms, but woke if she tried to put him down. She felt she'd never sleep again as the night became an endless tunnel she'd fallen into. Holding Raphael she wandered through the silent house, the empty rooms, saying goodbye.

In the attics, under rotted beams and holes full of sky, she opened the chest, took out an old book. Sitting down with the baby she began to read again.

We were in such good form – my darling happier than for days, our guests enjoying themselves out on the lawn. A perfect evening, Simon's quartet played like a dream. Then that little bastard climbed out on her window-sill, screeched to get attention and jumped. Everything ruined. I swear she's possessed by demons, barbaric. She torments my poor Charles, she's destroying him and I won't have it! He simply must agree to her being sent away in September . . .

Somewhere below, the old house creaked and stirred as if it was a long-dead creature roused. Or was someone

93

creeping about? Jodie listened until silence fell again, she could hear the shallow breaths of Raphael sleeping.

Putting back the diary she took out another and looked through the crowded, black-inked pages. The writing had grown spiky, distorted by angularity.

In India, that merciful tradition! The wife was permitted to throw herself on to her husband's funeral pyre. But here I am condemned to live on fire and alone.

Everything must be kept as it was, until I go.

The girl's been invited to the Hatherly place when she comes out, and Dr Spence approves. It is salt to the wound that I'm cursed with the constant reminder of this mad and hateful child.

Six years to the day and I ache for death. But it must come to me, my darling.

A cry tore up from somewhere in the garden.

Looking out Jodie saw the beginning of dawn. She gazed down on the walled jungle and something moved. It was a cat, several of the cats were there. And leading them, stepping through the undergrowth she saw Rachel, still in the black dress, staring into a stagnant pond as if something precious might be in it.

She could've been awake all night, wandering there.

Jodie felt tears on her cheeks. They were of pity and shame.

After that everything changed.

'I was dreadful,' Rachel said in the morning. 'I can't cope but it's easier with you here. You won't leave, you are happy really?'

She was so contrite, afraid they'd go. Jodie felt a sense of power mixed with relief; she desperately needed security and old Rachel was her best bet. 'It's just the booze,' she pointed out. 'You've got to try and stop, it makes you a flipping ogress.'

Rachel nodded. 'And – I shall give you an allowance, my dear. It's only fair.'

Jodie got a few pounds a week: she hoarded them for the future. Nothing was secure. Not ever – she'd learned that early on. But there were things Rachel said, like, 'You're the only daughter I have – think of me as your mother.' That made her feel warm, and it made her think.

What she'd never expected was how much she was starting to care for old Rachel. Moments when she felt washed away by tenderness. Like on the terrace when Rachel sat in a wicker chair that was round as a cradle and, with her wispy limbs and fine pale hair, seemed like a child in need of protection. What Jodie felt then was the beginning of commitment. She was being relied on: like a real daughter, she must stay and look after poor Rachel who was afraid of everything – of falling, or sleeping; of venturing outside or being left alone.

She was reaching out, taking the baby from Jodie's arms and he didn't mind now, he'd got used to her. Raphael shrieked at the cats that slunk round the terrace, he threw out his arms and trembled with excitement. Rachel laughed. 'This is Melchizedek, and this white lady washing her face by the statue is Bathsheba. You'd like to grab hold of all my cats, wouldn't you, darling? You'd like to positively devour them!'

Rachel couldn't stop drinking but Jodie coaxed her to eat more. She couldn't bear how thin Rachel was, and kept learning how to cook properly for her. Soon Rachel was buying them new clothes, and looking after the baby like a grandmother.

Under it all lay the thread of secrecy. Art's blond head bobbing past the French windows, that gave her a jolt. He was making a path from the terrace, down to what used to be a pergola. By now the garden was a mass of budding, multiplying weeds.

Sometimes Art turned up and sometimes he didn't. Rachel decided to have flowers in a bed by the windows, but she wouldn't let her gardener come around more than once a week. When Jodie was sent to Art with messages, he and she would speak like strangers. And if she went to his flat on Wednesdays, that distance still seemed to be between them, grown solid. She didn't feel afraid of him – she had Rachel now – but their lives couldn't be more different, and it was his choosing.

So she lived from day to day. Until suddenly it all looked like changing again.

'Although it's true I never had a child – I do have a stepdaughter,' Rachel confided at breakfast one morning. 'After years of silence, Chloe has written to invite herself here next Sunday.'

A real relation? A real daughter of sorts! Jodie stared down at her hands twisting with anxiety, realised how much she never wanted to go back to Junction Road. 'But if you'd rather she didn't come – '

'I shan't stop her,' Rachel interrupted proudly. 'Although perhaps I should. But why now, after so long?'

Jodie remembered, 'A man came here in February. Looking for someone called Chloe . . . I never thought it was important. I sent him away.'

Rachel frowned. 'Some professional adviser of hers. Snooping on the condition of the house, or trying to find out who lives here. That girl must be after something. There'll be trouble.'

Jodie slipped her hand through Rachel's. 'You've got me,' she reminded.

When Rachel went to rest Jodie crept upstairs and stopped at a door, listening. She turned the iron key and went in. Under years of dust the room lay shuttered and drawn so far into itself that she expected it to suddenly fall in on her – the uninvited – with a great shout of splitting timber, tumbled plaster. She closed the heavy door just to and stood inside with drumming heart.

It was the bedroom of a well-loved child, but as if that child had never grown past ten or so. As if it had died. There was nothing pastel here: the walls were scarlet, bordered with trumpety flowers in tendrils of gold; the ceiling deep blue with moon and stars. A tall brass bed lay draped in stuff all velvety with dust. Behind the shutters, stained glass showed birds and animals.

Jodie tiptoed between child treasures. A big statue, an oriental dancer with four arms, held little sunhats of battered straw. In a model farm stood cows and pigs. Dolls and teddy bears looked down from shelves of fairytales and picture books.

The dressing-table was as if an older girl, thirteen or so, had wandered out for a moment – then never come back. Dust and cobwebs shrouded the corpses of insects. A lipstick lay open. And a silver set of hand mirror and brush, black with tarnish, waited to be picked up again.

Jodie thought: how old will Chloe be now, and how crazy? For getting locked away she must be mad.

Touching the talismans of the unknown girl she whispered, 'She mustn't come back. Rachel mustn't want her back.'

10

'These are not my stories,' Jack insisted, tapping the bundle of neatly printed pages. 'Why do they have my name on?'

Ross Cammell looked away through the window at the Thames below. 'Don't exaggerate, Jack. There had to be a few adjustments. We can talk after the meeting if you want.'

Filing into the commissioning meeting were five hungry young men. Their faces were covered in determined smiles, their briefcases held the storylines. Jack knew he should walk out but he couldn't. This was the future.

Ross, congratulated on the stories, accepted these compliments. 'Before the fight for episodes,' he said mysteriously, 'there is one more change. The deaths of Cragge's family are being brought forward from Episode Ten, to Four.'

'Good. Fade out the old wrinkly and get things moving,' said someone.

Jack asked, 'What are you planning to call this show?'

'I'm sure we'll come up with a good title. Now – who's going for what?'

'I'll do you a great bombing raid ep,' someone got in quickly.

'The CIA story, that's mine!'

'I'm doing the hostages!'

There were many squabbles. The producer sat back and smiled, occasionally played the hand of fate. Other episodes – each violently action-packed, aggressively brain-free – were claimed. Each story belonged at its centre to Alain Duval, aka Pierre. Jack was asked to write the deaths of Cragge's family, which no one else wanted, and a later episode.

'My agent will be in touch,' he told Ross and drove home fast. His house was full of things from Putney, food lay waiting in the kitchen for supper with Justin and Anna. Upstairs Chloe was putting together a new dark-room. She turned off the infra-red light, let up the blind when he came in.

'Don't let me stop you,' he said.

She was fizzing with confidence, ambition he'd never seen before. 'I've got commissioned! A two-page spread for *Metro* magazine. And with my name on, a real credit.'

'But that's wonderful, darling.' He felt a brief stab of some other reaction, and pushed it away. It was the wrong moment, that was all. 'Wonderful. What's the subject?'

'Perfect for me, a photo feature on city farms – I shall wallow in metaphors.'

'Pigs among the high-rises?'

'Sort of thing. I'm going to use three farms – '

'Well that won't be difficult,' Jack said meaning it as a reassurance.

But Chloe quietened. 'It's a tiny job for a free magazine. Nothing to get excited about . . . How was your meeting?'

'Diabolical, disastrous.' He went to call Gideon and ten minutes later rejoined Chloe. 'Let's cook together.'

She wasn't to be put off. 'What did Gideon say?'

'I'm to rub along with Ross Cammell. He's the stepson of BA-TV's chairman Lex Bailey – who happens to be an old personal friend of Bill Bishop at XLTV.'

Chloe was furious. '*Cragge*'s your invention – and it's done so well for them.'

'Writers don't have rights – or this one doesn't. Ross Cammell's a new broom determined to make his mark.' He felt curiously calm, almost pleased. He could resign, shed years of investment and drudgery. A dizzy sense of freedom began. 'I could do anything, now.'

'Of course you could, darling, anything you want.'

Moving close to Chloe where she stood he kissed her, smelling the scent of her skin, feeling pleasure in her body through the thin fabric. 'Anything at all?'

'Hey, what're you doing?' she laughed as his hands stroked up under her dress. 'They'll be here any minute.'

She was kneading dough into a ball, hands white and dextrous with pliability. He stood pressed against her, watching as she took an empty champagne bottle from the sill and began to roll the pastry smooth, flat. His own hands were exploring all her soft places.

'We haven't got time. You'll just have to want.' Chloe wriggled, tried to push him away. She was taking a dish of strawberries from the fridge, and he wasn't letting her back to the worktop.

'This won't take long,' Jack whispered, taking the bowl away from her. He sought her tongue, slid his fingers round elastic and tugged, peeled off their clothing. She was growing hot and wet. Scattering abandoned food he grasped her buttocks, shoved her against the fridge.

'Jack,' she gasped, then gave a little sound of surprise or pain as he pushed into her. She steadied, hand against the wall, then stumbled, furniture upturning and in a muddle of its legs and their own limbs, still inside he backed her against the table. 'Ah . . . you're crazy . . .' She was laughing as he leaned over her, something sticky squashed on her face, he was licking it off, sweet sugary stuff then thrusting hard in her. An image of the day's

100

meeting flashed into his mind then was gone, banished. He didn't want to slow or wait for her. The door-bell rang shrill and he thrust shoving a kind of anger into his coming, his shout.

He was still entangled in her, their hearts and pulses thudding, hot breaths struggling when the door-bell rang again.

'Damn,' panted Chloe, tousled and half-undressed as they slid apart. 'Look at the table, the floor . . . and me! Shall we forget about them?'

'No.' Jack pulled up his jeans as the door-bell went on ringing. He towed Chloe to the door.

'Where were you?' quizzed Justin on the doorstep, looking from him to Chloe's flushed face. 'We've been waiting ages.'

'Urgent cooking.' Jack stroked Chloe's haunch in fare-well, so that Justin would see, and ushered in their guests.

'We were in the middle of laying the table,' Chloe explained with a distracted smile.

'Really?' Anna gave them a sidelong glance, righted a chair and stared at squashed fruit. 'Looks as if the pud-ding couldn't wait.'

Justin pretended to see nothing, was instantly opening bottles. 'So you two are an item?'

'Despite all your best efforts.' Jack smiled pleasantly.

'What d'you see in him, Chloe? I notice you've both avoided us. We want the latest instalment.'

Chloe asked Jack, 'Shall we forgive them or not?'

'He'll put us in his next play. Fortunately they're never produced.'

'We were only acting for the best,' protested Anna to Jack. 'After all, look at the way you dropped poor old Sarah.'

Jack's temper snapped. 'I did not drop Sarah. She

101

may've got fed up with my anti-social writing habits, but I never dropped her.'

Chloe remarked lightly, 'I didn't know she was an ex.'

'It isn't important,' Jack began, very aware of Chloe.

'There you are!' Justin was triumphant. 'Keeping secrets – don't trust him an inch.'

'As he says, it isn't important,' Chloe snapped back. 'Anna, you sit here. And Justin . . .'

Anna said, 'Isn't it good about Chloe's commission?'

'How did you get the job?' Justin asked in a voice full of innocence.

Chloe answered vaguely, 'Someone I used to know suggested me.'

'Oh Jack,' Anna remarked. 'We heard Paul's working for the BBC now.'

'Is he? What on?'

'No idea. Are we going to eat in the kitchen?' Justin demanded, collapsing into a rush chair which creaked. Jack prayed it would break. 'Chloe shouldn't eat in kitchens. She's an heiress.'

'Oh Justin, I'm not – how stupid.'

'Islington's abominable, Jack. Why don't you live somewhere civilised?'

Jack laughed, but he was stung. Justin picked up his plate. 'What's this?'

'Swordfish. Surely you've had it before?' Chloe asked.

'Good sauce, anyway. Yours?'

'Ours,' she replied firmly.

'I see *Cragge Mark V* went out largely unnoticed,' he continued. 'What's happened to *Son of Cragge*?'

Jack told them. Chloe added, 'They're turning it into *Boys' Weekly*, like most TV series.'

'What does Gideon say?'

'Nothing useful.'

'Sack him,' suggested Justin then began to crow,

boasting blatantly, 'I've got a new option on the first play. More dosh this time. We're getting the attic converted.'

'At least it'll save you from actually writing anything,' Jack said. Justin's gift lay in talking money out of people. Most of his work stayed unproduced, often unwritten. Producers flocked to pay for Justin's expensive tastes, while he himself slaved to keep proving his greater success with the public, yet earned less.

'Envy,' countered Justin with narrowed eyes, 'will get you absolutely nowhere.'

Jack turned to Anna. 'Chloe tells me you two go back a long way.'

'She and my sister were at school together.'

Chloe explained, 'I used to stay with them in the holidays.'

'Do you know Whitting House?' he asked Anna.

'We're going there on Sunday,' Chloe said, 'to see Rachel.'

Anna looked horrified. 'But why?'

'Why not?' he countered.

'For every reason!' Anna was staring across at Chloe. 'Was it his idea? You don't have to go along with that, love.'

Jack argued, annoyed, 'Chloe wants to go. What's the big deal?'

'Yes,' Chloe agreed. 'It's a good idea to visit Rachel. Don't worry.'

'Is there any coffee in this house?' Justin asked.

At this road junction, built to overlook the city of London and St Paul's, there was consecrated in 1829 the Church of St Pius. Its gothic design stretches from deep vaults, enshrining bones from the old chapel previously on this site, up to its many steeply aspirant pinnacles. It is a building not of this earth.

> A mystery attaches still to St Pius's Church. Amid
> the fervour of community in the war years, on the night
> after Christmas 1940, a young pacifist was found dead
> below the altar steps. The cause remains unexplained
> to this day. Some would have it that this victim was
> felled by the hand of God as he prayed. Others conjec-
> ture a more earthly hand, driven by motives we cannot
> know . . .

Images blurred in the pages but as Jack shut the book they
sharpened, displaced: a child evacuee among a crowd; a
woman in the rubble of her home; a soldier holding his
new-born baby; a pretty nurse dancing with a blinded
man.

Why a pacifist? he thought. Why laid out like a supreme
sacrifice? How, unmarked?

His thoughts lay like the stones of fruit – solid, not
vaporous as questions but fermentable. Stacked in the
back of his head, as he raked through a long sparse night
of obligation. He was giving Cragge a fiery send off and
the detective's few million fans wouldn't know if he'd
survived. Did it matter?

Chloe was awake all night playing music. At noon he
found her on the tow-path; her silence with him lasted
until they were almost in Highgate. She said, 'Rachel's
known me longer than anyone – and she hates me.'

'She'll be glad to see you again – stop worrying.'

'You're going to finish up hating me too, Jack.'

'Don't be an idiot – I know you pretty well.' She had
to be exaggerating in her mind.

They parked nearby – the drive was forbiddingly overgrown – and approached the place on foot. Jack caught
his breath, marvelled at it. Before them Whitting stood
silvered by the sun, innocent as a picture in a children's
book.

But Chloe stumbled the words, 'She's let it fall into ruins!'

She must have remembered it as a well-kept home. Now he began to notice the black stains in crumbling brickwork, timbers missing from its decoration, curls of paint that hung like skin from rotting sills.

They stood on the step. The door fell open to reveal the pale head and neck of an old woman. She seemed disembodied. The mouth was a twisted gash of a smile, the dark eyes gleamed. Jack saw her skeletal frame was clothed in black that merged into the hall behind her.

'So you came,' she said, and looked at him.

She wasn't all that old, maybe sixtysomething. White-grey hair was pinned up on her head. Cheek-bones ran like blades in paper to a neck unusually long.

'Rachel,' Chloe began, then stopped. He filled the awkward pause.

'I'm Jack Maine. Pleased to meet you, Mrs Rushe.'

Nodding at his outstretched hand she gestured them in. He felt a twist of excitement up his spine. The hall, unlit, was heavily handsome with carved cedar stairs and panelling, bizarre as a tree weighted in dark blossom. He caught glimpses, as they passed, of rooms like baroque fantasies undiluted by change into present time. They came to a drawing room painted green, French windows lit its gloom.

'A remarkable house,' he said.

'You're a surveyor?' Rachel Rushe asked immediately. 'Or a solicitor?'

Jack laughed, embarrassed. 'Just a writer of fiction. I dramatise.'

'Really? Sit down, don't stand there looking like spare parts.' And she acknowledged Chloe for the first time with a glance. 'So you're here after all these years.'

'You're looking well, Rachel,' Chloe said.

'Am I likely to live?' she gave a derisive snort then picked up a silver handbell. Its ringing brought cats, multi-coloured and ranging from elegant to ugly, then a rumbling tea trolley.

At first Jack didn't recognise the girl.

'Thank you, Jodie, I know it's early. Join us for tea.' There was a hint of pleading in Rachel's voice.

It was her all right but neatly dressed and changed in her manner, she belonged here. 'We've met,' he said.

'Jodie, this is Mr Maine. And Chloe Rushe.'

A murmur of hellos. Fragile bone-china cups, plates of cake were passed.

'I'll fetch Raphael,' Jodie said.

Drawing a gift from her bag Chloe asked, 'Do you still collect? We brought you a little thing.'

Rachel unwrapped the small crystal and silver jug, it matched the sugar bowl. Chloe sat watching rigidly. 'A milk jug,' the woman murmured then replaced it in the tissue wraps. 'Here's little Raphael, isn't he adorable? He'd like a biscuit, wouldn't you, darling.'

What was behind the exclusion? Jack could sense Chloe retreating into something impenetrable, something she'd trapped herself in a long time before. It was the reason she'd fled to Llanydd from him. As her stepmother cooed over the baby Chloe turned to Jodie, 'You call him Raphael? What a beautiful name.'

'Look, darling, lots of people,' Rachel purred, turning her back on her visitors. 'He's mother's little angel – just look at that smile.'

So they admired the baby. Jack felt angry. The woman was not stupid, not unaware of her effect. She hadn't seen her stepdaughter for years – and didn't want to now. How soon could they leave? He could sense the rage under Chloe's smouldering silence. She'd become a stranger to him during the past half hour, oddly unreachable.

'Dear Jodie rescued me, I was utterly alone.' Turning to Jack, 'I could've been dead, no one cared. But now I have Jodie and Raphael.'

Jack asked sharply, 'Why didn't you contact Chloe, Mrs Rushe – or answer either of the letters she sent you?'

She darted him a look full of spikes. 'Chloe was far too busy for years to remember me. Well, how are you amusing yourself these days?'

Chloe mumbled something and Jack cut in, 'She's working as a photographer, and living with me.'

Rachel's eyes raked to Jack and back again, speculative. She began to charm him, almost to flirt as if she were young and they were alone. Soon they were. Jodie went out and Chloe followed with obvious relief. He sat trapped. Rachel Rushe was trying to impress him, win his loyalty – perhaps away from Chloe. She talked of the past and Charles' adoration, and he began to pity her strange, desperate performance.

She showed him photos. Chloe's father was a matinee idol run to seed, smooth and blond, moustached. He had a self-satisfied smile, the charm of a Casanova and narcissist. Surely he was bored with a young child's company?

Charles had been electrocuted by garden machinery ten years ago. As she spoke of it the woman shrank to paper thinness, older than death. That catastrophe had destroyed three lives. Stealing the minds of this wife, that child, it had left them in a place where life couldn't root.

He shook himself: he mustn't believe that.

Crossing the terrace he stepped down to a bramble-covered walk where Chloe stood. 'Time to go.'

She looked up, answered, 'Everything's small ... But that happens to childhood – like using a telescope backwards.'

He looked up at the house, massive, a reddish-purple

in the fading light. Then to Chloe like a lost kid in that chaos of garden, her eyes puzzled and hurt. He tried to hug her, felt her struggling for control. Not tears but the rage that bubbled in a torrent through her.

Jack sat with her, held her hand.

'I'd give anything,' he remarked with a little laugh, 'to have a house like Whitting.'

'Really?' Chloe was astonished, eyes cleaving all through his expression. 'You like it, you'd want to live here?'

'And how.' He smiled again at the irony of it, and the impossibility. 'Chance would be a fine thing. I'll never have this kind of money.'

Rachel Rushe's voice floated down to them from the patio rail, 'Don't let us keep you. I'm not used to visitors, and you have to get back.'

Standing suddenly, Chloe looked straight at her stepmother, 'I want to restore this pergola, to clear it and replant. Will you let me do that?'

Jack stared at her, then swiftly at Rachel. Something struggled in the woman's face before she turned away. 'I shan't stop you.'

'We'll come next Sunday.'

Rachel Rushe disappeared into her house without another word.

'Why on earth?' Jack demanded. 'When she's been so – '

'My father designed it. You can't imagine how beautiful these gardens were. Full of roses – choked to death now.'

He still thought it strange she should want to return. She'd been made so obviously unwelcome. But to come back here . . . He felt a lightening and quickening of excitement.

'Come on,' she said.

They listened in the hall. No one was around to say

goodbye. As they went out he heard, up beyond the big staircase, a door slam violently as if from a draught.

He glanced at Chloe. 'OK?'

She nodded.

Driving through narrow lanes he looked for the church he'd read about. There ahead swam the spindle spires of St Pius, piercing a blue and white cotton wool sky. He drew in at the kerb. The place had a closed, battened look and he remembered churches were kept locked.

Chloe asked, 'What're you looking at?'

'Nothing.' Secrecy had fallen between them, he didn't know why. Driving on he saw a red signboard nailed to the church porch, *For Sale by Jackson*.

Jack started, smiled at the coincidence as Chloe said fiercely, 'I shall never have a child, never.'

Rounding Archway Junction, 'Why not?' he asked before remembering.

'I'm sure Magdalen never wanted to be pregnant, perhaps she knew I'd kill her. My mother had everything – love, beauty, fame as a pianist.'

Instinctively he knew she was lying again. But why now?

For a week they were skaters on thin ice – on the surface, almost as usual. He couldn't find out what she thought and felt. She'd moved away.

The deadline loomed for his last script. Struggling against sheer gravity – of other forms and shapes in his mind – he at last gave in and researched microfilm at the Newspaper Library. The pacifist, a sometime teacher then hospital orderly, had been found dead under the altar. The cause of death was never determined and an open verdict had been recorded. It was scarcely an unsolved murder story. And yet . . .

Driving south from Colindale he teemed with questions and inventions: why, how, who . . . Ignorance swelled his curiosity into a kind of passion. He sped down the A5 against a rush hour heading north.

Chloe was in the living room and all around her lay scattered photos of cityscapes full of animals. She scrunched them together so he couldn't see. 'I can't do it!'

''Course you can. Let me see.'

She shook her head, hid the pictures. 'You just missed Sarah on the phone.'

'What did she want?'

'You of course. We had a long talk – all about you. She sounds OK, why haven't she and I met?'

'I'll arrange something,' he promised vaguely, heading towards his study.

'We already did. If it's all right with you we'll have dinner on Friday.'

Jack felt annoyed. It would eat further into his writing time and he didn't think they'd like each other. 'I can't change *Cragge*'s delivery date. We're going to Whitting on Sunday, the run-up's from Monday and the director needs a draft.'

Chloe looked at him. 'I'll put her off, then.'

He thought for a moment. 'Let me try to get the script done before the weekend.'

She laughed, sounding relieved. 'For a minute I thought you didn't want me to meet Sarah.'

11

He didn't want her to meet Sarah, it was true. On Friday night they walked down Fulham Road to an Italian place. Sarah had booked one of their old haunts.

'Hasn't it got summery for April,' she remarked, seated on the familiar terrace. 'Jack's been secretive about you, Chloe.'

'Nonsense.' He wished Sarah would dredge up some tact from somewhere. 'Just busy.'

'I don't even know what Chloe does. Are you a writer? A Londoner? You're not what I expected.'

They ordered before Chloe replied, 'I'm a wannabe photographer, and a Londoner. What were you expecting?'

'Not that you'd be so – young.' Sarah stumbled over the words, clearly correcting herself. 'I've never seen him so devoted.'

'Oh but surely, when you were together – '

'That wasn't devotion, so I'm desperately envious.'

As they talked their way through three courses with three bottles, he thought how different they were. Sarah's direct ebullience made her a bossy big sister. Chloe's mood was elusive and she'd developed a brittle gaiety – a successful camouflage if you didn't know her. She was drinking too much, something he'd never seen before. It was easily done in Sarah's company.

'Have you learned to put up with his writing yet?' Sarah interrogated. 'The house could go up in smoke and he'd never notice. Don't let him neglect you. If he starts, you must bully him.'

'How should I do that?' smiled Chloe with a sideways glance at him.

'Scream and nag – I did. Maybe this is bad advice,' she mused. 'Have you met George and Mary? It took him a year and a half to introduce me. And the two of you are off to Spain – when?'

'Next month, for a holiday,' Jack put in.

'Meeting all the tribe?' she teased. 'It must be serious! Let's have some grappa, shall we?' Then she started chiding him about new ideas, pursuing contacts, wheeling and dealing for the future.

'I know what I'm doing next,' Jack stopped her. 'A second novel.'

They were both surprised. Sarah frowned. 'How many writers ever live off novels?'

'He should do what he wants,' retorted Chloe, firm.

Sarah raised her eyebrows. 'He's hell to live with when he's doing a book. Don't say I didn't warn you.'

Chloe changed tack. 'What're you working on, Sarah?'

'Oh, a couple of series.' Then she must've noticed Jack's curiosity: she was usually so full of her projects. 'The one about Japan, you know.'

'Set in Japan?' asked Chloe. 'Sounds unusual.'

'What's the other series?' Jack pursued, sensing her reluctance. 'Not that Wilder thing?'

'Mm, that's it. Goodness,' she exclaimed, 'I hadn't realised it was so late. Lovely meeting you, Chloe – glad you've forgiven me for enticing Jack into my bed.'

Chloe's expression fell. 'What d'you mean?'

'Oh – nothing. Sorry! See you both,' and Sarah hurried away up the street.

Chloe stared after her. 'What did she mean, Jack?'

'Come on,' he said, guiding her to the car. Damn Sarah! 'She's just drunk.'

'She meant that night – when you told me you slept on her sofa.'

'Chloe, a two-foot dwarf couldn't sleep on Sarah's bloody sofa. Nothing happened between us.'

'Then why did you lie?'

'I didn't want you imagining things.'

'What could I imagine – what else have you lied about?' Chloe seemed furious now. Jack was driving much too fast, he didn't care. How dare she preach to him about truth telling! She went on, 'You're still seeing her, aren't you? That's why she hates me.'

Skewing the car to a ragged halt he yelled, 'Don't judge me by your standards!'

'What's that supposed to mean? Since I've loved you I've never been with anyone. And never lied to you.' Jack felt his anger evaporate, instantly as it had overtaken him. He reached out to touch her but Chloe shied away. 'What's going on,' she asked, 'between you and Sarah?'

'Nothing, love. It ended ages ago.'

She looked frightened, pale under the street lights. He held her, she cried and he didn't understand why.

The next thirty-six hours he had to work but Chloe seemed to have dropped the *Metro* job. She got up in the night and from dawn played the piano obsessively. The sound left his nerves ragged. Abandoning the build-up in *Cragge's* third act he went through to the living room. His hands sent a shudder through her rigid shoulders. 'What's wrong?'

'What d'you mean?' She was sharp, brittle. 'Have you finished?'

Jack shook his head. 'I can't go to Whitting this morning. And I don't think you should.'

'Why not? You can't undo what you've started. Or is that your way, is that what you're trying to tell me? Doesn't it matter to you – I've got to go back, now!'

Angrily she went on attacking him. It was because of him that she'd gone back; he was leaving her stranded and didn't love her; he was going to abandon her as he had Sarah. Jack felt exhausted, his reasonableness cracked. 'Go then, if you want. I might come for the afternoon. You've stopped my writing, Chloe.'

Still furious, she got dressed and flung out of the house. The door slammed. He heard the power rev of her Maserati, its tyres yelping on the road.

Silence fell. Jack suppressed a vague sense of guilt. He'd encouraged her to meet Rachel again, and wished he could undo that: erase the text and start again from an earlier page in their story. He wanted back the more innocent first days of love.

Soon resentment hardened into anger. He returned to his computer.

SCENE 180. INT. EVENING. PARIS, HOTEL BEDROOM

(PIERRE and HELOISE in bed, entwined post-sex.)
PIERRE: She died . . . Never revealed who my father was.
HELOISE: But haven't you –
PIERRE: – every day of my life.

SCENE 181. EXT. NIGHT. NOTTING HILL STREET.

(CRAGGE's new Maserati roars down deserted street past alley, rounds a corner ignoring red lights. Tyres yelping. TWO UNIFORMS in patrol car up the alley.)

PS: Get that!

(They scream off in pursuit.)

SCENE 182. INT. NIGHT. PARIS, HOTEL BEDROOM.

(PIERRE sleeping alone. The phone rings, he wakes abruptly. Takes in the empty bed. He grapples for the phone. He listens.)
PIERRE: ... she is with the terrorists? They do – what?

SCENE 183. EXT. NIGHT. NOTTING HILL, CRAGGE'S HOUSE.

(Sirens. Over. Firebomb envelops the house. CRAGGE in Maserati slews into the kerb, jumps out. Stares up at the house, his face lit by flames.)
CRAGGE: *No-o* ...!

(Patrol car roars up. TWO UNIFORMS get out. PC takes out radio.)
PC: What the hell ...

(CRAGGE crashes through a downstairs window, jumps into the flames, is swallowed up ... Sound of approaching fire engines. Over.)

END OF EPISODE FOUR

'Bollocks,' grimaced Jack reading the text with a feeling of sickness. He set the printer, glanced at his watch. It was only five past eleven.

Picking out a directory he rang Jackson Estate Agents, remembered it was Sunday as someone answered. He explained and the voice said, 'We could show you that property – say at twelve?'

Shaving and showering he dressed in his only suit. Old jeans and a tee-shirt went into a bag with his camera and notebook. With twenty minutes to wait, making some coffee he sat in the kitchen to read Friday's *Broadcast*.

115

It was towards the end, a small item he might easily have missed:

The Wilder Affair. 3 x 60 minute drama now in production. With Paul Mann producing for the BBC, the series will be filmed in Italy and the South of France. To be screened early next year.

So Sarah had poached Paul for one of her shows, leaving himself and *Cragge* to founder. A sense of betrayal swamped Jack. How could she, an old friend who said she loved him, do such a thing – and say nothing about it?

He remembered her unease, her hasty denials that anything could go wrong with *Cragge*. Everything that could go wrong, had done – still she'd kept silent.

Bitterly Jack rang her at home, listened to her stupid message. His own voice rasped, 'So much for friendship, Sarah. Congratulations on destroying my life. Hope it's worth it!'

He slammed down the phone, slammed out of the house and drove to meet the agent on the hill.

'Mr Maine? Simon Marks. Here are the details. Would you like to view the outside?'

'Let's take a look inside.'

He got a curious glance, 'Are you in development?'

Jack nodded as the key grated, the church door opened with a stifled shriek. They stepped in, footfalls dead on the dusty stone. It was cold, dark at first, then his eyes adapted: white columns rose up a gloomy nave to meet in mammoth ribs over his head. Faint daylight illumined the empty altar space.

Marks shone a powerful torch ahead, its beam swung to the rafters. 'The windows are boarded up, they're very old stained glass. Lots of original features can be kept –'

'Where's the altar?'

'Fittings and fixtures aren't included. Hardly be appropriate, would they? There's planning permission for sixteen maisonettes in the main body and side – er, spaces.'

Now he could see more clearly. Pews were stacked against a wall, statues shrouded in white. Only a slab of marble lay above the steps. He walked to it. Here the pacifist had died.

A baroque pulpit and confessionals, painted wood reliefs of Christ's last journey. Side chapels with murals of the Virgin and some male saint. He knew little since his agnosticism had never faltered. Gazing back through the desolate belly of the church he saw a Christmas night in wartime, the blackout, a blaze of lights here inside and a buzz of people praying for life, peace, redemption.

'An exciting investment opportunity,' the estate agent said. 'A solidly constructed shell of stone. The beams are excellent, very nice original – '

'Do people want to live in a former church?'

'There used to be some feeling against it, but not now.'

'I'd like to take some photos.'

Flash swiped across the interior, the shutter like shot broke a depth of silence. He finished the film. Marks guided him into a vestry smelling of damp. 'Permission for a two-room cottage here – perhaps a porter for the block. The bell tower could house the bathroom, under it a reasonable size kitchen. They've been very successful, these conversions.'

An acrid scent of nettles stained the air. Jack forced a path round a greenhouse with no glass, its spiky frame was sepia with rust and fractured by a fallen tree. Distantly he glimpsed a cloud of blossom, perhaps an orchard still survived. Around him the earth seemed to shimmer and writhe in the primal energy of new weed life under a hot spring sun.

Behind a thicket of saplings she wielded a long-bladed scythe, whirling and chopping ferocious circles in the briars as if, set in motion, she'd never stop. Stout thorn bushes shuddered, subsided, clung to her and drew blood. She was covered in scratches. He felt dread drag his stomach, slow his feet. 'Hey,' he said. 'Steady.'

Taking the scythe he laid it down in slaughtered undergrowth. Chloe stood poised. 'Jack . . .' Then looked away across the sea of weeds, grabbed his hand and started pushing through. He was led in her wake, propelled by her urgency. 'You see all this? It was a lawn. And masses of roses, right along.' She turned to frown against the sun at the stark silhouette of house. 'Whitting would be filled with people, strangers from around the world. They'd come to parties or to dinner – I was allowed to stay up as late as I liked. There'd be a big marquee, lots of chairs. Musicians playing.'

He could see it as she spoke, and murmured, 'Yes, it must've been magic.'

'Enchantment . . .'

Hearing an edge of hysteria he said, 'You're worn out – we'll find a pub for lunch.' He wanted time to calm her, make her see the garden was a hopeless task.

Then the girl called, and approaching the verandah they saw a table laid for three. 'Rachel suggested lunch out here,' Jodie said. 'Everything's ready – chicken and salad, plenty of wine.'

'Is she going to have lunch with us?' Chloe asked.

'Rachel's resting, she isn't strong.'

They settled round the table, awkward and careful, Chloe saying too brightly, 'How nice. You made all this? How long have you lived here, Jodie?'

'Since last winter.' The girl's voice was proud, proprietorial.

Chloe countered, 'Not very long then.'

'Seems ages, I can't remember any other life. I've made lots of changes to help her out. She was living in a state.'

'I can imagine. That was true even six years ago. How did you find the job?'

'It's not really a job,' Jodie retorted. 'We're more like mates, friends.'

'How did you meet?' Chloe persisted.

'Oh – Rachel advertised, it was an ad.'

Jack intervened. 'Look at the view. There's St Paul's, and the Barbican.'

Jodie chewed at a chicken wing. 'The trees are starting to block it now. It's a better view in winter.'

'At least a few trees have survived,' Chloe blurted out. 'I can't believe how it's been left – '

'Rachel's an old lady.' Jodie flew to the defence. 'What could she do all alone?'

'Hire gardeners and a forester like my father did.' Chloe was trembling, with nerves or fury. 'And the house! Full of beetles and rot, fifty-seven varieties. It used to be – '

'And she's been neglected too. I don't see how you can turn up and – '

'There were good reasons for staying away,' Jack cut in. 'You probably got some idea, last Sunday.'

Chloe stood, knocking the table. Her glass tipped, red wine soaked the cloth like blood in a bandage. She didn't notice but started quickly down the steps. 'It's late – I'm going to get on with the garden.'

Jack rose slowly. Jodie was scowling after Chloe, 'Rachel's been wonderful, so kind to us.'

He looked into the girl's eyes, trying to see: what was she frightened of? 'You pretended, when I came here in February, that you didn't know who Chloe was.'

'I didn't know, either,' Jodie protested. She went on

more softly, 'This is our home, d'you see? Raphael's and mine.'

'Yes,' agreed Jack, beginning to turn away. 'But that's a bit tough for Chloe to take, at the moment.'

He glanced back to catch her reaction, knowing she couldn't understand. Her resentment was as justified as Chloe's. He added, 'That was a great lunch. Thanks.' A wide smile broke across the girl's mood, for a moment he almost trusted her.

Beginning to push through the garden Jack saw something – a servants' lodge or stable block – buried in the trees. Curiously he went to look: it was a small version of the house, elaborate with ornament and gothic roof. He swung open the heavy wooden door to reveal a gloomy interior, oppressive with low beams. Fuel was stored here and the walls were hung with garden tools, heavyweight stuff that looked disused. Idly, lightly he ran a finger along an old-fashioned sickle blade, was astonished when bright beads of blood appeared. The thing had been kept sharp as a razor.

Changing into his old clothes, Jack found matches and paraffin on a shelf, took up a rake and the sickle then stepped out into the dazzling sun.

The figure of a man, tall and angular, stood just inside the gate. He was staring at the outhouse and it seemed he hovered, not quite earthed but shimmering in a bright heat haze like some apparition.

12

He was wearing dirty jeans and tee-shirt; under pale curly hair that face was so impassive it could've been a mason's work. Something about him made Jack call, 'Are you looking for anyone?'

Without moving he seemed to change his stance from watching to furtiveness, hesitation. But then detached from the gate post and ambled up with a slowness almost drug-like. He stopped, close: he was a bit taller than Jack. Why did he look slightly familiar? A smile twitched his mouth, betraying tension, 'She wants me to grow flowers now, so I've bought new tools.'

Whitting House gardens scarcely looked as if anyone cared for them. Jack nodded acknowledgement and the man began to walk slowly with him. 'You're Mrs Rushe's gardener? We're just doing a bit of clearing up.'

He felt uneasy now, almost guilty. That was odd. Except it could be seen this way, that he was the intruder trespassing in the garden – in this man's territory. And Chloe was a kind of alibi so he was moving towards her, about to explain.

The gardener said, 'She likes the way it is,' then stopped. His watery blue eyes froze sharp.

They'd reached the clearing where Chloe was hard at

work, she hadn't seen them. But the man was staring at her. He looked shocked.

'My friend used to live here. She's family so it means a lot,' Jack began. Then spiking into him the eyes darted away again and without a word the man whirled off, his stride rapid and slightly stilted. The trees swallowed him.

Jack frowned to himself. Was he really a gardener, or someone pretending for some reason? Whitting House was vulnerable, and the odd encounter had disturbed him. Shivering, he lit a smoking pyre of brambles and watched Chloe feed the flames. He decided not to tell her about it. She was already irrational with need, obsessed: she shouldn't be here anyway.

The house was growing tongues of shadow, long and forking to the tumble of city below. There spires and roofs and tower blocks were almost lost, obscured by a strange covering mist. It was as if a great fire lay invisibly in that pit of people, making pale smoke rise towards the hill.

Behind him Chloe cried out softly. Under the brambles lay a gleam of white and peering down through ropes of thorns he saw it was a human arm. Flesh kept too long from the light . . . Carefully he cut the branches, gradually the arm appeared, then a long robed torso, head and face. It was an angel carved in stone, intact except for broken wings.

Chloe remembered, 'There were six statues along this walk. They must all be buried.'

'How hard you've both worked!' Rachel's voice drifted towards them, mellow as a blackbird's call through the misty evening. She was leaning over the parapet. 'You people must be tired. Come in, it's turning chill.'

Her friendliness seemed almost shocking – there'd been no hint of acceptance before. Raking the ashes, they locked away their tools and went in. The back door led into a dark passage and tiled kitchen full of oak, it was once fashionable *rus in urbe* untouched for years. Around the big farmhouse table, sipping mulled wine they chatted as Jodie fed her baby. Scents of meat simmered from dishes on the Aga. Rachel Rushe's good mood expanded but Chloe stayed close to Jack and silent, outside her stepmother's circle of warmth. He wished again for what seemed impossible: that the two of them might be friends, the past be forgiven. That there might be many visits like this.

Crossing to the window he rubbed at a pane of glass. Thick mist stayed clouding the dark evening, hiding trees and city lights below. In this room was Chloe's bed where she'd slept as a child. Everything had been freshly cleaned. He stared at the strong colours and design, leafed through childish books, smiled at the Shiva used as a sunhat rack.

Chloe said wryly, 'Lord of the Cosmic Dance – my father's gift when he brought Rachel home. Childhood ended right then.' She wandered around, searching cupboards and shelves.

'There must have been lots of happy years in this house.' Jack sat on her bed, watching as she found forgotten things. 'What's it like being back here again?'

She was avoiding him, took a while to answer. 'It's strange. I feel like a small insubstantial ghost because there's no bridge – all my strong times have been in other places.' Rummaging through a drawer she found a *diamanté* clip, fastened it in her hair before turning to him, still distant somehow, 'Shall we go downstairs? I expect dinner's ready.'

But there was an hour to fill. Chloe went with Jodie to the kitchen while, gin in hand, Rachel led Jack on a tour of her house. He looked into big dust-filled rooms, stared up at the elaborate cornices, questioned her on that extra-ordinary staircase and hall.

Outside the fog grew more impenetrable.

'I know nothing about architecture,' he told her regretfully, 'but this really is stunning. When was it built?'

'1865. Arkhurst designed it for himself. They say he was half demented then and died soon after it was completed.'

They stood in the cedar gallery, a lofty cavern of dark satin that echoed into the hall below. Jack said, 'It may be madness, but so splendid. Wonderfully overblown and imaginative.'

'An original,' she agreed. 'Unique. So I'm persecuted by conservationists – they want to have control and it's all double-Dutch to me,' and she glanced sideways at him. 'Not my natural habitat – I was raised in Leeds during the depression.'

He offered her a steadying hand down the stairs. 'You married late,' he ventured, curious.

'Ah. My fiancé, my first love – we would've been so happy together . . . I was eighteen when he was killed in '43.'

There was little connection really, but Jack was instantly alert. Yes: the death of the pacifist must be the culmination to a strong emotional story in the midst of war. The ending to a love affair, perhaps?

Chloe had never mentioned Rachel drinking – but she'd had a few gins by now. As they sat down to eat, maudlin sentiment took hold and she wallowed in self-pity about her husband. She was soaking it up. 'Charles and I never stood a chance. We were never alone, once we'd returned – '

Jodie stopped her. 'Rachel, you're getting tired. You know what I mean . . . Go on.'

'Don't try to order me about – my dear. Just because you've made a friend.'

Jodie and Chloe had emerged from the kitchen in a state of truce. How jealous and dependent Rachel was. 'You'll have to make up her bed,' she muttered, staring past the flickering candles at whited-out panes. No one had drawn the curtains and the strange half-night pressed in. 'They won't be able to drive home tonight.' It was as if she and the girl were alone together as usual.

Jack felt Chloe's glance, pleading. 'Perhaps it'll clear, we may be able to get home,' he said in reassurance. He could feel the heaviness of her heart, see her nervousness, as she played with the crescent-shaped clip in her hair. It was sliding out, and he leaned across and fastened it.

Rachel's eyes nailed into the fog outside, reflecting, veined with opaque. 'That garden, it killed him. Why should my garden be looked after now?'

'Papa would've wanted it looked after,' Chloe answered. 'He loved and cared – '

'How do you know what he loved?' Rachel cut in, viperish. 'You couldn't possibly understand – you were just a little savage bent on our destruction.' Jodie tried to cut in, Rachel ignored her. 'I'd sooner burn Whitting to the ground then let her have it! . . . This is what you came back for? Like everyone – after my property, my money. Everyone except Jodie – '

Chloe shouted, 'I'm not here for the house! Or the garden – '

'Ah!' Rachel pounced, pleased. 'Not because of the garden, then. Perhaps to see how I'm fading? Such a privileged one. And so young . . . The spoilt child. Your castle in the air will tumble into ruins – because I wish it so. It's the only ambition that I have left.'

Chloe tried to stop her, 'For God's sake – '

'You might inherit a heap of rubble – but I will not let Whitting pass on to you!' Then she hissed the words, 'Charles never loved you. He did not care at all for you.'

Jack started, 'Mrs Rushe. What are you saying? What are you trying to do?'

He was ignored. 'I think there's another way now...' Rachel threw back her head, suddenly laughing. 'Yes. Do you know what I'm going to do? I'll adopt Jodie and leave her my inheritance!'

Jack glanced quickly at Chloe. She wore a strange expression, intent and deathly white, twisted in the candle shadows. 'You wouldn't be allowed to get away with that,' she said too deliberately, too calmly.

The old lady cackled in triumph. 'It's time to forget all your delusions, Chloe. Charles never gave a tuppenny damn – didn't you know that? Poor Charles – he was sick to death of having to drag a whining, snivelling child around everywhere. Having to put up with all that silly, boring prattle. What did you ever have to give him? Charles needed a woman, he needed me – but you wouldn't allow that, would you?' She leaned forward, sharp with hate, 'You ruined his life. You killed Charles.'

Chalk-faced, Chloe stood up. She was shaking all over. 'That's a lie, that's a complete lie – '

Rachel hissed, 'Don't you know that you caused his death? Surely you remember how upset he was, going out to the garden shed that day. How you had taunted him and driven us apart. People have accidents when they're upset.'

'I wish it had been you, I wish you were dead!' Chloe screamed the words in a rage so violent Jack jumped up to stop her attacking Rachel as she must at any moment. 'You poisonous old vulture – it was you that should've died, not him!' And she struck the table instead, sweeping from it crockery, sharp cutlery and a candle that fell, threatened to incinerate them all but then guttered, was extinguished on the table. Jack tried to grab Chloe, she wrenched away and swore at him and stumbled from the room.

Shocked faces, a stench of the charred-wood dining table. Into the short silence Jack demanded, 'What the hell did you say all that to her for? Are you completely crazy?'

Reaching across, Rachel took Jodie's hand and said, 'It was time she knew.'

He left them there, went out to the hall and shouted Chloe's name. There was no answer, no sound or sight of her. He searched downstairs then upstairs, even called for her in the attics. She must've gone out. She'd be in the garden.

Outside lay dense white fog and silence. Feeling his way down the steps, calling, he heard his voice muffled and powerless, straining to make more sound as if in a dream. The fog pressed wet against his face. He pushed through a dripping tunnel of undergrowth and fat leaves slapped against his clinging shirt. Something loomed up on the path, sharp and angular: a wheelbarrow and other tools, long-handled and metallic. Edging past he tried to remember the way, searched the garden but she wasn't there, not near the verandah or the house, not by the ponds or at the cleared pergola where he stumbled into ashes.

Then he thought: she'll be in the car, waiting for me. It was so obvious that he laughed aloud. She'd want to go home to Islington straight away and one of them would drive – taking it very slowly, carefully – and soon they'd be curled up by the hearth together talking, comforting, putting this long day into perspective before they went to bed.

But she wasn't waiting in her car, nor his, and after standing in the silent lane he returned to the house. The kitchen was empty, the dining-room table cleared and all the lights were out. Creeping upstairs he looked in the bedroom to make sure Chloe hadn't come back. It was a bit after eleven. She might be home by now, had found a cab or taken the Underground.

An immense tiredness began to fall over Jack. Retracing his steps, quietly he left the sleeping house. Like a swimmer in difficult waters he made his way through currents of deceptive mist towards his car. With the foglamps on and the window down it was possible to make out the kerb, dense grey forms of cars, corners and junctions to navigate. There were few people trying to drive tonight, their lights came at him like late messages and the cars step circled round each other, random dancers in slow motion. Soon he was lost and directionless, eerily so blind and deaf the unfamiliar was imagined as familiar and he couldn't imagine that what he'd known could ever be again. Abandoning the car he drifted through the silent streets on foot, startled by walls and fences leaping at him. The thunder of his heart was the only sound.

It was half past midnight when he came to Noel Terrace. There were no lights on, Chloe hadn't returned. Heavy with dread Jack let himself in. He stared at the phone and willed it to stay silent; the instant it rang he'd know she'd had an accident or had harmed herself. In a moment of urgency he reached out for it to call the police, call local hospitals – but his hand fell back on to his lap. He sat hunched and shivering. Images of her body, dead or maimed, forced themselves into his unwilling head.

In the middle of that long, sleepless night a tiny sound cracked across the hall. A key turning.

Chloe let herself in quietly and Jack flew to meet her by the stairs. Her face looked exhausted, drained of colour and her steps grown uncertain as if she was suddenly old.

'Hey . . .' He enveloped her – alive, solid – in a long needy hug that was full of relief. She staggered in his arms, and he held her under the light to see. Her clothes were sodden, clinging to her as if she'd been swimming in them; her hair was wild and wet. There were scratches on her face, mud everywhere, torn sleeves . . . 'What happened? Are you all right?'

'I'm awfully cold,' she said. 'Yes, I'm OK. You disappeared Jack, and – '

'No, you did!' He began to laugh because she was all right after all. 'It's three in the morning – where the hell did you go?'

'I need a hot bath,' Chloe said. 'I'm frozen.' They went upstairs and he ran the bath. She told him, 'I went to your car – thought we should just go home. You didn't come and I felt – full of demons, awash with anger about the things that bitch had said . . .' He watched her undressing, climbing into the hot water. 'I didn't want to go back into the house. So I just started walking. Eventually I must've been up in Finchley somewhere, going in completely the wrong direction. Then I found the road south again.'

Jack's voice sounded false to his own ears as he sympathised, 'Poor love – you must've walked for hours! I looked for you in the house and garden, didn't think of the car at first.'

Colour was seeping back into Chloe's face, she sighed with weariness.

'All those scratches,' Jack said. 'How – ?'

'You know that area – those woods. Trees and bushes everywhere. I couldn't see the road and kept stumbling off.'

He knew that she was lying. Instinctively he knew. But why?

And where had she really been these past four hours?

'What a terrible day. A horrific day,' Chloe was saying as if to herself. She stepped out of the bath, Jack rubbed her limbs warm and glowing in the big towel. He made her a hot drink, hot chocolate with plenty of sugar. 'How I do hate her,' Chloe went on. 'That poisonous old woman.'

'Rachel didn't mean it. She was just drunk.'

Chloe's calm evaporated instantly and he could feel the vitriol flood her veins. 'Oh but she meant every word. You don't know her, Jack. She'd do anything to destroy me!' He said nothing, shocked by the violence of her anger. She could so easily lose control. She was dangerous.

'Rachel would finish our relationship, Jack – like she did with my father and me. Even his memory now. And nobody gets to do that. Nobody!'

It was morning when the police phoned.

Part Two

1

Waking late the next morning, opening his eyes he saw that Chloe lay watching him quietly. She smiled and snuggled close, kissed him. 'Darling Jack.'

The phone rang and sleepily he fumbled to answer it. A man's voice said, 'Mr Jack Maine?'

'Mm – yes,' he answered absently and smiled back at Chloe.

'My name is Detective Inspector Cairns,' the voice went on. 'Is Miss Chloe Rushe with you?'

He began to emerge out of half-sleep. 'That's right.' Memory was returning and he frowned.

'She's a relative of Mrs Rachel Rushe, who you both visited yesterday?'

Jack sat up. 'What's happened?'

But Inspector Cairns wanted to speak to Chloe. Jack sat watching her face as she listened. Odd sounds came from her, monosyllables, frozen. Then she put down the phone and suddenly he knew, and there was a stretched instant of extraordinary ringing clarity inside his head.

Chloe said slowly, 'Something terrible's happened. Rachel's had an accident.'

Jack sat at the kitchen table. That first shock was turning into a need to make the unthinkable real and to act on it. They didn't have much time. He looked at Chloe. Taut, fragile as glass in the harsh morning light. She was pushing down a kind of horror, 'I hated her, I loathed her but – not this . . .' Then, 'Why would she go to the ponds at night, so far from the house?'

'She must've gone outside for something,' Jack suggested.

'Rachel knew every inch of those gardens, she could never have stumbled into the lake.'

'That fog made distance very deceptive. When I was driving – '

She interrupted, 'Oh Jack, d'you think she meant to . . .?'

He took her hand, felt as if he was playing a charade with her, went on with it, 'I'm sure she misjudged – and there's no fence. Rachel was probably still drunk and never knew what was happening.'

A relaxation went through her; she seemed comforted, then was suddenly anxious again, 'Why do they want to come and interview us? And what are they doing at the house? If they're sure it was an accident.'

The forensics team would be at work from their white Scenes-of-Crime van. Measuring, taking photos and samples. Soon Rachel Rushe's body would be at the mortuary and a Home Office pathologist would do the postmortem, make a report for the coroner. He knew it all from reconstructions and now it was being enacted for real.

'Any sudden death has to be treated as suspicious,' he explained. 'It's just routine, to check.' Then hesitantly he asked, 'You didn't see or hear anything, I suppose?'

'I was never in the garden. I went straight from the front door to the car and then walked through Finchley by mistake.'

'Darling, when this detective interviews us . . . I think

we should just say we left together, around half past ten, when everyone – '

'Why?' She looked baffled, then incredulous. 'You mean they might – ?'

He stopped her quickly, 'It would save an awful lot of trouble. It sounds odd that we didn't meet up till three – '

'Odd for both of us,' she interrupted. 'But, you mean – Jodie will tell them Rachel and I were quarrelling? Oh, and what she said about changing my inheritance . . .!' Chloe began to laugh as if that was very funny, as if she was getting hysterical. He took both her hands, looked into her eyes that gleamed. 'They might think I drowned her?'

The idea sounded ridiculous as she said it. Ridiculous and so ugly – touching on the shadows in his mind – roughly Jack brushed it aside as a joke, 'A likely story. But you see, I know about these investigations. They'll drag it out and we want to go on holiday. Let's say you waited at the car, in your car after you'd gone straight to it. And around eleven I found you there.' He thought for a minute. 'We switched to my car because I wanted to drive. We got home around eleven thirty.'

'That seems wrong, to change – '

'Trust me. I know about these things.'

'It does sound odd. Four hours walking on a night like that. I didn't meet anyone, nobody would've noticed me.'

'Don't tell them anything about walking in the night,' he insisted. 'All these scratches on your face as well as your hands and arms, they're from working in the garden, cutting back those tall brambles yesterday.'

'I can see you're determined to rewrite a bit. Though I'm not entirely sure why.' And she looked levelly at him.

'Don't want to miss my holiday,' he reminded her.

Chloe was closer to crying than laughing now. 'It's so sudden. I'd just decided never to see her again. I feel as if . . . I feel guilty, Jack! But she was so expert at driving people away. Everyone except that girl.'

They stood close for a while. He felt the great strain under the way she was coping. What had happened still seemed like something that could be undone, might turn out to be a dream. But this was daytime, busily real.

How long before the police arrived?

Jack went into the bedroom while Chloe was washing her hair. Her clothes lay half over a chair, half on the floor where she'd dropped them early this morning . . . Or late last night, he reminded himself. He began to pick them up and saw again how covered in mud they were, how torn. As if she'd been pushing through undergrowth, had fallen or knelt on damp earth. She must have gone back into the garden last night, there was no other explanation.

In his mind, unwanted, he heard her voice, 'I felt – full of demons, awash with anger about all sorts of things she'd said. I didn't want to go back into the house. So I just started walking . . .'

But suppose she'd gone back? There was another quarrel and . . . He could only see it as sudden, passionate, unplanned. Perhaps they'd fought, and struggled. Or Chloe had pushed her impulsively?

Picking up her silk teddy he stroked its softness. He put it to his face – it smelled of her, her skin, her sex.

He heard her voice again, 'How I do hate her. That poisonous old woman. Rachel would destroy our relationship, Jack. And *nobody* gets to do that. Nobody.' Swiftly he gathered up her clothes, shoved them into the washing machine and switched it on. Returning for her shoes – her indoor shoes that were coated in mud – he suddenly realised that his own were muddy too from searching the garden. He found a knife, started to scrape it all off.

136

The door-bell shattered through the house, slicing his nerves into fine shreds.

He'd thought they'd have more time.

Shoving knife and newspaper deep into the rubbish bin, he opened the back door and hurled both pairs of shoes deep into the bushes. A second loud ringing. Voices in the hall. One of Chloe's shoes – still muddy – lay by the path but there was no time to hide it.

The DI was plump with a creased grey suit and small eyes sharp in a smoothly ironed face. A young DC called Olde hovered by him. They accepted coffee when Chloe offered it. Jack saw she had dressed demurely for the police, with her hair drawn back and no make-up. She looked like a nurse or novice nun, in black and white skirt and blouse.

His nervousness made him feel a fool. Surely they must see how he was sweating, how much his hands trembled? Yet Chloe seemed so calm now. Even when they took her into his study alone, closing the door. The interviews were to be carried out separately. Now how would he know exactly what she told them?

Darting down the fire escape, Jack glanced up checking empty windows then hid the shoe. Furtiveness and guilt pressed in on his anxiety. What was Chloe saying, what were they thinking?

The phone rang and he jumped, picked up the extension. A voice said, 'Detective Inspector Cairns.'

A puzzled secretary hesitated, 'No . . . *Cragge*. The production office. Jack?'

He noticed Cairns didn't hang up.

They wanted Episode Four and he said it was ready. 'Thank God – Ross needs a copy. I'll send a courier.'

So Rick Cragge's fate was collected from him. Time dragged unbearably. Why were they taking so long? He interrupted twice – anything more would have looked too fictional. Tucked up cosily among his scripts, the detective had stopped talking at once when he knocked and looked in.

When Olde came out with Chloe, there was no chance at all to talk with her or compare notes before his turn. He thought she looked paler than before, and subdued.

Cairns phoned someone, made Jack wait in his own visitor's chair, paused to browse in a leisurely way through an American paperback of his novel. '*Caught*,' he mused at the title then ran a fat thumb with a chewed nail across a row of videotapes before sitting down at Jack's desk. 'Do well out of it – these murder stories, the TV show?'

Jack shrugged. 'People assume I'm a millionaire. As you can see I just do OK.' His mouth felt dry and his guts were churning. He'd worked half a decade with plain-clothes officers like Cairns, yet now he felt like the conman or dealer, the thief or murderer. 'I don't exactly write murder stories, *Cragge's* a detective show.'

'My wife watches it,' said Cairns. 'Same difference – you don't detect a fiver gone missing. For that matter, rich widows don't croak in their own fish ponds.'

An army of fat female frogs hopped into Jack's head. Fairy-tale frogs perverted, black veils trailing as they leapt from lily-pads into open jaws of fish. He cleared his throat and said abruptly, 'We were both shattered when you called. How could Mrs Rushe have fallen in – and during the night?'

'Mm-mm. We haven't established the exact time, but we will. Of course, it's not your average goldfish tub. Seen the place, have you?'

'Last Sunday, and yesterday. Chloe and I walked all round the ponds, we were gardening.'

Olde looked at his notes. Cairns went on, 'Then you'll know what I mean. Ten feet deep in parts. It's a lake, that bottom pond. Steep sides, and thick weed in it.' He sat looking at Jack for a full half-minute. 'Bit of a puzzle though, how she never managed to climb out. Not that feeble . . . People have an instinct to survive and your girlfriend says her stepmother was a good swimmer.'

'Then it's inexplicable.'

'It's never that,' smiled Cairns. 'For example, can we be quite sure about the cause of death? Not yet. But you know all about post-mortems and analyses.'

'Only a little.' There was another pause and Jack asked, 'How was she found?'

'Young girl at the house.'

'Jodie Delancey,' contributed Olde from his notebook.

'Saw the body from a window this morning. Tried to get her out, went to call an ambulance.'

They'd interviewed the girl, she'd have told them about the years of hostility – all from Rachel Rushe's point of view. His heart fell: perhaps she'd mentioned Chloe's psychiatric history, maybe they could learn about it in details he himself didn't have. And they'd know by now all about that violent last quarrel and Chloe's threats. Unless of course the girl had any reason of her own to keep quiet? But no – why would she.

So he laid it on about Rachel's drinking, how unsteady and irrational she'd got. They asked over and over about the time he'd left with Chloe last night. How did he know it was before eleven? Who'd seen them go, who'd seen them get home together, how could he verify any of it?

They had to suspect something. Jack tried to stay cool, then to distract them. There was that intruder, the strange man in the garden yesterday after lunch.

'Who else saw this man? Who did you tell about him?'

'Nobody. I didn't tell anyone . . .' And hesitant, as he gave a description he realised how opportune it sounded, just as if he was making it up to protect Chloe. That's what the police were thinking now, he saw the glance that passed between them. 'He might've been a gardener there,' Jack insisted, remembering. 'He said he'd brought some tools with him. And late on when it was . . . when I went out for a minute, I saw a wheelbarrow on the path. It wasn't there before. A wheelbarrow and a couple of long-handled garden tools . . .'

Now both detectives were watching him closely, carefully as he stumbled into silence.

'Interesting,' Cairns said. 'You went out into the garden, late. And interesting because the girl says there was no other help at the house – it was only her and Mrs Rushe. And interesting – a wheelbarrow? Was there anything like a wheelbarrow around?' He looked at Olde, who shook his head in agreement.

Jack stayed meticulous about his story but he felt shaken, they must've sensed it. Cairns had a way of coming at the same details from opposite angles of questioning and that made it hard to give the same replies. Jack answered slowly, was impressed. If he was still writing *Cragge* he might've tried out the technique.

The detectives had him sign a long statement then they rose to leave. Cairns picked up the copy of *Caught*, his eye attracted by a banner on the cover. 'Soon to be a major film?' he queried.

'Soon is a long time,' Jack explained.

'As long as a foggy, foggy night,' commented Cairns. 'I'd like to take this and have a look, if that's all right. By the way, are you engaged to her – to Chloe Rushe? Or anything like that?'

'We just live together, that's all.'

A kind of lightness fell over them as the police left, and he found himself thinking that surely the worst was over

140

now. Their statements had been taken, Rachel's drowning would be confirmed and her accidental death recorded.

Perhaps it really had been an accident? But in his heart he didn't believe so.

Chloe was hungry and he realised they hadn't eaten for twenty hours. She put together a tray of food and they ate on the living-room sofa, from the same dish, feeding each other mouthfuls of veal and ceps, then chocolate mousse. She was all over him, wanting closeness, kissing and stroking him while he felt a passivity, complicit and quiet. Whatever happened, whatever became of her in the future, they were in it together. He'd lied to the police for her and knew he would perjure himself in court if it came to that.

When the door-bell rang they leapt apart like people shot at. It must be the detectives back again. Jack said, 'We don't have to let them in, we could leave it.'

Giving him a funny little glance, a sort of amused questioning, Chloe went to look out through the window. 'It's not the police, Jack. Shall I get it?'

Sarah stood on the step and Jack almost shut the door on her, but not quite. 'What d'you want?' he accused.

'Oh come on,' Sarah gave an uneasy laugh. 'All's fair in love and work, isn't it? Let me explain.' She came striding through his house as if she owned the place and he felt like hitting her.

Chloe asked, puzzled, 'Explain what? What's happened?'

Jack said, 'Sarah stole my producer for her series. That's why *Cragge*'s a disaster now.' He felt his own unforgivingness, heavy as a stone that filled and choked him. Why had she come? They could never be friends again.

Uncertainty touched Sarah's expression, then Chloe exploded, 'You did what? You mean, Paul's working with you instead of Jack? Why!'

141

'There's nothing else to it, Chloe,' Sarah answered, mysteriously. Then to him, 'You don't understand. I never dreamed of affecting *Cragge*. My show lost its producer and we'd been trying to get Paul interested for later. Then when he was emotionally committed, our co-producers got the schedule moved forward. I don't have any power, I couldn't tell him to say no. What kind of a kamikaze stunt would that have been anyway?'

Jack hated her, but he almost understood. Pouring wine he handed her a glass and threw himself into a chair. 'God preserve us from our friends.'

'Paul Mann has let Jack down very badly,' Chloe snapped at her, sharp. 'And so have you – without any warning.'

Sarah ignored her, went on at him, 'Paul hadn't committed to another series of *Cragge*. He wanted out, he'd done it for too long – that's the truth. Couldn't the shake-up be to your advantage somehow?'

She was almost pleading. Jack laughed bitterly and Chloe accused, 'Don't try to soften it! Ross Cammell's a catastrophe. We don't think *Cragge* will survive him.'

'What would you have done, in my shoes?' Sarah asked angrily.

Chloe was silent and Jack replied at last, 'I suppose, I'd have done the same.'

'There you are. Life's not a rehearsal – you know that, Jack. You've got to take what you want.'

He looked at Sarah with more attention. There was something different about her, a clarity or calm determination, not her usual muddle. She seemed happier, and younger. Was she having an affair? Probably with Paul . . .

Sarah demanded, 'Are you writing *Cragge*, or what?'

'More like what.'

'You've got to forgive me, both of you. It wasn't

intended.' And after a moment, 'Anyway, Jack, aren't you going to do that novel?'

She was steering the conversation away and he decided to let her. 'Probably.'

'D'you think what people make up – or what writers write – can influence real life?' she asked.

'Writers don't create real events,' Jack retorted firmly. 'Probably, real events conspire to make up writers. What's happening with you, Sarah?'

She smiled evasively. 'Nothing much. Jack, let me know when there's anything at all I can do.'

He saw her out, and supposed he'd forgiven the unforgiveable. But he wasn't going to let her be sure, not yet. Coming back alone into the living room he suddenly realised they hadn't even mentioned Chloe's stepmother. He didn't want to tell anyone: it was all too new, and too complicated.

'Bye bye, *Cragge*? Off with the old and on with the new,' he mused aloud, bitterness seeping through him.

'She'd get away with murder,' Chloe said.

'Who?'

'Sarah, of course! You've been strange today, Jack. I've never seen you so nervous.'

'It's been a shock,' he began. Then wanted to talk about anything else, did not want to know any of it – whether she'd been there, whether she'd been responsible. One day they might talk, but not yet. Because he'd have to be ready to hear whatever she might answer.

Jack looked down at her from where he stood by the mantelpiece. Chloe was sitting opposite him on the sofa, seeming so oddly neat and scrubbed in those monochrome, tailored clothes. Except for the sheer black stockings she wore, and the way she slowly moved one long slender leg, drawing it up – with a slight whispering, a

143

soft rustling sound – to cross the other thigh. And in the midst of his detachment, all his thoughts, he desired her.

She said carelessly, 'Jack, whatever am I going to do with Whitting House?'

2

For a minute Jack didn't understand but stood there waiting for her to explain. 'Whitting belongs to me now,' Chloe said.

'Are you sure?' On some level he'd known. Yet he hadn't even thought of it, and was astonished.

'Oh yes, it comes to me. That albatross,' she added with a wry grimace. 'But then, you really liked it, didn't you?'

She was studying him intently. Jack felt stupid, unprepared for this – too much had happened too fast already. And she was beginning to laugh aloud at his naivety, his disbelief that something he had coveted so hopelessly was about to become hers. 'Charles left me everything in trust,' she explained. 'That place was only in Rachel's care for her lifetime, don't you understand?'

'But Chloe, what she said – at dinner last night?'

'You mean about changing her will? Pure fantasy, poor thing. There wasn't any way she could disinherit me, ever. Even the building insurance was paid by the trust, my father saw to it. The only thing he didn't foresee was the way she let the place fall into ruin. And surely, at least in part, she was doing that because it was the only way she could spite me.'

He sat down then and watched her, practical and slender in that secretarial blouse and skirt, taking out the supper things, tidying the living room before they went upstairs for the night. Standing there, quizzical, then crossing the room to him and perching on the arm of his chair. She ran her fingers playfully through his hair, tugged at a stray lock of it. Kissed his face all over, tenderly.

'Whatever are you thinking about, Jack? I'll give you a penny for them.' And she laughed.

'I've not even a pennyworth of thoughts,' he told her, dishonestly. His head felt awash, running confusedly in fast circles. Nothing was as it had been.

She pressed her warm body against him, inviting, staying close. When she drew back after a minute her face was unreadable. Perhaps he'd never known her. 'Coming to bed, darling?' she whispered.

'I'll be up in a while.'

'Don't be too long.' She shrugged, hesitated. Jack watched her go out, listened to her footsteps on the stairs.

He craved aloneness, and maybe to turn back the clock. And to sort out something in his head – he had to be away from her.

Pouring a Scotch, tasting it Jack paced around his silent, empty living room. Images of Whitting House, fragments of each separate sight of it came to him now. His excitement, his sense of recognition there, the longing for what he knew could never be his. Stray ideas pushed at him. How Chloe had once loved Whitting, how it had in some way – for her and for Rachel too – represented the bond between father and daughter from an earlier, happier time. Surely it was true that Rachel had been intent on destroying the symbol, like the bond itself. But Chloe had stayed unaware of this until he had so casually, so self-indulgently, happened to bring the two of them back together again.

That was scarcely a week ago, and Rachel was dead.

Jack put down the whisky glass on the mantelpiece with a sharp crack. Conjecture and guilt would do him no good. He wanted to blanket out thoughts, to wash them away.

The bedroom was dark, he went past to the bathroom and there took off the clothes he'd put on so hastily this morning. Dragged them off like a sullied, outgrown skin and kicked them into a creased tangle in the corner.

Stepping into the shower he pulled the curtains, turned on the taps. The hot fast fall of water stunned the breath from his body and he turned his face up into its source, opening his mouth and feeling its fingers drumming on his skin, his taut shoulders, tense body. Cleansing, taking everything from him.

Then reaching for the soap he saw her through the white shower curtain. In the doorway, her shadow moving.

And suddenly the light went out.

He stood poised, sensing her approach.

In the hot darkness, heart pounding he felt her hands through the sheet of water glide up over his back to his neck and close around, kneading the muscles. And she began to massage, in deep and gently circling spreading waves his scalp and head, shoulders and spine, the flesh of his buttocks and thighs. Until he turned his tingling body to her and she stepped right under the jets of water with him, arms enfolding, holding him close. She was still dressed, the fabric of her clothing a strange barrier that clung to the shape of her, grazing against his own nakedness. Her caressing hands slid around his ribs and chest, his belly and genitals.

She was naked under that skirt. In the roaring of water in his ears and the press of it on his eyes he gasped swallowing, catching air, his fingers closed around her pussy and about the hair at the nape of her neck, tugging her backwards against the curtains and finding her

147

mouth, her tongue. He pushed her to the floor. She gave a fierce cry, tried to struggle and he held her crushed, bruising lips and bare arms with his mouth and hands and all of his body as he felt her heart thud crazily against him in the push of her breasts. She had to trust, he could do whatever he liked.

So he released her then and she writhed against him. Her legs wound round his thighs and he opened her hot swollen sex, felt her desire under his hand. She knelt over him, stretching his arms above his head and winding the spurting metal coil of the shower hose around his wrists, fixing it with the spray head so his own weight imprisoned him. He lay waiting breathless in fear and longing, in surrender to her – to ecstasy or to whatever kind of a death she might bring to him – hypnotised as she moved above, predatory, an unseeable felt darkness.

She crouched over his body and slid him into her, he was swallowed up, and she had him trapped like some creature wild and ferociously alive in driving out all separation, sterile thought, cold death. She bit him, scratched like a cat on heat drawing blood, sucking out their past, marking the future like a territory of ragged neon blazing signs white-hot. They started to shout not in words but feral screams that rose lapping them in waves into one monster – ravenous and huge and dangerously electrical – against whatever else lurked out in the unknown.

The spring continued hot and beautiful, a celebration of life and renewal. By the canal the trees were in fresh leaf, unmarred by time. The haves rubbed shoulders with the poor and Jack walked with Chloe under a bright sun between echoing tunnels as children played, couples strolled. Winter's harsh internment was quickly forgotten.

The *Cragge* production office called and a meeting was fixed between himself and Ross. Jack told Chloe, 'I've had it up to here with compromise, so there's about to be one helluva ruck between Cammell and I. And as for *Cragge*, I'm pretty sure it's finished.'

'You must do what you really want to do, Jack,' she assured him. 'Write what most involves you – I know it's the new book, isn't it – and then surely success will follow.'

He felt touched by such a simple view. He didn't share it but felt he had no choice, he had to follow his obsession.

On the morning before his XLTV meeting, Jack went with Chloe to Whitting House. Her solicitor had given her the keys, a big old iron ring of them although her ownership wasn't formally completed. The place was standing empty and she had access; there was on one else to look after it, to sort the contents or go through Rachel's stuff.

The inquest opened by the coroner had been soon adjourned. They needed forensic results and Jack knew that could take weeks. He and Chloe had heard no more from the police, and in their silence he wondered now about his own instinctive reactions. He might never know if she had been with Rachel or what had happened during that night. He never wanted to know.

It was the first time they'd been back to the house and it felt different now, the emptiness hollow, the silence total. Someone had curtained the windows and bolted the doors so, lightless and airless, the place had become a kind of sepulchre. There were rooms long disused and dust-sheeted, others slightly familiar to him and possessed by Rachel's things. Her cardigan casually thrown down by a work-box, waiting to be picked up again and worn. A game of chess abandoned. And, incredibly, dishes from that shared last dinner, washed and left to drain.

Slowly they stepped, not touching, pausing on the threshold of each room. Chloe just looked, wide-eyed and unspeaking.

They altered nothing until they reached the enclosed space of Rachel's study. Shuffling through her desk Jack wondered what had happened to the two letters he'd drafted and Chloe had copied and signed, not very long ago. They weren't there – had Cairns got them? Chloe took some unpaid bills and an address book. A few relatives, although distant and long estranged, had to be notified and invited to the funeral.

The visit seemed to have shaken her and she didn't want him to go on to his meeting. They drove to XLTV together. She decided to visit a gallery then wait for him in a nearby bar.

'This meeting won't take very long,' he promised grimly.

Ross said they should make Cragge directly responsible for the deaths of his wife and children, the revenge arson attack wasn't enough. 'He should be to blame for the fire, by some oversight, then fail to save them. He sees their screaming faces at an upstairs window – '

'What is this, who is this?' cut in Jack.

'You've missed every opportunity,' Ross accused. 'It's flaccid. Dullsville UK.'

'I didn't invent *Cragge* to be a comic cartoon for adolescents. I haven't made it lurid, puerile or obvious – until now.'

'Inability to take criticism is the hallmark of a bad writer,' snapped Ross.

'Little boys with big daddies,' Jack retorted, 'should sort out their inferiority complexes.'

They ended the meeting.

Later Jack called Gideon who, combing through their agreement, confirmed that Cammell was obliged to offer him the scripting of five further episodes.

'I wouldn't touch them!' shouted Jack down the phone.

Gideon replied calmly, 'In any case, according to my spies Ross Cammell is commissioning himself to write all the scripts. Says no one else's writing had been acceptable. Nice work, hm? Listen, Jack, let me trade with them. You'll waive the option if they'll give you a consultancy credit and fee.'

'Would that give me any power?'

'Of course not. Cammell would have to show you all his scripts, and take notes from you – but he wouldn't have to act on them. If you want power become a director.'

'No thanks. Get me that consultancy, Gideon. I'm going to shred that little prick on a very regular basis. One condition: they fly me out to six major European locations – three in different areas of France – with expenses paid.' He listened to the pause. 'Otherwise I'm going to script the show – my way – and get them blacklisted if they change one word.'

'Jack – '

'Go for it, Gideon.'

He put down the phone. He'd have his revenge. And the locations – which he wanted for the novel – could be in any areas infiltrated by British secret agents. To view this arena from the perspective of *Cragge*'s film production would add a surreal update that he might even use in the book.

Rachel was buried on the eastern side of Highgate Cemetery, in the plot reserved for her beside Charles Rushe. It was an afternoon late in May, bright between scudding clouds and heavy squalls of rain. A gusting wind snatched the words of the vicar and tugged at his robes. Jack stood among a small group of mourners at the grave with Chloe and the Fairbrothers, Inspector Cairns and the family solicitor. A couple of neighbours had come from the village and a handful of Rachel's relatives from Leeds. They prayed together. The coffin was lowered, earth and flowers fell on it. The rushing air seemed vibrant with life and shockingly ripe with nourishment.

The dark-clothed figures turned away from the grave-side and Jack followed the young law partner Hartsledge, who walked with an arm linked under Chloe's arm, supportive or proprietorial. Then something made Jack glance back. Under the urgent tossing trees he glimpsed a small figure darting between tombstones, approaching the mound of freshly turned earth and bouquets.

Quietly, leaving the mourners he threaded his way back among stone angels and marble slabs to the new grave.

It was Jodie Delancey, placing a bunch of bluebells on the ground. As she straightened up Jack grabbed her. The girl spun round.

'You're a little late for the funeral,' Jack told her. 'Or was that intentional?'

'Let go of me! You've got a nerve, you and her – driving Rachel to this and then spewing out prayers. I wish it was both of you in that box.'

He shook her. 'What d'you mean – what've you told Cairns? Tell me.'

'Like hell I will! You're to blame – just so's you know that . . .' She spat at Jack, wriggled out of his grasp and fled across the cemetery. He followed but she was too quick for him and vanished through a gap in the fence.

Justin and Anna were waiting by their car. 'What happened to you? The others have gone on to the house.'

'Right.' He wasn't in the mood for explanations. They drove in silence a hundred yards up the hill to Whitting House where the mourners were gathered for drinks. Justin was agog at the interior, 'Great film set. Lurid, wonderful bad taste. Did Corman use this to shoot any horror films. Poe adaptations or – ?'

'For God's sake, Justin.' Jack disowned him, hurriedly refilled the sherry glasses of elderly ladies. Within a minute the strains of a tango were swamping out the wake. Striding to the music centre, switching it off he hissed to Anna, 'Can't you keep that idiot on a leash?' and turned back to Chloe's guests.

Into a silence the unabashed Justin boomed, 'Let's dance – let's be genuine and celebrate the afterlife. Chloe, come on . . .'

She swept him out of the room on some pretext of showing him around.

Jim Hartsledge and his wife Lily had left; the few relatives followed early to catch their train. Jack thought Rachel must've struggled to rise above her origins – and the sweeter air hadn't lasted long. He said the goodbyes. Where were Chloe and Justin? He made himself ignore their absence.

'How well did you know Rachel?' he asked Anna.

'I only met her after her husband's accident. She was depressed, on the booze. Poor Chloe. Every time she came to stay with us she'd relax and get happier – then go back to Rachel or that school.'

'Mulhaven, with your sister. What was it like?'

'Madly progressive. Lessons not compulsory, drugs, everyone smoking and bonking.'

Jack wished he hadn't asked. Now he had a new, unwanted image of the young Chloe – experienced, knowing things too early.

Anna asked, 'What happens to this ugly old house? What will Chloe do?' He gave some reply that he didn't know what she'd want, it was too soon.

That night he couldn't sleep but got up and walked through the silent streets, uphill and so far that he found himself passing through the gates of Whitting. Dawn was blotting the night, seeping behind the spiked edges of those roofs and chimneys, the secret trees and undergrowth. There was no sign in the garden of their efforts, everything was just as it had been. Had he dreamed their second visit, Rachel's death and funeral?

As he wandered through the dew-soaked dawn the cries of birds were densening to a shrieking wall of sound. A giant crow flapped out, flew overhead. It ripped the sun which tried to set and a yellow beak scythed between those black ragged wings, tapered and long as a night angel's: they rolled over the sky blocking out the light. He tried to run to the sun but his feet were rooted and he saw he'd grown into a tree, top-heavy in full leaf. The sun had shrunk, it became the egg of the bird and smashed, it bled hot gold over him.

He woke because Chloe was hitting him. Switching on the light he saw her eyes glittering with panic. She'd had the first of many nightmares: Rachel rising from a watery grave; Rachel accusing and following in pursuit; hooking into her, unshakeable. She was towed to an abyss, fire raged beneath. She always woke at the edge.

When she'd grown calm they talked about her sense of guilt. Chloe said it was because she'd ill-wished Rachel and felt that to be powerful. She talked about social rituals, blessings and spells, about belief and how it was used by everyone, unconsciously in everyday life. About the modern voodoo spoken through the media. 'We use mass belief to move events.' She'd read about the results of thought with emotion, of faith, and said it was possible she'd caused Rachel's accident.

Now he knew what he'd been trying to forget – she was responsible. And telling him so, giving a false reason.

But dawn came and the sun wasn't dead. He told her, 'Superstition means nothing, it has no power.' He made coffee and they drank it in bed.

She argued, 'There are dark forces, whatever you say. And that house is an evil place. My father wanted to fill it with children, music, life – look what happened to him, and now to her! I'm going to knock the house down, sell to developers.'

Like St Pius's Church, arid with air-conditioning, carpets and Neff kitchens? He couldn't let her do that. 'Wait a while,' Jack persuaded, 'then see how you feel.'

Two days later Cairns dropped by as Jack was about to visit Mary and George. His suspense novel was being returned. 'I could've sworn the detective did it,' Cairns commented, perching on the sofa and tasting a Pernod.

Jack smiled. 'I had you fooled?'

'Mm. Never thought it would turn out to be the hero. Motive seemed too clear – with his wife in line to inherit. Crime writers, they must have their heads stuffed with ideas. Incidentally, how well did you know Jodie Delancey?'

'Hardly at all – I met her a couple of times.'

'Girl seemed frightened. And she's disappeared now – left a false address.' He paused, went on, 'Funny, said she heard someone moving round the house, well past midnight. Could it have been you?'

'I left before eleven and Chloe with me. Maybe it was Mrs Rushe? By the way, we're off round Europe for three or four weeks very soon.' Cairns, about to go, stopped and regarded him. 'We both need a break,' Jack added.

'Leave a contact address,' was all Cairns said.

His parents seemed more put out by their altered plans. 'For a whole month?' his mother queried. 'Michael's only expecting you in June. What about your writing? And Chloe, isn't she working?'

Her photographic job hadn't worked out but he wasn't going to talk about that. 'It's the best time to go. There's so much we want to see.'

George put in, 'Michael's planning to expand. They're doing very well.'

How he hated the way they kept on about his brother,

the elder son who achieved so easily. Anger left him silent and Mary must've sensed something. 'How's the series?' she asked.

He told them he planned to write a novel set in 1940. His father pondered the wisdom of it and Mary agreed. 'You had such a terrible time before the lucky break with TV.'

'*Cragge* wasn't just luck,' Jack took her up quickly. 'It deserved to succeed.'

'Oh but I didn't mean – '

He cut across his mother's backtracking to ask George for new titles. He'd be researching life in the Blitz and the work of undercover agents.

As he set the table Mary asked, 'Are you serious about Chloe? You never tell me anything! And this stepmother who died – where does her family live, what're they like?'

He didn't want to answer and as if to co-operate Chloe arrived, she'd come by taxi from seeing her solicitor. Mary sped into a flurry of activity, proffered drinks and put on vegetables, offered sympathy on the bereavement. Chloe looked uncomfortable. 'I didn't know Rachel very well,' she said finally.

'I thought you lived with her, dear?'

'That was a long time ago,' Chloe, brittle and edgy, was clearly afraid of interrogation.

Mary smoothed it over but Jack thought some instinct had been roused in his mother, a suspicion or resentment. There was more talk about Michael and the grand-children, the villa and the booming business. Chloe looked dutifully at snapshots.

They made their escape and roared off home in the Golf. He felt full of a pent-up desperation. 'Let's leave tonight. Let's never come back!'

Chloe laughed. 'We could just go – to hell with it all! They don't approve of me, you know.'

'They can't understand – I don't give a damn about it. Chloe, we can go anywhere and stay as long as we want.'

'To Paris – and the Massif Central . . .'

'Across the Alps . . . How about Monte Carlo? And Milan . . .?'

'Madrid, Alicante. Down to beautiful Granada. And along the coast to Valencia?' They drew up outside his house. Chloe smiled through the half-dark before he kissed her. 'What else would you like to do, darling?'

'Have you something in mind?'

3

Blood red, pink and yellow, like fat soldiers in uniform they marched across the earth. Rotted stuff had gone into them. He'd poisoned slugs and snails, sprayed greenfly, watered and pruned. Under their leaves the fresh mud of the flower-beds was greedy and grasping.

Washing his hands in Nora Smiley's kitchen, Art saw her glance out through the window. 'That's very nice,' she said approvingly. 'Those roses are as good as the park.'

'We strive to please.' Art took the two fivers she held out, noticed her hand jump away from his and her breathing stop. He gave her a grin and touched his forelock, mocking. 'See you next week.'

Walking home he stopped motionless and turning away from the sun gazed north, uphill, his face uplifted in shadow. Whitting House lay beyond his sight but he envisioned it waiting for him. In the deepest sense it was his home, he was aware of everything happening there. All his life he'd been caught up in the house and its occupants while fate wove him into its fabric. The place was his, his inheritance. But the cops were still around and for some reason far too interested. He had to wait.

The skip was full in Nightingale Place. There was a useful dining chair with no seat, easy enough to fix but Jodie kept throwing out his best stuff. She was back at least – she and the baby – they were his and the old bat's trying to take them away had been a neat warning. He must always be part of the triad, the family.

He went in and the baby was on the bed playing with a toy farm she'd brought with her from the house. Banging things together to make a noise it would chuck them across the room or gnaw them like an animal. In the back room Jodie was washing clothes at the sink.

'I bought us a few things,' he greeted her.

Jodie looked in the carrier bag. He'd got tins of baked beans and corned beef, packets of mash and crisps.

'That corner shop's a waste of money,' she complained. 'We could get proper food down at the market, meat and fresh veg.'

What was wrong with her? She was always moaning these days. 'That kind of thing's too pricey, we can't afford it.'

'It works out cheaper and the baby needs real food, not rubbish.'

Always the bloody baby. He could hate it so much. 'Why don't you shop with the nobs, then.'

'You know I can't go out now,' she retorted as if it was his fault. 'I suppose you want that for your tea.'

'I don't ask much. After doing a day's work.'

Jodie clattered the frying pan. The sickly, hollow smell of the gas brought an image of his mother's cooking, her face, her presence powerful even when she'd slept among the dead ... Art backed off faint, leaned against a wall. In a swamp of nausea he heard her voice disembodied like a tape recording gone wrong, 'If I'm going to stay, there's got to be some changes. For a start we need both rooms. All this junk has got to go.'

She didn't understand, couldn't recognise him because Rachel Rushe had undermined all his influence. Those words 'If I'm going to stay' ... But she had nowhere else

159

to go. He must humour her but it was getting more difficult, she would go on with her stupid mourning. He could
tell her everything – but that wasn't allowed, that was
taboo and it was easy to see why. She wouldn't
understand.

During the evening things got worse. 'I liked it there,'
she went on. 'Spacy, quiet. All those rooms – you never
saw half of it. And she was so generous – poor Rachel, if
only she was still alive.'

Biting back words, Art said in his soft reasoning voice,
'It had to happen.'

'No, it didn't. She wasn't that old and was getting better,
I helped her. She might even have given up the drink. It
was that girl Chloe, hounding her – specially on the last
night.'

Jodie was sitting at the table polishing stuff. Art took
up the carving knife that was from the house, it had an
ivory handle and long shiny blade. He thought: remember
her, remember the child. He said, 'I reckon she's got it
coming to her, doing that to the poor old bag.'

'I'm glad I took these things,' Jodie agreed. 'She won't
get these.'

Art frowned. He could sense someone moving behind
the wall on his left. 'Don't talk so loud.'

'Why not?' she cried. 'Who's there to hear, or care?
And don't go turning the TV on – I'm sick of it. I want
to hear music or nothing.'

'Quiet!' hissed Art.

'Rachel was kind to me. And you're jealous. I think
you're pleased she's gone.'

'Shut up about her!' Art was deadly serious now. Someone was listening, behind the wall near where they sat.
Goldman.

'I need to talk about her. Why shouldn't I? You spoiled
it all for Raphael and me.'

It was almost as if she knew, was about to blurt things out. He jumped up from the table resisting an impulse to hit her, silence her properly. 'Mustn't do that!' Had he thought or said the words aloud? It didn't matter, it was right, he had to protect the family. Stepping to the TV he turned it on and the volume up. Contestants in a game show were looking out at them and he threw a cloth over the set.

'Godsakes, turn it down!' Jodie screamed. 'We'll get complaints.' She sat staring at him through the blare of noise, then her face crumpled and she started to cry. How he hated her crying.

Then the baby was howling too on the bed and Jodie snatched it away from him. 'Raffy's frightened of you.' She began to soothe the baby, rocking it.

'He's my son. Don't you forget that.'

When the baby had quieted a bit she said, 'I haven't forgotten, but he isn't used to you so don't – '

'I'll do what I like.'

'He's not been well. He needs to go out, and now I can't it's driving us both mad. That's why he doesn't sleep. He was better at Rachel's – '

'Shut up.' Art heard his voice sounding cold and dangerous. That left her quiet. It was time she paid him more attention, gave him respect.

After a minute she said, 'If that rash gets any worse he must go to the clinic.'

'The police would send you back into care and take the baby away. Cairns, the cop you keep on about. Why'd he question you like that unless they suspect something? Now you've run off they're hunting for you.' Jodie shook her head but she looked scared. He went on, 'They're not sure about you at all. They'll get you, Jodie.'

Now he was back in control. Lining the partition wall with newspapers, Sellotaping them, he said it was for

161

insulation. She watched in silence, nursing Raffy. He knew Goldman was spying through cracks and reporting back to the landlord. And Cooper wasn't what he seemed, anyone could tell that. He needed information and advice, a new direction and on the third dawn a sign came. Walking into the kitchen, stepping to the sink he saw them. A knife, a fork, in the perfect symmetry of a cross. He was to go to St Pius's Church.

Leaving the flat he set off uphill. Early Mass was at seven, the church kept locked when there was no ritual on. He'd sit in the Virgin's chapel and ask when to return to Whitting, how his place would be handed over.

They must have changed the times for services. No one there and the door closed firm against him. Art looked for the noticeboard but it had gone. Someone must've stolen it. He tried the side then vestry doors but they were locked. Stepping back he studied the building and saw every window had been boarded up.

Why, against what? It looked as if there was a war on. As if bombs were expected.

He must get in. The vestry door had simple hinges. He'd come back after dark with a screwdriver. Deciding this he felt slightly better and turned to go.

Then he saw the sign nailed on the porch and its big red letters: FOR SALE.

Shock drove through winding him, making it hard to breathe. He lurched against the fence. Someone stopped to stare. Art read the sign again and again – those seven letters, their significance drilled into him.

He couldn't stand there for ever but began to walk and was soon at the gates of Waterlow Park. This at least was open and he went in, meandering numb through the designed landscape and past that sign: *a garden for the gardenless*.

Sitting on a bench Art looked across the lake. Weed covered, it reminded him of Whitting's gardens.

The little squares of the city below were smudged with early morning mist, nothing clear yet. Trees half obscured the lines and blocks of the gameboard but he knew it by heart. Closing his eyes he saw its subjects passing through lives directed by the powerful, the invisible. Art's left hand in his pocket closed on the edges of the twin dice. He'd done all he could to carry out her moves, had acted with faith and trust, patience and courage. There'd been no mistake, surely?

Fear stalked the sunlit park. He stayed all day until dusk fell, driving out the innocents, mothers with babies, kids and old folk. Tiny strings of light emerged, gold linings to London's deepening cloud. The keeper got him out, locked the gate. Still no explanation of where he stood! He went a different way to Junction Road avoiding St Pius's. His world was shrinking, closing in.

Jodie sat sifting through her treasures from the girl's room. Her mind was off in the past again. Peering into the hand mirror, she pinned a *diamanté* clip in her hair.

Art said, 'Let's have a look – is it the girl's?'

'Same as the one she was wearing that last evening,' Jodie answered.

Examining it he questioned her, 'Exactly the same? That last evening?'

She nodded. 'It must be worth a bit. But I'd rather keep these things.'

Art murmured agreement. 'We'll keep this – you never know.'

'They're all I've got left,' she started again. 'Rachel was really generous. If only she hadn't had that accident.'

Something alerted Art. 'Then what?'

'I know you got fed up but she was so kind. That last evening . . .'

163

'Go on,' he prompted. 'What?'

'Rachel wanted to adopt me properly so Raphael and I would be her relatives. She wanted to change her will and leave us all her inheritance. D'you understand now?'

He was just beginning to.

Art took hold of the girl and shook her. 'Is that true, you haven't made it up? She was going to leave you everything! Was she?' And he started to laugh at the clarity breaking in his head, stark and blinding.

'Art . . .'

He'd done right – and been betrayed. It was one terrible mistake. Fate's trickery was taking his breath away.

She had turned into his adversary.

Art dropped his hold on the girl and she backed off. He said, 'You're the only friend I have.' He saw the walls encircling him sway then tilt, steep like in a ship at storm before the tide sheered up and blinded him.

4

'Where are you?'

Art's eyes were afraid as Jodie bent over him. 'I'm here.'

'They've blinded me, I can't see! Don't go away!'

Jodie filled with pity. She tried to tug him up from the floor. 'You've got a fever, you need to get to bed.'

All next day he was flinching away from something invisible, jumping at any sound. He begged her, 'You mustn't listen to what they say.'

She reassured him, 'I'm here. It's OK.' They hadn't got a thermometer but she could feel it was a bad fever, his head was on fire.

The front room reeked of fear, fetid and rank. Outside the sun scorched a brilliant path towards midsummer. Jodie opened windows to cool the human oven but the lorries roaring past made Art scream. He wept and told her, 'You don't think so but they're hostile, they want to burn your guts.'

Hot days and hellish nights. The baby cried a lot, since the shock of Rachel's death she hadn't been able to feed him. He always seemed to suffer around his father. Now she nursed them both and fought revulsion because she couldn't bear to lie with Art again. Making a bed in the back room she slept there with Raphael.

The food ran out. When she went to the door Art staggered up, violent like a drunk to stop her. What was in his mind, what could she do? More than a year ago she'd bought some travel pills and she remembered how they'd make you drowsy. Art's fever kept him thirsty; he drank the sugary water and soon slept.

It was five to ten, the corner shop was about to shut. She'd only got a couple of pounds and reluctantly Jodie packed her keepsakes. The mirror and brush, the carving knife, a Victorian teething ring that Rachel had given Raphael. The *diamanté* clip was missing. What had Art done with it?

Tiptoeing out with the baby she felt like a thief and a dark shape loomed from the landing, scared her half to death. It was only Mr Goldman coming out of the shared bathroom. 'How's the nipper?' he asked.

'He's a bit fretful with the heat.' Jodie skipped out, went scurrying to the shop. She bought milk and rusks, came back then turned down the alley. Tony hadn't drawn the curtains, he was reading by a lamp and she could hear music playing.

'Hey,' he smiled, looking pleased. 'Thought you'd been spirited off again . . . All right, love?'

'Yes,' Jodie managed, feeling weak with relief.

He ushered her in. 'Frankly you don't look it.'

'Art's ill. I can't stay long in case he wakes up.' And she told him about the fever, how Art wouldn't see any doctor. She'd told Tony about it all: Whitting House, Rachel's accident, even running away and how scared she was with the police. He seemed safe to her. He'd done things like being an actor then sailing on a cargo ship round the world. And he made her laugh.

Reaching into the bag she showed him the treasures taken from Whitting. 'Trash ain't what it used to be,' Tony mused. 'I have to wind down this place.'

'*A'Laddinscave*? You can't shut down!'

'The lease ends in November, Cooper wants everyone out. Developers hover with flapping wings.' Her face must've fallen because he went on softly, 'But your Mr Adams is a sitting tenant, you've nothing to fear.'

She reminded him about the eviction threats, how she hadn't wanted to come back partly because of that. 'And what was the other part?' he asked shrewdly. Jodie grimaced. He asked again.

She began, 'He's Raphael's dad –'

'Come on, anyone can tell it isn't right. You and the baby look worse every time I see you.'

'Well, thanks very much!' She hesitated. 'Sometimes he scares me.'

'Scares you how?'

'Things he says. And – kind of jumpy.'

'Art doesn't know you've been coming here?'

Puzzled, Jodie shook her head. 'Why would that matter?' Tony didn't answer. She picked up the teething ring. 'You won't want to buy anything, 'cause of closing.'

Pulling a box from the desk he asked, 'How much d'you need?'

'Oh no, I didn't mean . . .' She felt uneasy now, and put the things back in the bag.

'Take it as a loan,' Tony said. She glanced at the notes he held out but she didn't want to take them, not from this friend. 'Go on, the baby needs it.' He put the cash in her pocket, she dropped the bag in confusion. What he was lending her looked too much.

'Don't know when I can pay you back. But I will – before November. Why don't you keep these, see if you can sell them anyway? I've got to get home. Thank you, Tony.'

Jodie kissed him. He held her for a moment, then let her go. 'Take care. Come and see me soon.'

With Raphael clasped tight and the money warm in her pocket she sped back along the alley, in and up the stairs. Her feet slowed heavy as she climbed.

If only she hadn't panicked and come back – but at least Art knew how to avoid the cops, and she'd nowhere else to live. The allowance from Rachel had gone on food but Tony's hundred quid felt like a fortune, solid as a passport to be kept for the future.

In the evenings, keeping a look-out for police she'd call at Tony's or just walk, tasting freedom. The detective Cairns would soon lose interest in Rachel's accident, then she'd be all right. And what about Art? The edge of violence had just been because he was sick, out of his mind in some way – but trust had gone.

Art wouldn't get up, not even to wash. It was the illness, summer flu or whatever – but after a week she got angry. He'd lose his jobs, what would they live on? She nagged him to get out, to phone and say when he'd go back.

'You're no bloody good!' she yelled in frustration. 'Doesn't it matter what happens to your kid? Don't you care about him?'

'Shut up!' he hissed, and the look in his eyes silenced her. 'I've got a lot to work out, a lot to think about.'

Jodie bit back anger. She felt unsafe with him. The baby cried when they quarrelled, it set off Art's temper so she must keep him quiet until Art was himself.

It was the Wednesday before midsummer that she realised she didn't know what Art was really like and she probably never had. After that day, she never wanted Raphael near his father again. She'd left Art lying in bed after breakfast. In the back room she sat down by Raphael and began to sort his clothes. She'd heard of a shop that exchanged kids' things.

Visitors were so rare it took a minute to recognise the

knock. Then instinctively she moved to pick up the baby. It might be authority, might mean trouble. Putting her ear to the closed partition Jodie heard Art move stealthily in the front room.

A man called from the landing, 'Mr Adams. Open the door.'

Another knocking. Then a sharp click. Art had put on the second lock. The man on the landing would've heard it too, now he'd know someone was home.

She jumped back as Art pushed through, she felt his wired intensity like someone about to run a race. Opening the drawer he took out a carving knife. 'Don't make a sound.'

'Art? What're you going to do?'

'They've come for us. I knew they would. Stay here and keep Raffy quiet.'

'Who is it?' she asked, frightened. He went back into the front room without speaking. From the doorway she saw him hide the knife behind his back. Out on the landing voices murmured; it was at least two men.

The same one called, 'Mr Adams, we want to talk to you. Unlock this door.'

That was an order. Now she knew the police had come for her. They were three storeys up with no fire escape, outside the kitchen window was a flat roof two floors down. If it weren't for the baby she'd try to jump. She thought: they know we're here and I ran away, they'll break the door.

Holding Raphael she crept to the tautly waiting Art, whispered, 'It's the detective. What can we do?'

He took no notice.

A key turned in the lock. The voices muttered again. Then a second key.

They both wore sharp suits, and something told her at once they weren't the cops. They had a different air, a different purpose. She felt relief, then a new fear. Whoever they were she didn't like the look on their faces. From behind Art she demanded, 'Who are you? Why're you breaking in here?'

'Scarcely breaking in, sweetheart,' came the oily reply. 'We need a little conversation and it's tricky being subtle through a door. Mr Arthur Adams, I presume?'

Art stepped forward. Now they couldn't come in without pushing. His voice was quiet, deadened, 'Who sent you?'

'Can't you guess? Associates of Mr Cooper, we are. We'd like to have a talk about the future.'

The words seemed to trigger some change in Art and a kind of cunning crept into him. If only she could get the baby out. The room felt stifling with menace. Something was about to happen, so terrible it would cripple all their lives.

Art – suddenly radiating charm – put out his left hand to pacify, 'Any associate of Mr Cooper is a friend of my own fate.'

It was an odd thing to say and left them uncertain, glancing at each other. 'Mr Cooper has a message for us to deliver. We'd like to come in.'

'No!' screamed Jodie as Art stepped back, left hand welcoming and right hand . . . 'He's got a knife!'

The man stopped. The blade in Art's hand flashed.

She threw herself across the baby.

A shout. From the floor she saw through bars of a chair blood running down the man's face, crookedly to an astonished mouth.

Art heaved himself forward as she screamed again and buried her face in the rug. A crash, and the chair fell on her. All blows and shouts. What was happening?

'Bloody cretin,' said a voice, breathless into silence.

'Cooper only wanted to do a deal. You've done it now, Adams. Had all your chances.'

There was another thud and she heard Art moan. She uncurled, raised her head slowly so they wouldn't see. 'The deal's off, OK. Clear out of here or we'll be back. You got that?'

They went away down the stairs and she saw Art lying on the other side of the room. Way down in the hall the front door slammed. Jodie got to her knees, her heart echoing the baby's cries.

Was Art dead? The knife was nowhere to be seen. She started to crawl fearfully towards his body. 'Art?'

He opened his eyes. They were cold and bitter. She saw that he was all right, and that he hated her. If he still had the knife he'd probably kill her and Raphael now. Staggering up she stumbled to the open door.

Like a shot he was up and there before her. He slammed the door, lurched against it. 'Whose side are you on?'

'What were you doing, trying to kill them? They only wanted to talk.'

'Keep your mouth shut,' he hissed. 'Little fool! You haven't a clue what's going on.'

'Like what? Tell me.'

'It was for you and him I had to see them off – don't you know that?'

She'd got to reassure him, lull him back to security by dredging up the right things to say. 'They didn't get too far. They won't dare come back, not after you put up such a fight.' But she felt he could almost read her mind and when he was near she concentrated on stopping her thoughts, living out a passive acceptance. Only Raphael gave them away by trembling at every sound, by clinging on to her.

It was like being in a siege. Secretly, while Art was in

171

the other room at night she made her plan of escape. There were sixty-six pounds from Tony's loan and it had to keep them until she found a way to live.

Waiting for her chance Jodie told Art she wouldn't go outside – not for a long time. The food cupboard was empty. And he took charge again in a couple of days, announcing he'd got things to do and people to see, he'd be gone for a while.

From the window she watched his tall figure weave its shambling walk towards Archway. With Raphael and a bag of clothes she crept downstairs, at every step afraid he'd reappear and catch her leaving.

Outside the bright noisy day was unreal because they'd been shut in so long. She'd tell Tony, arrange contact about the loan – and never come near Junction Road again.

He was sorting a tray of jewellery near the back and she felt a stab of regret because she'd miss Tony and their talks. 'I'm leaving Art,' she said. 'We've got to go quickly in case he comes back.'

He hadn't been expecting it. 'Where will you go? You could stay here.'

'Tony, thanks – but it's too close.' She started telling him about the knife attack on Cooper's men, how she was afraid Art might turn on her next. 'He mustn't know where we are. He's dangerous. Don't you have anything to do with him.'

'Where will you stay, Jodie? What will you live on?'

She was going to answer when the shop door-bell chimed. Someone was coming in. Tony said, 'Customer. Wait here, love.'

It must be Art. He'd come back, found them gone and guessed . . . Tony would be in danger now. As he went to the front she slipped round to hide behind some tables.

It wasn't Art.

'Morning, constable,' she heard Tony say loudly. 'What can I do for you today?'

Heart thudding, Jodie eased round the tables towards the door. They were walking slowly back up the shop, the constable saying, 'There's a check on for stolen goods. Had anything in recently?'

'I'm winding down my stock,' Tony answered. 'Closing soon, so I haven't been buying. But feel free.'

'I'll take a look round.'

'Come through by the back, maybe you'd like a cuppa?'

'Thirsty kind of day,' the voice agreed.

She was near the door now – but it would chime when she opened it. The cop couldn't see her but he'd hear, might look after them and recognise her description.

Then she heard the high, bell-like tune of the music box starting up. Clever Tony! In one quick movement she was at the door and dragging it open, darting out to the road.

Running through mean streets, skittering round corners on a panicky course she zig-zagged between the staring pedestrians and didn't dare stop even when the baby's weight and the bag thudding left her slowing, gasping for breath. Hurtling among market stalls she lost herself in the crowd and tunnelled towards the mouth of the Underground.

5

Jack put his foot down and the Saab leapt faster, smoothly obedient to his touch, eating kilometres with an almost silent power. Chill air tore through them in the scorched, sun-bruised plain. His new white convertible had speed and elegance, the dashboard of a jetplane and upholstery of the softest, deep maroon leather. What if there was a huge debt waiting back home? No need to think about that yet and meantime he could feel like someone in a movie.

He glanced across at Chloe beside him, she gazed straight out at the passing strangeness. Her arm lay along the top of the passenger-door, left hand tapping to the beat. A musician's hand, supple and long-fingered. The gold band, new and shiny, meant she was his. And yet . . .

The truth was he didn't know much about her, even now. As the cassette ended he asked, 'When did you last take a journey like this?'

She turned to him, the huge sun-glasses hiding her eyes and half her face. 'Never,' she answered. 'There was nothing like this.'

Who was she kidding? A girl like her. 'But touring, driving about. Have you crossed western Europe like this before?'

'I only went to music festivals with Charles when I was little,' Chloe said. 'In Paris and Vienna, Marrakesh.'

'Marrakesh? But what about since. In the last six years?'

Chloe shook her head. 'No. Travelling's best with someone you care about, isn't it?'

'But you've had lovers,' Jack began. There were things he wanted to know that he hadn't felt able to ask before. 'Were there droves of them, before me?'

She flashed him a glance. 'Only two. Not like your droves of old ladies.'

'You're joking.' But she wasn't. 'Who were they?'

'We're not in Spain yet. Why the Inquisition?' She sighed. He waited. 'OK, Bryan was my music teacher – '

'At Mulhaven?' He felt appalled. 'And were you under age?'

'Only the first year. Anyway he was living with Ginny who taught pottery.'

'How very cosy! No surprise you had a breakdown.'

She was annoyed. 'We cared for each other – '

'Don't give me that,' Jack cut back. 'What a little fool.'

'I didn't start confiding in you so I could be judged!'

He felt her withdrawal leaving him cold and alone. 'I'm trying to understand. The second one – was he married?' Bringing out the words finally he asked, 'Was it Justin?'

A second's silence then Chloe yelled, 'What d'you think I am! Anna's husband? I hope that's a joke.'

She was protesting too much, it was false. 'Who was it? You can tell me.'

'I promised not to, and that still stands.' She stared at him, a sort of disappointment was in her voice, 'It shouldn't matter now. Stop putting me down.'

Jack took her hand, put it to his mouth and nipped the fingertips one by one. 'My vulgar curiosity, the Writerish Inquisition.'

'Uh-huh,' she relented. 'Think we're ever going to get there?' He'd slowed right down without realising. 'Maybe I should drive,' she suggested, sly.

'Like hell.' And Jack sent the car zipping ahead fast.

Then they were silent and thoughts crowded his head. Chloe was so secretive. He wanted control... With a schoolteacher, from the age of fifteen – hadn't anyone suspected? And how long with Justin, if it was him?

The blurred blue dream of hills ahead grew dense and solid, real, as he began to tell her what he'd learned of this country in wartime, of courage and betrayal. And soon the Saab began to climb, winding over tumbling outfalls and through ancient tunnels in black rock, until they emerged at dusk to gaze on the fields and towns of France far below.

Chloe took photos in the fading light. 'Is this about the new novel?'

'I must be transparent.'

'There's an incredible intensity when you get close to a new piece of work. Going to tell me?'

Jack hesitated, then started slowly, 'The character's a secret agent who disappears – British HQ believe he's dead.'

'And he isn't?'

'His wife, working in a London emergency hospital, has got involved with a conchie. But Massey isn't dead, he's a prisoner of the German SD.'

'So what happens?' she mused.

But he smiled non-committally because not to tell felt rare and precious. And to analyse might mean to kill.

He thought: Massey's training and experience have turned him into a murderer.

Linking arms they walked to the village, to a tiny *pension* on the ravine. A million stars grew bursting with fertility close overhead, dimming lights in the dark pit of the plain.

Chloe recorded the man-made ruins overgrown by landscape. After a couple of days they headed for Perpignan, abandoned the car to walk in Pyrenean foothills. It was desolate and wild and his mind ranged over thoughts about Massey.

Crossing the border they drove to Barcelona, staying in the gothic quarter. It was the next day as they climbed steps from the cathedral crypt that Jack realised they were being followed. Chloe was ahead when he glanced back. The man stood out a mile, Spanish in appearance, in a suit and a tie on this hot day. As Jack stared he stopped to light a cigarette. Tourists wandered past and he was gone.

He bore the stamp of a plain-clothes cop but would be a city businessman at his place of worship. And yet, all down the length of his spine Jack could feel he was being watched.

Out in the glaring heat they crossed the ramblas to a shady table and ordered drinks. Again he felt observed and cursing himself for an over-imaginative fool, turned to look. The man sat in full sun across the street and seemed to be reading, but they were clearly in his sight. Then he shifted to face away.

'That bloke,' Jack said casually, 'was in the crypt just behind us. And why's he sitting in the sun – unless to keep some distance?'

Chloe had grown very still, staring at him as if at some intricate pattern. But he could swear it wasn't him she was seeing. 'Darling, you think we're being followed?' she mocked. Then she turned to look.

And the man got up, walked back towards the cathedral.

'There he goes. Didn't even order.'

'We scared him off?' Chloe hooted with laughter. 'Why would anyone follow us – do we look suspicious? Too much cloak and dagger, my love!'

Jack smiled slightly. Maybe she was right.

Whispering overhead, the butterfly settled its shimmering wings on a scarlet poppy. The field lay shadeless under a hot sky, the grass was studded with wild flowers and bees purring lazily close then distant, underlining the layers of noonday silence. Breathing in raw scents of blossom and baked earth, Jack stretched out on the rug and Chloe's skirt touched his arm, soft as a wing.

He shaded his eyes to see. She was watching the bright creature and as it hovered over one then another sensuous feast of a flower her lips, slightly parted, curved in a smile. Finding the folds of her skirt he crumpled it against her so that she turned and looked at him.

Like a negative her skin was darkened, hair bleached pale. She stared down with mischievous eyes, laughing at his need for her attention. Desire scorched through Jack and his fingers tightened on the loose light skirt, sliding it up over the ridge of her briefs. Caressing her through the cotton. He couldn't bear to lie still but it was too hot to stir and they stayed motionless, looking into each other's eyes, daring silently like cats.

She ran a hand deliberately over him then pressed him back against the rug. Stroked down over his bare chest, unfastened his belt and the zip on his jeans. Her fingers worked to release him, closed hard around his bursting prick. She knelt, bending over him with a teasing, flickering, too-expert tongue. Then her mouth pushed down, sucking and thrusting deep into her throat and it happened faster than he'd have believed possible with red pulses building, roaring through his body to ejaculate wave on exploding wave into her throat.

Then a slight sense of betrayal began. Because Chloe was darting through his shimmering vision, uncatchable, untouched, and somehow satisfied. And looking at her smiling face he felt cheated for no clear reason.

Chloe smoothed damp hair from his forehead, he touched the curve of her cheek. Later, as she lay on her stomach, chin propped on one fist and studying him, she asked, 'How well do you get on with your brother? Are you close?'

'We haven't been around each other much for years,' Jack replied, managing to avoid her question. He didn't feel like making the promised visit to Michael now.

'You grew up close, only three years apart.' She was packing up the remains of their picnic and getting ready to set off. 'I feel terribly curious about meeting him, about seeing you with him.'

After weeks on the road alone together, everything was about to change. There'd be questions and comments from relatives, past and future were going to intrude. Why had he arranged it?

They crossed the province, wound through dried rust fields of olive and citrus. The heat felt stifling. From the village led a track of pot-holed, blood red clay where dead needles from thirsty pines filled cracks ribbing the earth. There'd been no rain for weeks.

The villa loomed long and white with red tiled roof, its garden circled in a clay wall. Then a rush of barking dogs. 'Vicente!' Jack called to a nephew and soon there was a swarm of children – thin, black-eyed and olive-skinned. Maria appeared, then Michael from the garden where sprinklers worked on lawns. There were kisses and hugs, introductions. Dragging battered luggage from the dust-caked car, in a chattering entourage they went up the wide stone steps.

On the verandah gifts were unwrapped and news was

exchanged over long cold drinks. The children, their English struggling, went off to the pool where shrieks and splashes rose in the hot evening air. Chloe rhapsodised about the kids and the villa, its trees and the massive scarlet bougainvillaea. 'So exotic a family!' she smiled.

The dogs clamoured, bounding down to the gate and Michael yelled to a girl by the pool, '*Elena!*' so she sped barefoot across wet grass. A man was delivering a huge flat white box. 'Friday is Maria's only evening off from cooking,' Michael explained. 'I insisted she keep to it.'

'Is that a pizza?' Chloe asked, amused.

'Paella. We always phone out for take-away paella – so exotic, huh?'

Cragge's blue eyes lanced across the shuttered living room. He leaned against a door, motionless. Conflict played over his features... They were more youthful and more dangerous than Jack remembered. Slowly the detective stepped into the bedroom, bars of light illuminating him. He shrugged off his jacket wearily, unbuttoned his shirt revealing a lean, surprisingly muscular body. As he sat on the bed his wife stirred under the covers.

'*Cariño? Rick, esta's bien...?*'

Rick Cragge looked down at her, unable to answer because his close-up froze and credits began to roll across it.

They'd gathered in the living room for part of *Cragge*'s first series. Jack mused, 'I'd forgotten how naïve and young he was.'

'He's likeable – and handsome,' commented Maria with a glance at her husband. 'He is popular here and it's only been on three weeks.'

Chloe put in, 'You should see him years later. A lot of disillusionment – a battered man.'

180

'But I prefer him as a proper hero! Why have you changed him, Jack?'

He shrugged. 'Events changed him – and the actor has weathered. There had to be some direction.'

The children dispersed to the garden and Michael switched off the commercials. 'Were you surprised to see it here?'

'The world has bought *Cragge*. I often wonder, what the hell do viewers in Iceland or Zambia make of these Brit cop shows? But it's the human experience which connects, since we're more alike than different. Now the moneybags insist on a mix of cultural detail – Euro puddings! I won't write *Cragge* again.'

'George said you're doing another book. They don't understand you chucking in that hard-earned security.'

'A man alone in a desert full of ravening jackals would feel more secure than a writer in television. I hear things are going well for you.'

'We're expanding next year, trade's good,' Michael agreed.

Soon Chloe began to question him about the company, his English boyhood and change of country. Jack listened. Through school then university, he was by birth the follower. Now Michael had achieved all this: a business with money and success, a big house with gardens planted by him, years of marriage and a horde of kids.

Was Chloe attracted? She seemed interested in Michael. Suddenly Jack found himself remembering small favouritisms: his older brother's bigger bedroom, later bedtimes and new clothes then handed down to him. The desk, the piano lessons. To the ten-year-old Jack these injustices had been cause for war and even now they lingered in some way. He wasn't worth it, he could only ever come second.

Even their wedding – spontaneous, with just two

witnesses and five minutes for a simple vow – became tawdry under Maria's questioning. As if they'd had something to hide. No pictures or mementos, no real celebration. And Chloe was admiring the wedding group photo on the mantelpiece. If she'd married Michael it would've been her big wedding, smart house provided. Nothing second best.

Then questions about where they'd live and what work he'd do if . . . Flippantly Jack answered, 'We'll decide all that next week.' He knew Chloe saw straight through him, heard the cause of his silence – she'd chosen in him just an echo, insubstantial.

On past visits he'd slept alone in the cool tiled guest room that overlooked Spanish gardens, distant hills. Now Chloe slept with her arms round him but he lay restless, awake a long time. Below, he knew, Michael and Maria talked on about his inadequacies.

In the morning the sun shrank these dark fantasies. They drove into the hills for a picnic, swam at the beach in the afternoon, dined in the city. At Elena's First Communion children sang under a gilded statue of the Virgin as the little girl, in long white frock and veil, was married to her parents' God. Chloe had been her father's partner until at this age she lost him to a second wife, then to the Reaper. Listening to alien prayers, watching the ritual like a tourist at a bullfight, Jack felt its violence under the pageantry. It devoured real flesh, spilt real blood, as Christ hung nailed to a dead tree of life.

That heavy, sometimes erotic symbolism – it was there too in the pictures at the print-works. 'Little Britain,' Michael mused, 'is beginning to blink her cold grey eyes at mainland Europe's Catholic heritage. Some mystery, some sensuality, might one day start to penetrate.'

Jack laughed. 'Hear the expatriate longing for his

homeland!' He felt again Chloe's fascination for the family, romanticising out of her lack.

It was their last night and Jack joined Chloe at the window, photographing the kids under the algarroba tree. A gecko hung motionless on the shutter waiting for them to go. The dogs were barking, listening, calling like wolves to their pack far across the province.

A hundred questions lay between them. Jack chose one, perhaps because of the children's voices crying out through the garden. Twining his arms round Chloe's waist, feeling familiar desire he asked, 'You were playing with Paquita this afternoon – you've enjoyed the kids?'

She grew tense and sharp instantly. 'You're asking if I've changed my mind? You know how I feel!'

It was a rejection. She didn't want his children – ever – and he tried to imagine them over the years, growing old without a family. He said nothing, watched his brother's children.

'You don't love me,' she accused. 'I'm not enough for you.'

They smoothed it over. Of course they loved each other, they were best alone together. It didn't matter where or how they lived.

Jack embraced Michael. Across the driveway Chloe laughed with Maria, kissed each of the children. Their departure was full of shouted exhortations and barking dogs. Speeding north a kind of urgency took hold and they hardly spoke till reaching the Normandy coast.

It was dusk the next day and they walked along a flat pebbled sweep of beach. Out across the Channel the horizon was invisible, sky and sea merged in deep trans-lucence. The tide was out, the shore lay slippery and treacherous under dark strands of weed. Jack climbed over clusters of sharp rock. The stained concrete landing platforms from D-Day stretched out before them into the ocean towards home.

He turned to Chloe where she stood staring out to sea. 'Where are we going?' he asked. 'Where is home?'

Carelessly she picked up a stone, threw it in a wide arc out to an invisible fall. 'I don't know. Anywhere!' She was sifting pebbles, finding a pale gleaming shell. 'Your house? Or mine in Putney?'

'We need somewhere to mark the change.' Jack took her hand, they wandered further down the beach. Lights were coming on all along the shore, sharp and small and bright. He suggested, 'There's Whitting.'

Chloe glanced at him sharply in the near darkness. 'I've never wanted to live there.' The tide was making little slapping sliding sounds.

'But it might be fun, worth a try.' He felt her shrug, or shiver, and put his arm round her shoulders because she was cold. He went on, 'It would be temporary until we decide – we've got to go somewhere.'

Chloe laughed suddenly, surprising him. 'I feel so happy, Jack – too happy to care. We could stay there a while. How shall we decide?'

Then reaching into her pocket she drew out a French coin: it glittered silver in the early night. Chloe laughed again. 'Let's toss a coin. My house or Whitting. It doesn't matter to us – we'll let the fates decide.'

'Wherever they tell us to go? Crazy . . . OK!'

'You call.' And she spun the coin.

'Heads,' he called.

Like children, not caring or believing that it could make any difference to them, they peered through the dark at the franc. 'It's heads,' Chloe said and slipped the coin back into her pocket.

Jack never got to see it. But they would live at Whitting.

6

SCENE 203. EXT. NORMANDY, DOCKS.

(The Lancia screams over narrow twisting cobbles. PIERRE at the wheel, expert nonchalance.

Closing in on Mercedes.

Outside a wood shack, an OLD FISHERMAN mending nets, he looks up.

Mercedes streaks past OLD FISHERMAN. He jumps back, falls.

PIERRE dive-bombs Lancia straight through shack, decimating it. Cutting into path of Mercedes. Cars collide at great speed.

KOPEC hurtles out from Mercedes.)

SCENE 204. EXT. NIGHT. NORMANDY, QUAYSIDE.

(KOPEC runs for his life. PIERRE in pursuit, Beretta in hand. KOPEC up blind alley: nowhere to go but the narrow quay . . .

PIERRE takes a shot. It zings past KOPEC's ear.)

SCENE 205. EXT. NIGHT. NORMANDY, OBSERVATION TOWER.

(Quay ends in observation tower under renovation. Scaffolding, cranes, hardware.

KOPEC is trapped, desperate. Scrambling up a hundred steps ...

At foot of steps PIERRE aims, takes another shot.

KOPEC screams, winged: slides round shield of scaffold platform at top.

PIERRE brushes dust from lapel of his Armani suit. Steps coolly into cab of yellow bucket crane.

Crane moves towards observation tower. Bucket swings closer to KOPEC's tall perch.

KOPEC raises both arms in terrified surrender.

PIERRE sees this. Rams lever home ...

Bucket swings, knocks screaming KOPEC through glass. He hurtles into jaws of machinery below.

Sea swells and froths, reddening.

CS: PIERRE permits a tiny smile. Takes out slim silver cigarette case, lights up.)

Sinking back among papers and boxes on his study floor, Jack let the script slide from his lap. It was printed on yellow paper, the title page was most intriguing. '*Kops*,' he mused aloud with a cynical smile. 'Rehearsal draft.'

The thirteen scripts, pink and yellow, green and blue, had no writer's name. Had Ross Cammell penned these then feared censure for self-commissioning? Or had the eager virgins on his writing team coagulated so instantly that this lollipop jelly was no one's responsibility? The stories' subjects – the usual terrorism, drug syndicates, political shock horrors – bore no relation to viewers' true experience. They'd be fed this weekly for three months.

He picked up a lime-green romp through someone's idea of the Mafia. Rick Cragge, warrior for justice and long beloved by millions, lay embalmed inside. It seemed a bad idea to have his own name anywhere near. A few scribbled notes caught his eye, their pencil faint on the photocopy. Was the handwriting slightly familiar?

He went to the phone. 'Bill, please. This is Jack Maine.' The Head of Drama was unavailable. Redialling direct, Jack got through. He kept his tone neutral. 'I've suggestions you may find helpful, Bill. We need a meeting, and with Gerry Forbes as first director.'

'Where'd you hear about Gerry?'

'From him. He's a great choice for this material. Gerry mentioned our co-producer Giraud's in town with Duval and I've set up a meeting – tomorrow at eleven. Ross Cammell too,' he added.

The bluff worked. Bill Bishop would be there. Quickly Jack phoned Cammell, Forbes and Giraud, telling them Bill had arranged the script conference. He didn't ask Richard because the actor would do best to get out fast.

Jack made some notes, sorted mail and returned calls. He fielded questions about the secret wedding and prolonged honeymoon, asked everyone to visit them at Whitting. Then loading scripts and clothes from his flat he set off in the Saab.

A heat-wave baked the streets in rank decay, rubbish towered from a council strike. Car horns blared, violence simmered, the scorched metal traps edged fuming between lights. Noise jarred in the heat and nerves frayed with effort while beggars and dogs lay at ease in the shade. Inching uphill between juggernauts he turned for Highgate's leafy lanes.

He parked in the newly cleared drive and seeing it as home, looked up at the steep sides of Whitting House. Jack expected a mellow, sun-drenched mood and felt a sense of shock. Those windows were too small and blackly glittering, malevolent. The narrow tower sheered dizzily with dagger spire, the red brick face hung runnelled like an ageing drunk in stormy mood.

Then Chloe appeared in the front porch, small and slight. She wore denim dungarees and her face was black from cleaning. Jack climbed the steps, gathered her up and carried her wriggling across the threshold.

They went into the cavern of the hall, its blackness, its silence and he laid her down gently on a rug, stopped her laughter with kisses. They'd arrived home for the first time and he wanted to celebrate.

Collecting his security tag, Jack crossed reception. The lift doors whispered open and a familiar figure stepped out. Justin Fairbrother, arranging a bundle of white scripts under his arm, didn't see him at first.

'Well!' Jack exclaimed. 'I thought you no longer frequented this kind of joint.'

Dismay flicked across Justin's face, covered instantly by a friendly grin. 'You've caught me now,' he admitted, glancing around to make sure no one important was nearby.

'Not hard at work in illustrious theatre?'

'House mice could not survive on it, let alone my animals. Needs must.'

'What're you up to?'

'A trilogy, m'dear. I'm off to the darling south of France. Congratulations by the way.' Justin was avoiding his eye, edging away and Jack recognised jealousy – he'd just married the man's mistress. An airy, jerky wave of the hand then, 'Must rush, old mate – regards to the missus.'

Jack stared after Justin's rear, took the lift to the thirteenth floor.

Bill Bishop and Ross Cammell, the elderly director Forbes, a narcissistic Alain Duval and co-producer Giraud. Whatever they'd been discussing was suddenly redundant as Jack walked in.

'Good morning. How's the run-up?' He looked at their faces: they wanted confidence. They were about to employ hundreds of people in months of huge effort, to produce thirteen hours of film that would be valueless to everyone who watched it.

Forbes responded, 'We're all tremendously excited.'

'We expect you at the read-through,' added Ross in his designer crumpled raw-silk suit. It was Italian, an Armani like the fictional Pierre's. So Ross had wielded the pen, the sword.

'Of course,' Jack smiled across the conference table. 'How's Richard doing, by the way?'

'For some reason he's being a pain in the butt.'

'Shall I have a word with him?' Jack offered sweetly.

Bill Bishop took the meeting. 'You've one or two script suggestions, Jack?'

Handing out wedges of notes he began. 'Basically each script needs a quick rewrite. None of the stories goes far enough.' They were looking understandably puzzled as he went on firmly, 'Every idea's a missed opportunity – bland, dull! Frankly old-fashioned, domestic and insular. I'm surprised, Ross. Your writing team looked meaty in approach – '

'We ditched the writing team.'

Adopting a stricken expression Jack looked at Ross, 'Sorry . . . It's your scripting? I'd no idea!'

Ross said curtly, 'I didn't write them.'

'Oh. Who did?'

Glances passed around the table. Forbes sighed. 'A new young writer called Ben Ashe. You won't have heard of him.'

'Ah.'

Bill Bishop, watchful, cut across, 'So give us a for instance.'

'For instance in the story about the French cop, German soldier and Dutch drugs baron, the Greek heiress should be released from her Italian kidnappers by a Czech manufacturer – a new character.'

There was a cautious silence. 'Why?' Forbes ventured.

'It's obvious. We've left them out. Another for instance – what's all the pussyfooting between Cragge and his son?'

'I wouldn't call it pussyfooting,' objected Ross, annoyed.

Jack insisted, 'But where's the culmination to all their fighting? It's obvious that Pierre ought to kill his father.'

A deep silence lay over the polished veneer of the conference table.

Giraud murmured, 'Alain, his character will be thrown into jail? And we have no future show.'

'Not if he frames someone else for the murder,' Jack explained.

'Oh but – '

'No really . . .'

Forbes and Cammell were getting ready to leave, Bill Bishop looking at his watch.

Suddenly Alain Duval pushed back his chair, fingered the paisley chiffon scarf at his throat and shouted with an inspired gleam in his eyes, *'C'est magnifique!* I like this.'

Horror dawned on the faces round the table.

'Yes. Yes, I like this too,' echoed the star's producer from his side. 'It has many balls, no? You explain more the ideas – please.'

Jack hurried home that evening but Chloe was in town and it was after eight when she got back, excited and full of her day. She'd visited galleries, bought a new display portfolio – she was going to try again with photography. Then she remembered his meeting and Jack, hazy from a solitary bottle of wine, told her what had happened. 'So we're blazing a trail for patricidal cop-killing, by our new hero, across the world.'

'Surely they won't go through with it?'

'What Duval wants, Duval gets. They're in too deep to

pull out. Oh yes, one more thing – they've asked to use Whitting as a location.'

'To film *Son Of Cragge*? When?'

'A day or two in December. It would be total chaos – shall we say yes?'

Chloe frowned. 'But this house will be sold by then. I really feel – '

'It wouldn't get sold by December. And we need time to decide where to live. You agreed to that. And it's a fun story – Son Of Cragge saves the day for the Keystone Kops,' he bulldozed on deliberately. 'Ross's stepfather owns BA-TV, that's why my series got rubbished to death. Cammell and Forbes want a look at your house – '

'Our house,' Chloe corrected him. She'd gone quiet now, he'd won. 'You'd told them all about it?'

Jack frowned. 'I've never mentioned it at all. That's another mystery.'

Cammell and Forbes brought location manager Steve Mabe. The location was perfect, the producer would rewrite events to fit and nothing must be changed until after the shoot. XLTV would pay good money.

It was a hot July day and Jack found Chloe on the terrace. London shivered below in wisps of haze then shifted like the contents of cheap glass. He leaned back in a chair, swirled ice cubes in a long drink. Out of this place the new novel was emerging. It was a natural home for the book's heroine – darkly eccentric and vulnerable, under nightly threat from the Blitz.

Chloe was marking contacts of a ruined church on a wild hillside. 'Could I have some prints?' She nodded absently, intent on her task. 'Why don't you ever photograph people?' he asked idly.

'They're too difficult.'

'To aim a camera at?'

'You think that's all I do? Thanks a lot.' Chloe glared at him. 'People freeze – they sweep around with their eyes like wild animals, you can't catch them unawares.' She went on, 'I suppose it'll be dozens of crew, truckfuls of hardware coming?'

'Just for a couple of days. How better to bury my hero. We can't change anything, we'll have to live like you and she –'

'Jack.' Her face had darkened. 'We've got to sell up soon, and start in a new –'

'We will, darling.' He squeezed her hand. 'It's just not the right moment.'

Chloe said slowly, 'You want things to stay the same. It's funny, when we met I thought you were secure, confident.'

And she'd been wrong. Suddenly Jack knew she minded very much. She'd needed someone strong and he'd fooled her. Putting down his glass he felt cold like a man receiving sentence. Some time she would leave.

Then she was kissing the top of his head lightly, towing him to the kitchen, 'I'm starving. Pie and salad? Spanish wine . . .'

'Save the Rioja for the crew?' Jack suggested vehemently so she laughed. Then there was a silence.

'Jack?' He turned, saw her looking puzzled. 'The pie was on this shelf . . .' Then quickly checking, 'There were four pints of milk. Two loaves of bread. Who's been taking things?'

'Hm. They don't normally starve the producer –'

'I'm serious! And – the biscuit tin.' She was biting her lip. 'What's going on?'

'A very hungry burglar? Sorry, darling,' he soothed her. 'It is odd, but it's only food.'

'I hope so.' She was very troubled. 'Oh come on – I'll make an omelette or something. Maybe it's only a tribe of giant super rats.'

'A comforting thought.' They laughed it off then looked gingerly round the house. Nothing else seemed to be missing. As he went from room to room he thought: she's got to agree to stay, it's too extraordinary to ever sell. In time she'll come to love it again. She must.

That night she woke him whispering, 'I can hear footsteps.'

He listened beside her in the dark but heard nothing. Then a soft creak, like dry timbers shifting. 'It's just the house. Old houses always creak.'

'No, listen.' She was very still, gripping his arm. There was another faint settling sound. 'Didn't you hear that?'

'Nobody's there, love. You're imagining it. Come on, lie down.'

He wrapped Chloe in a comforting hug but she lay rigid, scarcely breathing and he thought: she's afraid it's a ghost, it's Rachel come back to haunt her.

After all, he should never have persuaded her to live here. Her past was full of pain and terror, stirring again to stalk the dark places in her mind. He cursed himself for stupidity, for selfishness and nuzzling against her frightened body he tried to melt away her imaginings.

Then he too heard the footsteps.

7

The footsteps trod lightly, carefully across the floor overhead then away. The sound was distinct. It couldn't be
anything else.

Chloe whispered, 'They're going towards the tower.
Jack, let's call the police.'

He was in the doorway now, listening to the silence.
'No, we don't want that. Stay here,' he added as she crept
to his side. 'Tell me how to get up there. Is it through the
attics?'

'I'm not staying here alone,' she insisted.

Jack stepped along the dark passage. Chloe followed.
Under his hand the panelling gave way, he edged round
a corner and a dank chill of rot began as they climbed
the attic stairs. The only sound was of their shallow
breathing, the slight protest of floorboards. Surely the
tower lay to the left? But Chloe tugged his arm and
obediently he turned right through a narrow door to the
largest attic. The dried decay smelled sweet and dusty.
Moonlight shone through the rafters touching old furniture and junk. The rooms formed a circle across the house,
he realised. Starting at shadows, straining to hear they
reached narrow spiral stairs that led up. The heavy door
to the tower was closed.

Chloe pulled at his sleeve. 'He may be armed.' From

behind the door there came a wail, and his spine prickled with alarm. She whispered, 'What is it?'

He opened the door.

Crouched in the window, silhouetted in light from the moon a cloaked figure was rocking to and fro. From this the moaning spread in a wave. Jack fumbled at the wall. Chloe found the switch first and electricity jagged out white.

From the window she snarled down at them: a she-wolf with her young, cornered and dangerous.

Jack lurched across the echoing floor with a sudden release of fear. 'What the hell are you doing here!' The small circular room was packed with baby things – an old cot, clothes, toys and food. Fury possessed him. 'How dare you, scaring Chloe half to death!'

'Keep away from me!' Jodie yelled back. 'I've got more right than you have. There's nowhere else to go and Rachel wanted us here!'

'Rachel's dead – this house belongs to my wife. How long've you been up here creeping around, stealing food and who knows what else?' And he said to Chloe, 'She could've done a lot of damage, at least we've found her.'

But Chloe was ignoring him. 'What d'you mean, you've nowhere else to go?'

Jodie gave a bitter laugh, a kind of bark. 'You haven't got a clue! Ever been on the streets? Not likely. Wrapped up in cotton wool and spoon-fed all the way. Ever noticed people are starving? You don't care.'

Jack began, 'Come off it – no one starves in Britain today. What about Social Security? You're not our responsibility.'

'Next time you go down the Underground, through the city, by the embankment, under the bridges, try opening your fucking eyes – there's hundreds of us.' She was snarling, shaking. 'You're like the others, pretending to yourselves. You've had every kind of chance. What about my little boy? Nothing's his fault. This is the only place – ' Her voice broke, the anger gone. 'Rachel cared and she didn't have to. My baby's never had a home. Why should he be punished?'

Chloe crossed quickly to the crying girl and baby, put her arms round them both. They clung together.

Tentacles crept through his flesh as Jack stood watching. It was an absolute presentiment of disaster, sharp as if the girl held a knife to Chloe's heart.

'Don't trust her! It's emotional blackmail.'

Chloe mumbled, 'I don't care. Life's unfair and I've been lucky.'

'Lucky?' he countered sharply. 'I wouldn't say that. You must see we can't let them stay, it's out of the question. You'd regret it.'

His words fell into silence because she didn't answer. Then Jack realised, it was her house and he had no right to decide who lived in it.

The voice went on in his head with its muffled shout of alarm. Chloe cleared out her old room, arranged it for Jodie, explained – they had so much and happiness was something to be shared. She'd made up her mind, seemed to think she owed it. To Rachel, he thought with a sinking heart.

So he tried to give in with a good grace. 'We are having children after all,' he joked wryly. 'Two of them and instantly. Think we'll survive?'

'What nonsense. They'll help fill this great barn of a house. We won't be tripping over each other.'

But it was different. They weren't alone together now and as visitors began to call on them his sense of invasion deepened.

Anna Fairbrother was first, calling by while her kids

were at nursery. Justin, she said, was in France talking to producers. Jack showed her a postcard arrived that morning, 'From Sarah filming in the Dordogne with Paul. Bitter, am I? 'Course not!'

'Sarah – she's such a carnivore. Paul Mann won't do well out of that show, he's made a mistake,' Anna promised, biting into an apple and glancing across at Chloe.

'I'm sure they're all having an amazingly glamorous time,' Chloe said with a sly smile, and Jack wondered again at her easy friendship with Anna. There seemed no shred of animosity between them. Didn't Anna suspect anything?

She was answering wistfully, 'Maybe I'll give Justin a surprise visit, dump the kids with my parents. How've George and Mary taken it, you getting married without telling them?'

They'd taken it badly. Their feathers were ruffled and Chloe set out to make amends with a large, complicated dinner. But it was an uncomfortable meal, tensions grappling under the surface. Raphael, delighted by extra attention, crowed and plastered chocolate on everything with fat little hands while his audience watched with varying nausea and indulgence. Jack could hear the unspoken questions, whose baby was it, why was this teenage girl living here? He wished he knew the answers.

George had brought war diaries for his research. Mary, given a tour, hated the towering trees outside and the dereliction inside. Chloe told her it was temporary but Mary was puzzled. 'Don't you want to make a nice home, dear? It's not exactly comfy and must be so hard to clean.' And turning to Jack, 'I do hope the two of you will be happy.'

'Don't worry, Mama, we intend to be.' With mixed affection and exasperation he waved their Volvo down the drive.

'We're never alone,' he complained. 'Since we got married.'

Chloe laughed and ran a hand lightly across his body, along his back and down over his buttocks. 'Come upstairs,' she murmured with rampant suggestiveness. 'No one will follow us to bed.'

But they as good as did.

A furious banging on the bedroom door. Jack started awake, scrambled out of bed. It was morning. Dragging on a bath robe, befuddled and still half asleep he opened the door.

Jodie said urgently, 'That detective's here – he's snooping outside the window.'

'D'you mean Inspector Cairns?' Jack felt a flash of anger shot through with fear. He'd been trying to forget everything – what was Cairns doing back here again?

'You mustn't let him see me!' The girl sounded terrified.

'Why not?' asked Chloe coming to the door. 'What's the matter?'

Jack thought quickly. 'The cars are in the drive, Cairns will know we're here.' He added, 'Anyway, we've nothing to hide.'

'Just don't tell him I'm here, all right.' Jodie was backing away, hanging on only to catch their answer.

Chloe said, 'Wait a minute – we can't lie if he asks where you are.'

'Don't tell him, don't let him come in and see the baby's things. Please, Chloe!'

She seemed to take Chloe's silence as agreement from them both, went scuttling off like a frightened mouse.

They looked at each other. Jack said, 'I'll go and talk to him. You stay here. It'll be all right, it'll be nothing.' And pulling on his clothes, with a kind of grim satisfaction

198

he added, 'That girl's got a big reason to hide. She's not what she seems, I told you.'

'But she's so scared, Jack.' Chloe looked into his eyes and he saw her fear, her silent pleading to have things turn out. Giving her arm a reassuring squeeze, he went to look for Cairns.

The detective was on the side path, staring thoughtfully up at the house.

Jack watched him, feeling as if the man was his enemy. 'Good morning,' he called and heard aggression grind in his voice.

Cairns turned too abruptly at that tone, after a moment he approached. Some ambivalence, some distance in his manner. 'Mr Maine. So you've moved in here.'

'You got our message,' Jack replied levelly, 'about the change of address.'

'A good holiday? Quite the grand tour, wasn't it.'

His heart jumped as memories flooded back: Barcelona Cathedral, the cafe on the ramblas. The man following.

Cairns went on, 'You've made it official, congratulations are in order.'

'So what happened about the inquest, is it over?' His question was brusque. He hadn't intended that.

Raising his eyebrows Cairns replied, 'Couldn't very well go ahead without you and Mrs Rushe's stepdaughter, could we?' And he went on heavily, 'The inquest resumes next Monday at ten, same place – you and your wife are required to attend as witnesses.'

Could the detective see the sweat that beaded his face? With every ounce of control he could find Jack said, 'Then of course we'll be there.' And he forced himself to ask, 'Did the forensic results come through then?'

Cairns gave him an unfriendly look, he shouldn't have asked. 'You'll hear all about that, won't you. At the inquest.' And with a nod he left.

Except, he paused at the gate for a backward glance. Jack drew hastily into the house and found Chloe, gave her a version of their encounter which missed out his sense of things unsaid. 'It's going to be OK, everything will be over soon.' He took her in his arms, stood holding her. Danger pulsed through him. If he should lose her . . .

Then Jodie reappeared, demanding to know what had happened. 'We'll ask the questions,' he snapped. 'If you want to stay.' Jack watched the girl pouring juice for her baby. Devotion to her kid was the only thing he liked about her. She was trouble and he wanted her out. 'If you're on the run, why – what've you done?'

When she began to explain it sounded innocent enough. She'd been an abused child placed in care, but ran away, then had the baby. The authorities mustn't catch up with them. Chloe argued it would be best if they did; she and Raphael would get looked after. But Jodie seemed terrified they might take the baby away. 'They'd put him in care too – they'd say I'm not fit but I am. He's mine and I won't let them take him!'

'They wouldn't keep you apart,' Jack told her firmly. 'You're imagining the impossible worst.'

Jodie begged, 'Please, please, Jack – I'll be eighteen soon, it's only till then. I can't risk losing my baby!' Her fear might be unreal but it was overwhelming, and he could see Chloe wanted to give in.

He asked, 'And where's Raphael's father? Who is he?'

'He's out of the picture, nothing to do with us now.'

'You can stay here,' Chloe told her. 'That still stands.'

Jack was on a short fuse, 'What about the inquest? If they ask, why should we protect her.'

'Please.' Jodie turned to him. 'They've got my statement, lots of it. They don't need me any more.'

'You can't live in hiding,' Chloe reasoned. 'Shouldn't Raphael be meeting other kids, for one thing?'

'After Monday everything will be all right,' Jodie said.

Angrily Jack hoped that was true. Fears lying dormant since their holiday now flooded back in a wake of superstition. He and Chloe were happy, could it last? With the girl here, he felt haunted like her. Had a sense that what was hidden might rise up to devour them, destroy their new life. He didn't want to let Chloe out of his sight.

But she decided to take Jodie and the baby to a playgroup, and that afternoon Jack went up to the big front room that was his study. Books and papers lay waiting, unsorted because Massey's story grabbed at him every time he came in here. He gazed out through a ragged wing of cedar that hung still in the blaze of white heat. Long hot days had followed each other endlessly and might have given a sense of well-being, of peace. Why did he feel such foreboding? The sharp light, too bright and starkly delineating, reminded him of a film set and the march of inevitable action. It was merciless.

As he watched, a foreshortened figure appeared on the path below. The hair shone, a white-gold halo in the sun and for a moment Jack thought Chloe had come back alone. But whoever it was approached and rang the bell.

He opened the door to Rachel Rushe's gardener – if that was what he'd been. Odd and awkward with his veneer of self-conscious charm.

'What can I do for you?'

'It's more a question,' the man said, 'of what I can do for you.' He smiled at Jack confidentially. 'I worked for Mrs Rushe here – God give her peace.' He inclined his head like a ham actor, and suddenly Jack remembered how disturbed he'd been by their efforts to help. He was so different now. 'The gardener for seven years I was, doing what was needed. It wasn't like this – I kept the orchard and vegetables. I'm good with my hands.'

Jack frowned, thinking back and trying to remember.

What was it the police had said all those months ago? But maybe a gardener didn't count as household help. And he hesitated, because he wanted to call in builders and landscape professionals but Chloe would have none of it. He felt a strange reluctance to send the gardener away, to see him disappear for ever. Perhaps because he belonged to Whitting and its past; he was some tiny part of its elusive history. That history felt vital to the story he was working on.

'We could try you, I suppose.' God knew the place needed looking after. And it wasn't as if he'd ever come into the house or be a nuisance.

'Tuesday afternoons? It always was.'

'All right, sounds fine. What's your price?'

The man told him and it seemed reasonable. 'After lunch on Tuesday then. Wait a minute – what do we call you?'

'Adams,' replied the gardener.

Jack smiled at the name's serendipity, watched the man walk away down the drive. Then he forgot all about it and sank into that other world, the compulsive fiction in his head.

8

The number rang on emptily. Tony had never closed the shop on a Monday before. What if he'd already left London? She'd never see him again.

Jodie went out down the steps with the baby on her hip. Summer weeds were waist high, brambles tore at her skirt and grass seed clung. Settling Raphael in the shade she picked wild strawberries for supper.

It was after three. Jack and Chloe had been gone all day and she tried to imagine what could be happening at the Coroner's Court. The cops knew about Rachel's insomnia, how she'd walk round the gardens in the dark. Why did there have to be any inquest?

Dazzling sun bleached out the bushes and undergrowth. The ponds. When she shut her eyes it all came back ... In the early morning light, black skirts ballooning half submerged in weed. That icy, slippery weight she couldn't pull out and – choking on terror and effort – the realisation it was just a dead body.

In her nest of tall grass Jodie cried for Rachel. She missed the old woman. Reminders were everywhere of her kindness and their life together. She buried her face in her hands. But the baby touched her bare arm, tried to prise her fingers away. Scrubbing off the tears she made it a game, peeping out so he shrieked with laughter.

Raphael was plump and jolly, pink from the sun and strong. He could push himself up to stand now. She'd breathed happiness into him and banished the bad times, done everything she could to help him grow. She imagined him older, running through the garden, making friends who'd come and play. There'd be a good school nearby . . . If only they were left alone.

Ages later the car drove up. Suppose the detective was with them and come to get her? Jodie sat out on the terrace steps, too scared to go in.

Until they came through, just the two of them – and Jack was opening champagne. He looked triumphant.

'You're probably off the hook,' he said to her. 'The inquest's over and no one asked about you.'

She breathed out a long sigh. 'They know it was an accident? Of course they do.'

Chloe took a glass of champagne, put it down without drinking. 'They think Rachel fell and hit her head on the side, that's why she couldn't climb out. But they aren't sure why she fell.'

Jack said, 'They gave an open verdict.'

'You mean, they haven't done with investigating?'

'There's not enough evidence. She could've fallen because of high blood pressure. Might've felt dizzy, her doctor said.'

'Then why –?

'The verdict's just a formality. It's over, after all these weeks.' Raising his glass Jack looked at Chloe; they both drank.

That grated on Jodie. Relaxing in Rachel's house, putting her into the past, they felt glad. 'So that's all right, she's over and done with!'

Jack snapped, 'It's not your place to criticise. You were the only person here when Rachel died. And you're mightily afraid of the police – I'm still not convinced as to why.'

'What d'you mean?' Jodie remarked.

'Nothing – except you were looking after Rachel when she died. You were alone –'

'She'd never listen to me if I asked her not to do something.'

A breeze shivered round the deepening shadows of the garden. 'Rachel never listened to anyone,' Chloe said.

Jodie couldn't stop herself, 'If you'd stayed around she might've been different.'

Chloe shook her head, and Jack said, 'You don't understand. So just leave it.'

Jodie drained the glass of champagne that stood before her. 'Maybe,' she suggested, 'it's you that doesn't understand. I want to show you something.'

Chloe ought to know what Rachel had been through. They went up to the attics, curled into a *chaise-longue* together, leafed through the diaries. What was Chloe thinking? Her hair screened her face, now and then she moved restlessly.

Eventually she looked up. 'Of course it was awful for her – but what about me? I was only a kid!'

'You've made Rachel into some villain – she was only difficult. A real old bag sometimes, but there was good in her. Will you read these?'

'But they're full of hating me. Why should I?'

'You were both jealous, insecure, that's all –'

'It's like me saying go back to your father, your family instead of hiding with us.'

'That's different –'

'It's the same except you never got driven mad.'

'Not yet.' Jodie smiled. 'OK, a truce. No more wicked stepmothers? And I'll be grateful to you and Jack.'

'That'll be the day. I admire your cheek – elbowing into our honeymoon. We'll put up with the two of you . . .'

She'd got to be kidding. Chloe was fond of Raphael by now, and liked seeing how close they were. After all, she'd never had a mother, only money and the best of everything. And the little boy, like a bridge, tugged at their opposite memories of Rachel.

Together they took him to the Tuesday playgroup. His world was usually full of giants but now he crawled among other dwarfs that grabbed and gabbled like little mirrors. He'd never leave until everyone else had gone.

It was after six when she'd bathed him and they went downstairs. Voices rose from the kitchen, but she knew Jack was out. Who was Chloe talking to?

It was only Anna Fairbrother, sipping wine at the window seat.

Jodie set the baby in his high-chair for tea. 'Aren't they pig-like at this stage,' Anna smiled, watching Raphael smear strained peaches on to everything. 'Sorry, Jodie – I've got two of my own. They go through a kind of mini-evolution from tadpole to fish to reptile through various forms of mammal. Some people get stuck,' she continued, 'at the dog or the sheep or –'

'What a horrible idea,' laughed Chloe.

'But it's true. The woman I'm playing is a goat. Giddy and crazy, greedy, she'll devour anything –'

'Is this a person we know?' asked Jack coming in, dropping books on the table.

'Anna's doing a radio play.' Chloe embraced him. 'Good research, darling?'

Why did Anna look embarrassed, as Jack approached and kissed her? He and Chloe didn't seem to notice anything. He was saying, 'You're back in business, Anna. Sorry I couldn't get you a part in *Son Of Keystone*, I'm not flavour of the month. It's a turkey now if that's any consolation.'

He was looking at Chloe, she was pouring wine and they didn't see Anna's confused blush. Jodie thought: she isn't the blushing kind, what's wrong with her? Anna chatted on about the play, then about the kitchen where they sat. 'That wonderful old fireplace, the cooking range – you'd never think we were in London. What will you do with the house?'

'Sell it,' Chloe said quickly, 'and buy a new place together. Won't we, Jack.'

He answered, 'We can't until after the filming.'

Suddenly Anna gave a little whoop, 'Hey, you should have a Whitting House party! And celebrate getting married.'

'We celebrate every day,' Jack groaned but Chloe was smiling at the idea.

'A party . . . With masses of people.'

Jodie said, 'Terrific! Music, dancing on the lawn.'

'What lawn?' asked Jack.

They ignored him, catching enthusiasm. 'You could hire a dance floor, put up lights everywhere.' Anna turned to Chloe. 'Parties here were always heaven – this time it would be yours. You must.'

'Go on, Chloe,' Jodie urged.

'The lights everywhere,' Jack said drily, 'would have to be very dim, considering the state of the place.'

'Oh go on, it'll be great. And I'll help a lot,' Jodie offered.

'We could hire a marquee,' Chloe suggested. 'Have it mostly in the garden – get that cleared.'

Jack said in an exasperated way, 'And who would we invite to this huge, expensive wilderness party?'

'Everybody! Friends and doubters, your relatives, col- leagues, everyone.' Chloe went on persuasively, 'If Anna and Jodie and I organise it, you won't know it's happening until the night.'

Jack muttered he wasn't in the mood and wanted to bury himself in books. They badgered him. It would be a wedding celebration, a beginning.

That evening Jodie realised Jack had been the writer of *Cragge*. She'd always watched the series, with her brothers and sisters at the start, and had seen the detective change from sensitive beginner to obsessive rebel. It was exciting. She questioned Jack but he was vague, didn't know where his ideas came from, was caught up in other writing now.

Every day he disappeared. They had to field callers, put off visitors. If he emerged they weren't supposed to start talking to him. How could anyone stand such a peculiar way of life? He was getting invisible. And he wouldn't let Chloe change anything in the house – that was for his new novel, giving him the feel and detail of the place. Surely Chloe must get lonely? So Jodie drew closer to her during the next week or two.

Then everything changed.

It was a Tuesday. Jodie was doing the washing when Jack came through into the kitchen. 'Where's Chloe?' he asked.

'She's taken Raphael to the playgroup.'

'On her own? She's getting very fond of him, isn't she. I'm glad she's got you both.'

He'd been so suspicious before. Now it was as if he trusted, valued her. And she wanted to be relied on, it was important. 'Chloe needs us. Is it always this awful, writing?'

Jack looked up at her for a minute. He asked, 'Am I impossible to live with? But I think Chloe did know what it might be like.'

Jodie grinned mischievously. 'Maybe she'll put up with

you then – for a while.' It was no bad thing if he worried about Chloe. Putting the pegs on the basket of laundry she straightened up.

The basket slid through her hands, wet clothes rolled across the floor as she gazed out at squares of glaring aridity, the sun-scorched garden. And the tall figure of Art walking towards the outhouse.

Jack, too, glanced out to where Art was disappearing between brambles. 'It's only the gardener.'

'You mean he's working here?'

He nodded, looked curious. Jodie was shaking, she tried to stop. 'He startled you,' Jack prompted.

'You get used to seeing the empty garden – not a stranger there.'

'He's been working on Tuesdays, the last couple of weeks. He worked for Rachel while you lived here.'

'I remember now, there was a gardener but I hardly ever . . .' Then she saw Jack was picking up some books. 'You going out?'

'The London Library – back this evening.' And he was half-way to the door.

She wanted to say: Don't go, don't leave me with him . . . She wanted to tell Jack everything but it was impossible. Dully she listened to his footsteps through the hall. The door slammed shut on her like the nail in a coffin hammered home.

Then the Saab hummed off down the drive. Art would hear it and know they'd both gone.

She flew to the back door – but locking it would anger him. Art had been working here, while she'd been out at the Tuesday playgroups. With a surge of hope she thought: He's only come back to his old job, he doesn't know I'm here.

Then with a sharp grating of metal on wood, the door

209

was unlatched. Art stood in its frame looking at her and his face was stone. He said nothing. Detached thoughts flew through Jodie's mind: how he was thinner, and the clothes hung loose on him; about the way he'd attacked Cooper's men with the knife. There were knives here and she might find one before he did. She would defend herself.

Art walked in, glanced at the high-chair and toys. 'Where's the boy?'

'Why d'you want to know?' Jodie countered.

His eyes were so cold. 'They've gone out now – I've been waiting.' And he crossed the kitchen towards her.

Jumping back she braced herself. He mustn't know she was afraid. 'They'll be back any minute.' She began edging towards the drawer with the carving knives.

But Art went to the sink, turned on a tap and filled a glass. He sniffed it, then hurled the glass at the drainer where it shattered. 'Don't drink any water. Don't eat what they offer you. They're not our friends, don't trust them.'

She thought: he's crazy, he could do anything – thank God the baby's not around.

'It's clever, Jodie, you being here. Makes it easier.'

She said, 'Jack's only taken the car to the garage and he'll walk back any minute, see you talking to me.'

Glancing sharply – surely he could see straight through her – he stepped close, in his confidential way, 'Good thinking. It isn't just them, we're surrounded. So much danger but I've got an idea.'

'OK. OK.'

'They're in our way. I'll take care of everything. It's us, the family, if we're together then it's all right – and we are. Aren't we? Together, Jodie?'

' 'Course we are – only you've got to go now.'

To her huge relief he turned to the door. Then he

210

paused. 'I'm never far away, Jodie. From you and the baby.'

In a small voice she asked, 'Where're you living then?'

'I'm never far away,' he repeated. 'Don't you ever think I am.' And he headed out, going towards the side gate.

Now every nerve in her body hummed with danger. Her first impulse was to race to Jackson's Lane, pick up Raphael and run from Whitting, to anywhere away from Art's poor crazy violent self. Why did he want to harm Jack and Chloe or make trouble for them? Could it be because she lived here, was it jealousy? But what harm, really, could he do? She'd only seen Art respond against what he saw as an attack – violent, unforgiveable, but only in response.

If she ran from Whitting, where could she go? This was Raphael's home, it was the only bit of security he'd ever had. She couldn't break that for him. And besides, if she left it could be worse – Art might follow and find her, or he might attack the others to learn where she was.

She must stay, and watch out.

Chloe came back with Raphael, proudly: he'd learned to go down the slide alone, he was so good with the other kids. Jodie wanted Chloe's trust – hers and Jack's – more than anything else for herself. How could she tell them about the baby's father now?

She tried calling Tony again – he'd understand and give advice – but no one answered at *A'Laddinscave*. She imagined it shut up with ghostly, dusty things listening to that one repeating sound.

Now the party was a week away. A JCB appeared outside, cutting undergrowth already dying from summer drought. A platform was built with railings and a marquee; the house was rearranged. A band was coming and caterers, and over a hundred guests.

Perhaps, she thought, the party was just right – a way of boxing old shadows and shouting out a future here.

9

It felt unfamiliar, milling with strangers now. From rooms below drifted sounds of people calling, a shrill whining and hammer blows. He was marooned, besieged. He couldn't concentrate.

But of course, it was like this in wartime . . .

The house is an emergency hospital, bustling with medicos, crammed with victims of the Blitz. Charlotte still living here has a servant's room – those attic stairs are impassable for stretchers or invalids. The lower rooms are wards of iron bedsteads, nurses hurrying through hall and passageways. Patients are brought for assessment, immediate treatment . . .

Jack took up a pen and scrawled:

WHO THEY MIGHT BE – THE CHARACTERS

FRANCIS. A conscientious objector working here as a ward orderly. Early 20s. Nervous at damage and gentle. Bisexual. A poet. Observer who believes neither force nor action can change anything – connives with fate. Superstitious.

MASSEY. Courage, with necessary action. 12 years older than Charlotte, they married at outbreak of war in Europe. Cell leader, field work in occupied territory. Control of events. Imprisoned and interrogated – experiences death of his sense of power? Escapes and eventually to England. A casualty then of comparative peace?

CHARLOTTE. Wealthy background, shaped by previous order and intact class system. Limited experience. Becomes a voluntary nurse. Position of women changing radically and fast – perhaps this is the key.

. . . Massey, secret agent and trained killer, can't tolerate normal life. And finds out his wife's got a lover. But he's far too obvious as F's murderer. What if . . . what if it's Charlotte, kind and gentle-seeming Charlotte who does it – ?

A man in overalls barged into the study and barked, 'Sorry, guv, wrong door,' and banged out again.

Then the idea was just an idea hanging on its broken thread. What had he meant by it?

Cursing, Jack gave up. From tomorrow *Kops* would swallow his time and energy. Could the novel wait or would it slip away?

Doubt sucked him in. Watching friends revolve between deadlines – wanted and needed, with a job to do – he'd struggled out of the machine. The consultancy was nothing, just cold turkey. He was isolated and depressed, woke cold with panic each night. He felt abrasion, a rawness that made him want to do harm, altering the pain and giving it focus. He told himself it was only his head, and a selfishness that was being frustrated.

Next morning Chloe passed him in a hall packed with caterers' gear. She must've been up for hours. 'Talk some time?' She sounded wistful.

Giving her a quick hug, 'After tonight?'

He got caught in the rush hour. Hot sun baked through the windows of the rehearsal hall where forty chairs waited around the central tables. Veiled like a diplomat he greeted actors and heard their worries. Today's read-through should allow some fleeting sense of dramatic logic before character development was abandoned. Thirteen hours of drama were to be filmed out of sequence.

Alain, the star, read in a world-weary throwaway tone. Richard sat glowering, trapped by contract and necessity, as he missed some lines and snapped out others. Actors with minor parts made much of each word to prove they deserved more. Gerry Forbes presided genially and chain-smoked his cast into a bitter-smelling fog.

Dialogue batted to and fro in macho homage to a hundred TV series past. Jack thought: I don't believe in it now – so I've no integrity in being here, I deserve to suffer . . . Ben Ashe was a fiction. Who'd been stupid enough to write these scripts and wise enough to prefer no credit?

Breaking for lunch they fell on champagne and smoked salmon sandwiches. Richard had counted his lines through the thirteen scripts and compared them with last year. It was breach of contract in spirit if not in letter, he insisted, commandeering a bottle in a corner. Other actors were upset about their characters' fates, not knowing who was responsible. Jack mouthed about commercial necessity, European co-production, global sales and American fashion.

Poor valiant actors, he thought. The room was a shelter for the displaced, a therapy group for the mildly psychotic. An actress, hired to be killed immediately, flirted for her next character. She'd found a wonderful heroine, might he adapt the stage play? 'I won't be doing anything like this again,' Jack said and she melted from his side. He thought: I'm the displaced person here.

215

Someone else approached. It was Steve Mabe. 'Coming to the party tonight?' Jack asked.

Mabe nodded. 'Hope you haven't changed anything there?'

'We'll reassemble it. By the way, who told you about Whitting?'

'Fairbrother, of course.' Mabe, reaching for another sandwich, missed a sharp look from Ross Cammell.

After a moment Jack pursued, 'Do you mean Justin Fairbrother?'

Mabe's face distorted with dismay. 'Oh my God – ' he began.

'Justin Fairbrother . . . He wrote these scripts, didn't he?' asked Jack in a dead calm voice.

As he came in Chloe ran to meet him. 'Hey, how'd it go . . . What's wrong?'

'Nothing that can't wait,' he decided grimly.

She ducked to avoid hanging wires, followed him to the drawing room. 'Are you sure?'

'Just rehearsals – you know.' He couldn't begin to separate the strands to Justin's betrayal of himself. With Chloe, now with *Cragge* . . .

She must've known, from Justin, about the massacre being done to his work. Yet she'd said nothing. It was much worse than duplicity. She was drawing a circle of destruction around them both.

'What is it?' she asked again with an edge of alarm.

He couldn't cope with this yet, the little fragment of knowledge was too new and too deadly. 'Nothing. Want a drink?'

'Hey, steady!' she laughed, as he splashed whisky into a tumbler. 'Don't think I'll start yet. Sure you're OK?'

'It's just *Son Of Kops*,' he cut in, curt. 'I'll be glad when it's over.' He changed the subject. 'The house looks – '

216

'Chaotic,' Chloe supplied, laughing again. 'Perhaps we'll be ready, perhaps not. We've a couple of hours.'

Swallowing whisky Jack gazed out towards the marquee and dance floor. A red and white striped awning had appeared and beyond it clouds lay heavy, yellowish and sultry. The heat was oppressive, the sky too close.

Infinite cloudless, luminous skies had stretched across their summer. 'Is it going to rain?'

'Absolutely not! The forecast says tomorrow morning, but it's beginning to look very strange out there . . . Jack, who is that man?'

He followed the direction where she pointed, to the men arranging chairs round the dance floor. 'Oh, you mean Rachel's gardener. You didn't meet him?'

She was looking troubled. 'I'm sure, sometime . . . Why's he working for us?'

'I must've forgotten to tell you. It's only one afternoon a week. Don't you like the look of him?'

'I've been trying all afternoon to remember where I've seen that face. Anyway, it doesn't really matter. Some people look familiar when they're not.' Chloe shrugged. When Jodie skipped up she smiled and they were like sisters, excited and giggling.

Tonight belonged to Chloe, it was a late celebration of their marriage. She was happy and he would try to play a part.

An oddly early dusk settled over Whitting as lights blinked on round the garden, a soft glow filtered through the rooms. People started to arrive and music lapped through open windows. On the terrace a blaze of chatter grew.

London lay briefly visible far below in disturbed geometry, lit threads that netted and snared the city's dissoluble fragments. Bits of wall and roof slid into the horizon as dark fell, until only the snare was left.

Waves of people, reclaimed after years ... Jack ebbed through the hall. Paul Mann was arriving with his wife and in thickening crowds Jack steered savagely towards them. With surprise he saw Chloe kiss Paul hello.

Smug, sun-tanned, satisfied Paul was saying, 'Congratulations. This is my wife Grace – Chloe Maine. Jack, how're things, old mate?' Chloe disappeared to greet new guests as Paul went on, 'What an amazing place. You're doing not badly, obviously.'

Jack saw Gideon, beckoned him over and said to Paul, 'I didn't realise you knew Chloe.'

'We'd met – she did typing or something, didn't she? Well, Gideon, shall we hold a ritual mourning for *Cragge*, or welcome the new like sensible people?' Gideon smiled queasily. Paul continued, 'Jack and Chloe keep turning down our dinner invites – we're gatecrashing tonight.'

'What nonsense.' Jack kept his voice neutral. 'Red, white or something stronger? Gideon is welcoming the new, he's got plenty to celebrate. Excuse me, I must ...'

He wove through to the terrace, nodding to Jim Hartsledge and his wife Lily. Here the music was louder, the air slightly cooler. A mix of hatred and despair engulfed him as from the parapet he looked down on the floodlit garden. The place buzzed with people, noise, music, words, all meaningless. Gideon passed like a net, catching only the big and succulent guests.

Chloe walked on to the crowded floor below. She began to dance with Justin Fairbrother. Flaunting. Taunting him.

They were moving together with practised grace between other couples. Jack saw Chloe's laughter, watched the sensual flow of her white dress. Justin's arm was round her and he fooled about, swirling her away between other dancers then spinning her magnetised back

218

into his orbit. They didn't know he was watching. But they must know that everyone else – all of their friends – were watching, and knew.

'Jack darling! How beautiful it looks. The dancers, the lights, the music. How clever to arrange all this.' Sarah's arms went round him and he turned towards her kiss. She was sun-tanned, smug and satisfied like Paul.

'I didn't arrange anything. Is the party going well?'

'Everyone's having a marvellous time, high as kites. Sorry I couldn't get here earlier.'

He grabbed a bottle and refilled her glass, his eyes strayed back to where Justin and Chloe now danced very close. Sarah asked, 'Want to dance?'

'Maybe. All right.'

They pushed their way down the steps to the garden, music thudded and a press of people writhed. Cool breaths of wind whispered unexpectedly across the hot night. There were no stars above, no moon, only bright electric bulbs in imitation rainbow colours. He could never feel the same way he used to about Chloe, about himself. Everywhere he saw hot faces lit by strange shadows and stretched in smiles he knew were false, bared teeth hidden beneath the grins. A nightmare, a rush hour of bodies seethed in swaying forced proximity, dizzying above thudding feet on boards that echoed above space. A foam of faces bordered the dance floor, their eyes and flashing teeth malevolent.

He couldn't dance. 'Let's sit down. I'm sorry.'

'What's wrong, what is it?'

'Nothing.'

'Don't give me that.' She found a couple of chairs at the rail, the ringside: for the screaming sounds and crowds and his sense of great danger about the space they revolved in had turned the dance floor into a boxing ring full of blows, grazed bone and blood, a sport for jeers and cheers. A sharp roll of drums produced applause. The band had stopped playing.

Sarah said, 'Oh God. Richard would, wouldn't he.'

Jack saw people turning away towards the house, others glancing across the boards with embarrassed smiles. Richard, who'd arrived drunk and was now much drunker, did not want the music ever to stop. He was slow-stepping, swaying his hips and drink-ravaged torso in a quiet fantasy striptease that was not pretend enough. His red shirt was whirled like a banner overhead and flung across the floor, over the bullring with its gnawing crowd. Teetering on imaginary stilettos, circling his pelvis pathetically, the actor began to undo his trousers.

'Better stop him.'

'Why?' Jack smiled for the first time in an hour. Then the smile faded. He watched the silent bellow of the actor's pain, a sharp blade of recognition held him pinioned. He thought: we're both failures, you and I – in our professions, in our lives. We're ghosts now, our turn is over, we should insult the present before we go. I'm living off my new rich wife, in her house – everyone here knows the score. My new, rich, faithless wife . . . He shook with silent hysteria. Sarah squeezed his arm sharply.

'OK, we got the message.' It was Justin, smooth and cheerful, in control. Pulling up Richard's trousers before they quite went down.

'Bugger 'em all!' bellowed the actor, staggering against Justin who stopped him falling. 'Bugger 'em all is what I say.'

'I agree,' soothed Justin Fairbrother. 'My sentiments exactly. But not here, fella – not now.' He was looking round for help, looking past and through Jack. Two figures emerged from the shrinking crowd. Forbes and Cammell. The trio, victors sandwiching the vanquished, staggered like a dying monster out from the empty circle of light.

Jack felt drops of rain begin. Cold and welcome, shocking after weeks of barren summer. He walked across the boards.

How plausible Justin was, how deceptively friendly. Cancerous and malignant. That reddened face looked like a sore, its beady little eyes darted aggressively. How could he ever have liked this man? Kicking aside a fallen loop of fairy lights, wondering if the rain might electrocute them all, he went up to Justin. 'You've really seen off poor old Richard. Well done.'

Justin blinked. 'Someone had to. Good party, Jack.'

'Enjoyed yourself, haven't you.'

In a small quietness, under the flicker of falling rain, Chloe started, 'Jack, what – ' but he was over the edge, there was no turning back.

He shot the words, 'Ben Ashe . . . Sasha and Benjamin. Must've been child's play for you, destroying my baby!' And feeling Chloe's touch he rounded on her, 'You knew. You've known all along – the mystery axeman, hired to hack up *Cragge*.'

Deeper silence, the heavying rain. Chloe answered, 'I'm sorry. Anna – '

But Justin cut in to stop her, 'Of course Chloe didn't know. And you don't understand.'

Gideon took up the defence, 'Yes, Jack, the circumstances – '

Jack whirled on his agent with such fury the man shrank back. 'I understand betrayal very well – now I know what's been going on!'

Gideon tried, 'Look at it from another point of view – '

'That's easy if you wear two faces,' growled Jack. 'I trusted you, thought you were on my side.'

Gideon snapped, 'I do have other clients to consider.' He walked off.

Chloe began to plead with Jack. 'Darling, don't let him go –'

'Darling?' he mocked her, hating her. 'And I scarcely need your advice,' he went on, then to Justin, 'If you really expected me never to find out, what kind of an idiot must you think I am?'

Anna tried to intervene, 'Jack, don't quarrel with Gideon – or us. We've felt terrible, it was so awkward but somebody had to rescue the scripts –'

'What d'you mean, rescue them? He's massacred my work, years and years of effort just thrown away! You're not a writer,' he shouted at Justin. 'You're a crap artist and a con merchant who's got found out!'

Justin froze. 'You want to know why they begged me to help? Because you were sabotaging a show they were committed to making. Because you're impossible, paranoid, with no idea of your own motives or your real nature. And they were desperate.'

'What the hell are you saying?' Jack was electric with rage. 'I made a success and you screwed it up. You want to destroy me in every way, you just couldn't resist the chance to!'

'I understand you're upset at finding out. We wanted to tell you. But making a scene like this? Come on.'

Anna stepped in. 'Calm down, Jack, we'll talk about it later. This is Chloe's night.'

'Chloe's and Justin's,' Jack snarled. 'Maybe we should all leave them to it. Oh, don't play the injured innocent now!'

Justin said quietly, 'Why've you been neglecting Chloe? Not only tonight, but ever since you got back to England together. Why marry the girl if you don't care about her?'

Chloe tried to stop him. 'Justin. Please don't.'

'Why not?' growled Justin. 'Jack's got what he wanted

– Whitting House and your money. He doesn't even bother to pretend now – '

Jack's fist flashed out and cracked on the bone under Justin's wiry beard. The man skidded across the wet dance floor, sagged into the railing. A scream rang out. Hurling himself after Justin, Jack started battering him back on to the ground as he struggled to rise, before people tore at him and dragged him off.

There was no dawn. The sky stayed black as a cave. Rain sheeting through long night hours stopped any natural lightening. Drumming on the roof, choking in the gutter it spewed through cracks to pound the debris of a hundred guests. Swirled chortling down steps to flood the dying garden below.

'I don't understand,' Chloe said later that night when they were alone. 'Of course you're upset about Justin and *Cragge* – how dare he, and behind your back! But what did you mean about him and me?'

Jack turned it aside, couldn't tell her he knew, wouldn't have it confirmed. His humiliation felt too complete. After she'd fallen asleep at last, he got up and paced through the silent house in his dressing-gown, breath puffing in the clammy air. Among the shadows of the garden something was moving, detaching and gliding through the trees towards him. A thin snake of fear coiled up his spine.

It was only Rachel's gardener.

'Why are you still here?' Jack's voice was ragged as his nerves. 'Everyone's gone.'

'It's you I want to see. A private word, the two of us alone.' The man stood on the top step, sculpted by the falling rain. A faint light shone and he glistened as if made of slime, emerging from the undergrowth in the night. He added, 'Someone had to check the electrics were off. Shipshape for the night.'

'What did you want to talk about?'

'The night old Mrs Rushe drowned. I'd brought her some tools that day, you know.' He paused, continued. 'Wasn't expecting strangers in the garden and hurried off too quick. I woke up that dawn – not far from here I lived – remembered I'd left all her brand-new stuff out by the gate. A foggy wet night, they'd get rusty and spoiled. Couldn't sleep again after that, so I drove back here in the van.'

'Wait – when was this? What time?'

'Around dawn – maybe five o'clock. I put the tools away, dried them all properly.'

Jack leaned towards him. 'Did you see anything, anyone? Have you talked to the police?'

'Not yet. All I saw, you see, was this . . . And I thought nothing of it at first.'

He was taking a clear plastic bag from his pocket. Inside lay a piece of jewellery. Chloe's hairclip, the one she'd worn on the night of Rachel's death. Its *diamanté* glittered like tiny eyes.

Adams leaned close, whispering as if rain could hear. 'It was lying all shiny there on the path towards the lake, that's where it was.'

The rain beat down. Jack heard Chloe's voice, 'I went out to your car . . . I didn't go back . . . I just started walking and walking . . .'

Staring at the hairclip, the gardener's hands, his face, 'Why should I believe you?'

'Why should I lie?'

Jack knew it was Chloe who'd lied – about Rachel, and Justin. And probably, about loving him. He thought bitterly how he would've understood, he could've kept on taking her side if she'd trusted him. He said, 'Well, thanks. I'd better take the clip. Please.'

The gardener turned it around in his hands to catch the

light, examining it as if he hadn't heard. Then he slid the clip back into the bag, replaced it in his pocket. 'She's a valuable piece, Mr Maine. I know a thing or two.'

Part Three

1

Coming from the house in the morning he stepped down the gravel drive towards Hill Grove and felt the sky like a sodden sheet. The gardens were all cried out, sap drained from the bushes that nodded to his passing as they shifted on their stalks. It was autumn, he realised, and then he smelled the smoke.

He looked back at the house and saw flames tongued up. The wall was gaping, tiles fell in sharp showers and the tower cracked cleaving like a pod to spill its mind. But he didn't see her.

She was trapped somewhere inside.

The thing twisted quivering in mist as he ran to it, breath rasping, hands bruised from battering until the wall gave way. He fell through into the long dark hall and on to something soft. It was the feathery ashes of her body in a pillow and there on it, cradled in it, her skull a planet newly discovered, her contours the light and shadow in a photograph.

Then she was gone, sucked out and blowing through the empty doors, aghast rooms in thick black cinder that caught his nose and mouth, seared his eyes, filled his throat squeezing out breath. He was suffocating –

Waking in a strange bedroom, windows open, raw and rainy. Lead light enclosing silence, subterranean. Outside the sullen ivy dripped. He banged windows shut, sat on the bed in crumpled clothes. Memory welled. His fists were sore, his mouth was ash.

She was making a fool of him with Justin. Images of them together, of the witnessing crowds were burned into his memory for ever. And she'd known Justin was secretly rewriting his work, at least she'd admitted that. But Rachel's drowning... If it was an accident, why hadn't Chloe told him in the past few months? He'd done everything, everything he could to protect her. And she'd been nervous of the gardener. Could she have sensed that he knew?

Jack flexed his hands. Chloe had wanted marriage, but it was never him she'd loved. They should've let him kill Justin last night: then maybe, somehow, Adams might never have wormed out of the wreckage to give him that last proof.

Dragging his protesting body downstairs he pushed open the kitchen door and heard Sarah's voice, 'You can make anything happen –' She broke off abruptly as he walked in.

Why was Sarah still here? She and Jodie sat either side of Chloe at the big table, the three of them staring at him in silence like some jury.

'By wishing on stars?' Jack spat out the words derisively. 'Or offering human sacrifices, maybe? Magical thinking is pure shit.' Then he thought gladly: they're afraid of me.

Sarah smiled, tightly. 'By having faith, Jack.' Was her irritating new radiance because of Paul Mann?

Chloe said, slow, 'She means a kind of trust. It's like having daylight, you can exist without it but not happily.'

Slopping black coffee into a mug, Jack snarled, 'Three damn witches, brewing up in the kitchen.'

230

'You're just full of sexist nonsense,' Sarah snapped. 'And about last night – '

The phone rang in the hall and Jack slammed out. Behind him their voices started up in argument.

It was Ross Cammell. 'Trouble,' he barked. 'It seems Richard went on to a nightclub. Somehow he bounced a bouncer and the guy's suing for assault.'

'Publicity stunt?'

'This we don't need. It's got to be kept out of the papers.'

'Is Richard OK? Where is he?'

'In the cells, waiting. We can bail him out. And try to buy the bouncer.'

Jack suggested, 'Cragge's a national hero, millions of people identify him with law and order. Why not talk to the upper echelons about it?'

'A CID chief? Mm, maybe . . .'

Jack took his hangover back upstairs and later in the day Chloe came to find him. 'We need to talk.'

'I don't want to,' he growled.

'You owe me some explanation.' She sat down and looked at him in a careful, controlled sort of way. 'You were impossible, Jack. The way our party ended – nobody understands and I certainly don't. Was it just drink? I've never seen you like that – and as for hitting Justin . . .'

He felt detached and hardened against her. An edge of chill cut through his voice, 'Don't you think I had good reason to?'

Chloe leaned towards him, urgent. 'Jack, I learned from Anna a couple of days ago about what Justin was doing. But I'd no chance to tell you, you've been – '

He laughed aloud at her pretence, so that she stopped. She'd known it from Justin from months back. 'And I suppose it was Sarah who fixed the job for Justin?' Or was it Chloe, he wondered suddenly.

'How could she, from the BBC?'

Jack shrugged. He strode off to the bathroom to get rid of her but Chloe followed. Why wouldn't she leave him alone?

'That call,' she asked. 'Was it Gideon? You insulted him, Jack.'

'I hoped that was noticeable.' He began taking off last night's clothes. 'He threw *Cragge* into Justin's grubby paws and said nothing – absolutely nothing – to me about it!'

'I doubt if it happened through him, Justin's pretty well-connected. Jack, you know how much you need Gideon.'

'I don't need him. Or Justin Fairbrother. Or anyone else who betrays my trust.' He stabbed a look of ice in her direction. Chloe stood white-faced, wounded by his felt condemnation. Stilling a glimmer of pity, he turned his back. Switched on the shower fast, so a wall of water ripped between them.

'I give up,' Chloe exclaimed in a burst of anger. 'If you want a war, then you've got one!'

But she didn't mean it, not then.

It was a big enough house but they couldn't avoid each other for long.

While he lay sleepless, staring up at the ceiling, Chloe crept into the bed he'd made up for himself. And he felt glad – he'd missed her last night – but made no move to welcome her. She was clutching an old black notebook.

Jack took it, 'What's this?'

'One of Rachel's diaries. That's another thing I've needed to talk to you about. But you were off in a world of your own.'

He opened the pages of black scrawled ink and read:

Even Charles is losing patience with her, ever since the

barbaric thing of that toad in my dressing-table! Even when we get away from her, steal time alone to be happy together, she comes between us now. Every day I remind myself: the child is very disturbed, she never had a mother. But this is why I thought it could work out. Instead she sees me as her enemy. But she won't drive me away, won't destroy us . . .

'Why are you reading this?' Jack asked, closing the notebook and dropping it on to the bedside table.

'Jodie showed them to me,' she explained. 'And I want to understand Rachel if I can.'

'I would've imagined that you'd want to forget her.'

'How can I possibly forget, after all that's happened? You persuaded me to see her again.'

Jack watched Chloe take off her robe and slide into the bed. Her body was warm and comforting to him, soft and familiar. He registered his own desire, felt a mix of love and hatred. And guilt. Why had he talked her into meeting Rachel again? Had it been simply the writer's curiosity to provoke change, to create a *what if* and to drive events as far as they could go? That made him culpable.

Maybe Justin was right. Maybe he'd wanted, through marriage, the bizarre and beautiful fantasy of this house, of everything that surrounded Chloe. Privilege and deprivation, the unknown, a sense of dangerous relation? Did he really love her, with all her secrets and all those lies?

'Hey,' she breathed softly. 'Put your arms around me, Jack,' and she cuddled close, in comfort he thought until she whispered, 'I know you want me.' Her hand moved over him and she began to lick, to tease. She would have him – his body, his loving – and wielded an armoury of knowledge and of memories which were happy. She filled his mind, his vision and senses that made the dark so dazzling bright, as her firm young flesh took him over, took him in. This is what people mean by fucking, he thought, caught in movement but still here, and the next moment he recoiled because she, the flesh of her had turned cold and heavy, dead. And he hurled her away from him. Lay panting, eyes unseeing, gripped by fear.

With a cry she rolled over and buried her face deep in the pillow.

Almost from the start he'd felt her madness shutting him out, leaving him isolated.

She'd been there that night by the lake with Rachel, bound together in the fog. Chloe had been provoked powerfully on that last night. He'd seen the extent of Rachel's threat to her mind. Images flicked past him of that day and evening, the imagined night. Chloe had been there. Had Rachel grown dizzy, or stumbled? Had Chloe pushed her in? He saw it each way. The dark webbed water pierced, the fall.

Yes, he loved Chloe.

But he could never be easy with her until he knew, until she confided. Jack banished the images but they crowded back. He looked at her lying in bed, at the shape of her body under a snow-white duvet, at her head averted from him. He took her shoulder and shook her.

'Listen, I know you were there that night.'

She turned to him and answered, 'What night? Where?'

If she chose to deny it now, could they ever be close again? 'By the lake, on the night she died.' Chloe had stiffened, she was frowning. 'There's no need to keep silent or suffer alone. Tell me what happened – just between us two.'

'Jack, what are you talking about?'

'Rachel and the way she died. I'll love you anyway. I'll protect you. I know how she tormented you and –'

Chloe sat rigid, she drew back. 'You think . . . Do you think that I killed Rachel?'

He looked away from her burning eyes. 'Please, don't pretend with me. You were there. How did it happen? I've got to know.'

'But I never went near the ponds! You don't believe anything I said?' Fury was on her face, outrage as she went on, 'Is that why you suggested lying to the police? About the time I got back to Islington, that we left Whitting together. Because you thought I'd pushed Rachel into the lake to drown?'

He tried to touch her and she jumped out of bed. He asked, 'It was an accident, wasn't it?'

'So even then, you thought I'd killed her somehow? You married me, thinking I'm a murderess?'

'Whatever happened, I've been trying to tell you it doesn't matter.'

'Oh but it does!' She seemed fragmented by shock – she'd never expected him to ask. 'It's horrible. How could you think that of me?'

So she would never tell him now, and he'd gone too far.

Chloe cried, 'You don't believe me, you don't believe a word I've said.'

Confused, he tried to hang on like a man drowning in flotsam, 'You often said things that . . .' Then quickly tried to take it all back. 'But of course I believe you. Chloe, come here.'

She stayed crouched out of his reach. Taut, endangered. She whispered, 'You can't believe that I'm all right, since I've married you. Or that I love you and tell the truth. Oh Jack, you've no idea what's just been done.'

She didn't trust him; she clung to her story of walking for hours in the fog. He'd sensed from the start it wasn't true. He pretended to believe her but somehow it was all too late. An ocean separated them and he felt angry, he felt like doing damage.

He was propelled between rehearsal rooms and notes for his book. Calling Gideon, he got an assistant and told her to change his consultant's credit: 'To Maud Keystone'. Solemnly she promised to phone the *Kops* production.

Gideon called back. 'Jack, what the hell are you doing.'

'We've nothing to talk about.'

'Right! But you're making a big mistake.'

Jack hung up, grabbed a notebook and scribbled:

BEFORE THE WAR BEGAN. BACK SETTING

Charlotte is moon-complexioned and slightly built, dark hair worn long and pinned up. She kneels at Mass: the Sanctus sung in Latin, the acolyte rings the bell. Deep silence, incense drifting. A large scarf thrown over her head becomes a cowl, her face half concealed. Receives the sacraments. She's well known here in the little church – in this parish the older worshippers knew her as a child.

She's schizophrenic, a split personality – take the narrative this way?

In the walled garden she plays with the cats, their kittens. Many fine trees, a well-kept lawn, rose-beds blazing. Charlotte takes a basket to cut flowers for the table. Guests are coming this evening, she discusses arrangements with the housekeeper.

The house: a strange Victoriana, an oppressive dark interior. The atmosphere of impending crisis.

The murder will be unpremeditated, a crime of passion.

The phone rang, stopped in mid-ring. He picked it up and Anna said, ' – crazy! Can't you persuade him?'

'Justin should never have touched his work,' Chloe answered.

'If Justin hadn't rewritten, someone else would've done a worse job. Jack's always been envious of Justin – '

Jack dropped the phone. He despised Justin, had never envied him! It was Justin who was jealous – of his marrying Chloe. How else to explain the butchering of *Cragge*? And what of Chloe with Anna, that friendship based on betrayal?

Chloe mentioned Anna that evening and Jack said, 'She can't think I'll ever speak to Justin again.'

'Anna's my oldest friend.'

'So don't worry about me.'

'How can I – ?'

'That's between you and your conscience, I suppose.'

Chloe didn't mention the Fairbrothers again. If there'd been a chance of contact it soon passed. Jack's sense of isolation deepened.

She'd abandoned her photography and while he wrote she'd play the piano, obsessive with nervous energy, furious at any mistake. Dissonant sounds night and day like madness shouting. She was unreachable and kept secrets. Phone calls, days out she never explained. She was seeing Justin and it wasn't doing her any good.

Eventually, quick with guilt Jack searched her cupboards, her pockets, her desk. He couldn't have said exactly what he was looking for. A note or love letter, a keepsake? It had been going on for years, she must have something of Justin's. He found a restaurant bill, a cinema ticket, a pressed flower. Suspicion deepened. She'd kept nothing to link the two of them specifically.

Then in a drawer of her desk he came across a folder of yellowed press cuttings.

Piano prodigy Magdalen Opie Rushe died today, twenty-four hours after receiving severe head injuries in a car accident. Police are still seeking the driver of a dark blue saloon believed involved in Thursday's crash on the A1.

Concert pianist Opie Rushe, 20 – described by critics as 'inspired by a divine force' – was eight months pregnant. A daughter was delivered by surgeons last night. Husband Charles Rushe, the music impresario and publicist, flew from Vienna to be at her bedside. The couple had been married for one year.

He was careful to leave no trace of his search, replaced everything exactly.

Eventually he followed her. Without thinking, as if it was his job. She left at eleven and he tracked her through the backstreets, heading south-west as he'd expected. Heavy traffic separated them, he caught up again and saw her ignore the turning towards Putney. Instead she drove down Fulham Road, turned at a side street and parked. He left the Saab round a corner and followed her on foot.

She rang Sarah's entry-phone, went in.

Jack waited in a bistro across the street. Would Justin join her, using the flat for a rendezvous? Would Sarah do that to him? As he thought of things she'd done since their failed love affair, suddenly he caught his own reflection in the cafe window glass: watching, spying, furtive. Self-hatred propelled him into the street, almost under a speeding bus.

He couldn't leave it alone but called Sarah – had she seen Chloe recently?

Sarah said in her forthright way, 'Poor Chloe.'

It wasn't the reaction he'd expected. 'What's wrong?'

'The poor girl came to me for help – about you. What could I say? She seems to imagine you don't love her any more.'

Jack put down the phone, stood at the window noticing autumn lay in the leaves like a burn. Slowly he went out of his study and paused on the landing. He must go to Chloe, must get through to her. She was playing the piano, the sound shooting jaggedly round the house. From the gallery he looked down through the cave of cedar stairwell, the glistening carved snakes of the balustrade. The drawing-room door was half-open and someone was standing still in that bright blade of light. It was the gardener.

Soundlessly Jack crept down the stairs. Nearer to Adams, and to Chloe. He hadn't seen them so close together before. Suddenly he recognised their similarity – and their opposing traits. Adams's larger harder frame and face, her smallness and softness. But they were two sides of the same pale coin: fused together they would melt smoothly into one androgynous being.

Adams was watching Chloe and she didn't know he was there. Some panic rose in Jack and he shouted something wordless like the alarm cry of a beast. Instantly Adams slid from the doorway into the blackness of the hall. Jack confronted him, steely, then gestured towards Rachel's study. They went in and he pushed the door to. Chloe's playing had stopped.

'What d'you want?' he demanded.

The man looked around the room, murmured with appreciation as he touched the clock, touched Rachel's carved black roll-top desk. He was filthy in misshapen clothes, he stank.

Jack dragged back the shutters, flooding the small space with light. He opened a drawer and took out the flat manilla envelope waiting there. Adams had seated himself in the wing-chair and was sprawled comfortably.

Holding out the two hundred pounds Jack demanded, 'Where is it? You said you'd bring it.'

The man got up, took the envelope and examined the money in a detached sort of way. 'You're going to have to trust me,' he said with a smile. 'It's in a safe place.'

Anger jagged through Jack, he moved forward but whatever he might've done was prevented. Chloe stood in the doorway. She was staring at Adams in shock.

'Until next week,' Jack said quickly.

'We aim to please,' the gardener replied. He darted a look at Chloe – a brush of obvious familiarity – then melted out through the hall. They heard him whistling a tune in the drive. It was aggressive and territorial, the song of a bird of prey.

Chloe stood very still as the sound strutted away. 'What were you doing? Why was he in the house?'

She must've guessed, but couldn't say it. Jack said, 'I'd forgotten to pay him, he came to remind me.'

Her voice cracked out of control, 'I don't want him anywhere around! Can't you understand?'

He shrugged, watching her carefully. She was straightening the desk, closing the drawer and shutters. She was acting like someone mortally afraid. And that was it . . . Suddenly he realised she was acting, for his benefit for some reason. Nothing was genuine. There was something about the connection between those two . . .

Chloe turned to go out. 'Aren't you working, Jack? I thought you were busy. Are you going on location tomorrow?'

She wanted him out of the way, she was going to see Justin.

'I suppose so,' he replied with a kind of hopelessness.

240

*

They were shooting at Tower Bridge from dawn, moving off as the tourists arrived. Fragments of a chase and fight were filmed along the Thames embankment. It was a cold and overcast day, a spiteful wind whipped out from the river and curled round corners, sneaking up.

Richard and Duval had been choreographed by a fight expert, rehearsed blow by blow. The event was filmed in seconds of action and reaction; continuity problems had cast and crew hard at work for most of the day. To keep their schedule Forbes cut a scene at a third location on the South Bank. Pierre's girlfriend, played by new discovery Veronique Audet, had little to do beyond standing on the sidelines, screaming, occasionally being rescued by Pierre from villains. Now she had even less. The beautiful young actress needed much consolation from her director and this was, Jack realised, exactly what Gerry Forbes had intended.

The light faded. Driving north across London, half-way up Highgate Hill he stopped before St Pius's. Its thin dark spire disappeared into a piebald sky. Jack walked slowly around the little gothic church. Could Francis fall from that spire, from the bell tower? How would it happen?

A muffled banging caught his attention, then a faint movement in the shadows of the wall. A side door was blowing against its frame in the wind. Someone had unscrewed both hinges and left them undone.

It was irresistible, the chance to go alone into the church. The street was deserted. Pushing the heavy door back against its padlock he slipped through the gap into near darkness. Jack's eyes adjusted to the small gloomy space of the vestry. He glanced up: the hollow tower was vertiginous, tall enough to cause death from a fall. His footsteps echoed in the cold barrel of the nave and finding he'd held his breath, as if someone might be listening, he expelled it in a sigh that resounded over the valleys and mountains of stone.

The gallery next to the organ space was high above the gap where the altar used to be. A fall on to thick carpet with stone beneath – could that cause a dislocation to the vertebrae, a severance of the spinal nerve with little other sign of damage?

He shivered, staring up and craning his neck uncomfortably, because it was cold and because for a moment he thought he'd seen a pale face peering down from the shadows. His foot slipped on the stone slab floor and he glanced down. Inscriptions on the old tombstones were worn almost smooth. And on one lay a darkness, a wetness, and a narrow crack of streetlight through the blacked-out windows revealed a gleam to it so that he half knelt and put his fingers into it and found them smeared with something that looked like fresh blood, although it couldn't be.

A hole in the roof, he thought: the rain's come through, mixed with timber preservative that's turned it dark and thick.

He was being watched. His heart was banging, locked in the cave of his chest, it was hurting.

He thought: children are taught of an all-powerful god that breaks into hearts and minds from outside, to judge. He said aloud, the sound cracking out in many fragments of a voice, 'I don't believe. I'm not a believer.'

2

'I don't believe, I'm not a believer.'

The words hissed around the pillars and curled under the rafters.

The man was creeping far below the church gallery and Art knelt watching from between a tracery of bars. His enemy was trespassing, hunting him even in this circle of protection. Had stepped on the tomb, had dipped his hand in midnight's sacrifice.

Standing in silent concentration, Art juggled the opposing forces.

In many ways the manifestation was perfect, it confirmed. He was bound and twinned. Their paths, their souls were linked, his strength drained by the outflowing cancer of his twin, enslaved to the adversary. She was betrayal, his fate reversed and now they were entwined so close one might survive if the other was weeded out.

Art drew the knife from his belt and gazed down on the head of Jack Maine, willing him to stillness before gliding fluid as a shadow towards the steps. He felt the rushing whisper of some approach outside where night and day were in collision. Some disturbance there, another thing not considered. He sent it away, focussed . . . But the wavering was to his cost. As he took the last step down the target moved, broke away from her influence, heading towards the bell tower. In there he'd find the coat that lay folded into a pillow, the bottle and part of a loaf.

Fear needled through to plough his stomach; he caught the face of the Virgin mammoth on the wall, her eyes snapped round him. The all-powerful mother smiling unperturbed.

With a huge effort Art drew protection to him, regained his purpose. But it had gone wrong. His quarry was disappearing, out through the trap he'd left in the unholy wall and . . . the defeated day had got through a remnant of its army at the last . . .

He stood paralysed, unbreathing in the small stone space.

The locks and bars and bolts shot back from the big front door and a powerful white beam penetrated searching the nave. He saw the silhouettes of three men enter against an orange glow before the door banged shut. They were inside. They laughed. The clear voice of one rang through the sanctum, 'A little piece of heaven is turning out quite popular with purchasers!'

A first frost came overnight. Art was a stooped and gangling figure grown ragged. The long hot summer and changeable fall were over and the world lay whitening, stiffened and bled out like paper as it emptied of human life. He couldn't go back to the church full of danger. He'd stumbled down the hill, his quarry long escaped into the sanguine sodium night.

To keep warm he walked the streets in circles round the small patch he knew. From empty boxes he made a cardboard cave and lay shivering, dozing fitfully, craving the loss of thought that sleep would bring. He'd saved Jodie from this life two winters ago and now she slept with their child up in the house.

Lorries, pedestrians brought the dawn. Flexing toes
and fingers he started to walk through streets white and
crumbling. For weeks he'd stayed away from Junction
Road, since Cooper's men – four of them – had turned
him out. He'd watched them board up the empty flats.
Now Art faltered but didn't turn back.

Something was to be done.

He went cautiously. Six doors on was the derelict building where he'd lived with Rose, where he'd grown up and
she'd died. The single eye of his boyhood home was
bricked up now with purple blocks under a brow of bud-
dleia and a red lettered sign: *Dangerous Structure*. From
here Art could see flats with blinds, a chain and padlock,
the window of *A'Laddinscave* beneath a banner: *Clear-
ance*. He'd lived his life in places closing . . .

Opposite he cast his consciousness around, found
danger – not substantial – hiding nearby. He waited in
case it changed, then judged it safe to go close. The road
heaved, rumbled and seethed, setting up a howl of horns
as he picked a path across. On the other side he looked
into the window.

There were the talismans from the house. The bronze
clock with cherubs on, a gilded spoon, the silver brush
and mirror set, the ivory teething ring . . . Art scanned
the objects. They had properties and he must return each
one, having first cast himself into its fabric, to strengthen
his position in the house and trinity.

He raised a fist to break the glass. The head of an old
enemy swam through the dusty clutter framed by gilt.
They were all around; although he'd escaped there was
no relief. As he stared into the window of *A'Laddinscave*
the head swam off, the door chimed open.

'Art,' said the man. 'What d'you want?'

He remembered him lurking among the stuffed bodies
of beasts, the under-stuffed chairs vacated by dead

men . . . His right hand felt the hundreds of pounds lying heavy as newspaper in the lining of his coat, his left hand pointed boldly at the things.

'Those, I want them.' He took out the bundles of money through a hole in his pocket, leaning over and working the notes up the seam. They came out crumpled and torn.

Tony Ladd looked at the money. 'Where did you get that?'

'It's enough! Get me those, they're Jodie's. Fetch them for me.'

'I know they're Jodie's,' he answered. 'You're in touch with her – you know where she is?'

'I'll return them where they belong. That's where she is – where she belongs. Go on then, I haven't got all day.'

Art kept his foot in the door feeling like a salesman, feeling clever. Tony Ladd came back out with a plastic carrier and in it were the talismans.

'Where are Jodie and the baby? Sure you'll be able to get these back to her?'

Art scowled at him. 'You don't inform to anybody that I've been here.'

'All right.'

A simple transaction? Art knew that transparency must hide trickery. He backed two fast steps, braced himself and fixed the other with his eye. Then hurling Maine's money into the face of this enemy he turned and ran.

He was drawn back to it. Winding up the hill, the slope, the path to the side where he stood watching, hidden deep in the undergrowth as dusk fell. Lights flicked on one by one inside. The house grew flat like a cut-out mask with eyes an only living dimension.

It was his by right. And it was his only shelter now.

Bars framed their window like a TV screen. Three heads hung technicolour solid inside. He remembered that other night when she'd been taken – his time of betrayal. The picture looked very different now, clear and brilliant with infinite visibility since he was wiser.

Jodie sat dining with them at the big table as if she was family. It was a fiction. He watched for long enough ... She gathered dishes to take them out and he went in quickly, stood braced, waiting with arms folded by the time she'd left the dining room and wound down the passageway and opened the heavy door.

'Art ...'

'I've only got a minute,' he answered. 'And so have you.'

In that new dress of summer blue he thought her beautiful. Putting down the plates on the draining board she asked quietly, 'What is it? What d'you want?'

Art held out the bag. After a moment she took it and looked inside, rather cautiously he thought, the talismans surprising her. So she'd given up hope of possessing them again. 'Are you pleased?'

She didn't say directly. 'You found them.'

'*A'Laddinscave*, that's where they were.'

'I had to get money when you were ill with flu that time. Don't be angry, Art. I had to. Did he give these to you?'

What was she talking about? He hadn't had flu for years. He told her, 'I took what's ours, I had to pay of course. I've always had to pay, Jodie. For the mistakes of others and their treachery.'

'What d'you mean, whose treachery?'

'You're well in with them.' She didn't answer so he went on, 'You're clever – '

But Jodie interrupted, all abrupt, 'I don't know what you're talking about. Don't you work in the garden? What are you doing in here and at night?' and he saw the man had come in.

Art said, 'Mr Maine knows why I'm here. Don't you?'
This man was afraid of him. He was turning to Jodie now.

'Do you know Adams?'

'He works for you, you said? I don't know him.'

'That's right,' confirmed Art.

'You'd better go back to the dining room,' she was told.
'Chloe will wonder where you've got to. There's no need
to mention this. Tell her I'll bring the coffee.'

They watched Jodie scuttle off down the tiled passage.
'How d'you know I won't stay all night, or for ever? I
like this house, I always have,' Art taunted.

'Did you bring the hairclip?' asked Jack Maine.

Art made a great show of annoyance at himself.
'Terrible memory! But it's safe enough.'

'What do you want? I'm not rich, I haven't got money.'

With a display of amusement Art asked, 'A poor man,
is that it.'

'You think I'm well off? Nothing here is mine. I've no
income to speak of. If you're hoping for regular money
it's impossible.'

'A man of means if not money, you can't deny. Belongs
to your wife does it, all of this?' Art allowed sympathy
into his voice. A warm cloak of elation was creeping
over him, he felt all-powerful. 'What matters most, I'm
wondering? You see I can't forget that night, and there's
others who can't forget either. Who can't help wondering.
It seems to all come back to your wife. What she did, and
what she owns.'

'So tell me what you want.'

'Perhaps you'll find out more about me as you get to
know me better and remember.'

There was a silence, the crackling and shifting of coals
in the Aga.

'Why should we know each other better?' he said at

last. 'I paid you to return some jewellery that Chloe lost. You haven't returned it.'

'Shall I have a word with her?' Art suggested. 'I know she's a bit nervous of me, a bit irrational in her way. But shall I – ?'

Maine stopped him, wasn't going to have that. Closing the door he stood against it. 'I don't want you anywhere near here again. There seems to've been a misunderstanding – I'm not open to blackmail. If you don't get out – '

'What will you do?' Art laughed, enjoying this. 'Tell the old Bill?'

He was clearly angry now, 'Yes, if you turn up again – '

'Then I'll shop her. You can't get rid of me, I've belonged here for years. More than you dream of. A banishment?' and he burst out laughing again. 'You can't escape what's meant for you.'

'Now get out!'

'Before you call the cops? Don't make me laugh. Oh I'll go all right.' Art opened the back door, the great cold dark night whirled into the house and lay between them. He saw that Maine was bewildered by his sudden going, and anxious. He laughed irrepressibly remembering Jodie's talk of the detective. 'I saw Cairns at the gate the other day, Tuesday. He was looking in at you for a long, long time.'

The man followed him out quickly, grabbed his sleeve. 'Wait. How do you know Cairns?'

Art shook him off and started down the steps. 'The detective and I know each other all right. He's still very interested in both of you. I can slip him the word any time.'

'Come back here.'

'Make up your mind! Goodnight, sweet dreams. Regards to the old lady, don't forget.'

He pretended to leave.

The dance to death had only just begun and Whitting would always be his home, he wouldn't leave again. It had so many hiding places. Finding refuge he locked himself in every night, left no trace in the mornings. He felt safely enclosed under the low beams, beneath the rows of tools, between those arched windows that should've belonged to a church. Here it had all begun.

He watched the house and its inhabitants, he observed. Jodie often went out alone in the evenings leaving the child. He didn't like that. What did it mean?

Something worried him and eventually he worked it out.

With despair Art realised. He'd kept her powerful by still following her earlier commands. He'd been told to tell Jodie nothing and so some time he'd have to tell everything. How might she react?

He dreaded telling her. He put it off. She'd know he was still nearby, watching over her since he'd promised to. But he avoided her and hid as carefully, when she came near, as he did from the other two.

For a while he felt safe.

Then came the morning when he woke with a start and saw the eyes of the mother glazing on him. He had been found.

3

... he's trained in their language and way of life, in combat and firearms. And to kill when necessary.

And trained in the character he must assume, taking on a fictional identity. Parachuted secretly overnight into enemy territory, he must forget his real self and live in the detail of a fictional character. His cover story becomes watertight and convincing, interrogation can't force cracks in it. While his secret, silent life is totally committed to defeating the enemy from within.

For the duration of his assignment he must forget life in England, personal loyalties, Charlotte and his marriage.

Shutting the notebook Jack sat immobilised. Every surface, half the study floor was covered with notes for research. Perhaps his idea was drowning in these thousands of facts and possibilities?

Downstairs Chloe wove her gritty fabrics of sound. From the cool November morning he drew sharp scents – damp earth, mouldering leaf fall – that were heady, dizzying. A bird sang a dissonant spiral into the near silence, the faint whirr of a passing car became its undersong. Last night's rain pattered softly down.

His feet sank deep in muddy paths encircling the ruined garden. It had become entrapped and limited; he followed the crumbling wall that bordered the road and saw only the ivy had kept its density, everything else had shrunk its flesh to sticks and bones that pierced the air or lay decaying underfoot. Cats appeared and began to follow. He'd stirred some memory in Rachel's chorus. A ragged tabby waved half a tail, a black and white matriarch stalked birds and a ginger tom stared down from a damson tree. Jack looked at the smudge of London below, the abandoned orchard where fruit lay wasting, the damp dark gables of Whitting House.

Someone – Jodie – was waving from the terrace and starting down towards him. She was vivid with high spirits as he trudged back to the house with her. 'We're off now, Jack. It's for a shop Tony's going to open in Edinburgh. He's got lots of contacts among the Brighton antique traders, that's why we're going there.'

She was shy about her new man, she was proud of him. Jack helped Tony load the van with bags and push-chair, while Jodie dressed Raphael in his coat and mittens. Reluctant to let her go he asked, 'One for the road?'

Tony glanced at Jodie. 'We ought to get off because it's Saturday and the traffic's building up. We'll be back tomorrow night.'

'Have supper with us then, if you like.'

Loneliness fell over him. They were so certain of happiness, caught up in it. The battered van puttered away while Chloe's piano played on, oblivious, shutting him out.

He decided to walk to the village and buy a paper. The High Street felt comforting in its normality and he put off going back to Whitting, wandered through the Merchant Chandlers, called in at a deli, the wine shop and patisserie. Laden with carriers Jack went back and arranged their brunch in the kitchen before going to her. He saw how febrile she was and tightly strung, there was no pleasure in her playing. Chloe glanced up, distracted. He placed a kiss on the top of her head and her hands crashed down on the keys in anger. 'Stupid, no concentration – I've got to do better than that.'

A sense of pity crept over Jack. She needed distracting like a child from what caused her pain. He said, 'Come on, leave this for a while. I've bought lots of edible treats to tempt you with.'

Reluctantly Chloe allowed herself to be prised away towards the kitchen. 'Aren't you writing?'

'Don't mention writing,' he warned. She exclaimed over the champagne and croissants, the sausage and fresh figs. For a moment he felt warm and thought: everything's all right, it's only my imagination.

Putting his arms around her slight body Jack held her captive. He breathed deeply, slowly, trying to instil calm in her, trying to make her let go. Chloe stiffened in his arms and pushed away. 'I can only stop for ten minutes.'

He sat her down, poured orange juice and started to open the champagne. 'You're exhausting yourself and it's all for nothing.'

Her face darkened with anger. 'No – it isn't for nothing! There's no other way to be good enough. Don't undermine what I'm doing.'

'Good enough for what, darling? Pass me that glass.'

'To be a concert pianist, of course.'

Her words jarred into him, crystallised in a shudder that almost made him drop the bottle as the cork popped. Champagne flowed over the table. A memory came to Jack of how they'd met at the Fairbrothers', of his first naked sight of her. He felt washed by tenderness, and by regret.

Now she was day-dreaming, avoiding reality – a woman

in her mid-twenties who hadn't studied music for years, lacking stamina or self-belief, eternally giving up on things. 'A concert pianist?' he echoed.

'Like my mother – she was quite famous.'

Why was she lying again? But suddenly he remembered it was true: he'd seen the press cuttings.

Chloe was watching him closely, suspicious of any slight discouragement – she'd see that as sabotage, he knew.

'It's what I meant to be, what Charles wanted. There were years of lessons, they said I had the talent. They said I could do it.' Her face grated sharply at him as if her life depended on this fantasy.

'You play very well,' he soothed, agreeing. She must make her own discovery and choose to stop by herself. He wouldn't reveal the chill he felt at a glimpse of hell turfed over with such hope, such irrational effort. 'And the photography?' he asked. 'You had people interested, the contact at *Metro* – ?'

'As you said, I just aimed a camera at things.'

He tried to divert her again. The contract had arrived for his house in Noel Terrace, and she seemed almost interested. The place had taken a while to sell and he wanted that money to buy time. But he didn't want to think about money or all it implied between them.

She said suddenly, 'Jack, I am going to sell Whitting.'

'We can't now,' he pointed out. 'It's the only home we've got.'

'We must go away together soon – travel, perhaps. We must.'

He glanced at her. 'But we've just got back, Chloe. We need to settle. Next year . . .'

She pushed away from the table. In a moment she'd be at the piano again. He was determined to make her rest, find pleasure in the here and now before she was completely lost. Bullying her out into the garden for a walk he admonished, 'Practising isn't everything. Music isn't only a keyboard.'

Chloe laughed suddenly. 'Because you can't write today,' she teased, 'I'm not allowed to play?'

There was so much truth in it that he protested, denied what she said. Then a kind of gaiety began at their joint truancy. Hand in hand they picked a path between the brambles naked as wire, spiked with thorns and orange rosehips. The lake had grown a rusty layer of leaves. They went through the open gateway to the orchard.

'So much fruit!' Chloe exclaimed. 'And we forgot to pick any. Look at all these.'

'They're spoiled – been on the ground for weeks.'

'I'm sure some are good.' She bent and picked up a few apples, turning them over one by one then letting them fall back into the earth. The underside of each was seething with maggots.

Jack took her arm. 'It's too late. Next year we'll pick them.'

She shook off his hand irritably. 'No,' she insisted. 'It isn't too late at all. I'll go and get a basket, we'll gather up all the fruit.' And she turned and hurried away purposefully, taking the path towards the outhouse. He stood staring after her. Couldn't she see that none of it was any good?

Jack walked a few paces slowly, troubled. He disembedded rosy-cheeked apples from their nest of decaying leaf and weed, stirring them with the toe of his shoe. Their pulp disintegrated. Minutes passed. He glanced up to see her pale-coated figure hurtling through the stark trees towards him, her face distorted with terror.

Chloe had seen some vision – the ragged figure of the gardener lying on sacking in the outhouse. 'The door wouldn't open but when I looked in through the window

255

– he was there, exactly like my father when – I found him . . .'

She was hysterical. He knew it was another strange working of her guilt. A hallucination of some kind. So he led her trembling back to the building and showed her – it was empty.

'There's no one here. Look all round, Chloe. No sign of the gardener or anyone. And the outhouse door wasn't locked – it just sticks, you know that.'

'He's run away. I tell you, he was lying there! And then he opened his eyes . . .'

She seemed in a state of shock. She'd been faced with a part of herself so dark that she couldn't accept it. He should never have taken her into the garden or past the lake. He should've recognised that warning, the apples she refused to see as decayed.

In the warmth of the kitchen he made tea, tried to hold her. Chloe could not stop crying, hallucinations ran through her mind. Wonderingly she said, 'He was there today and – the day my father died . . . He was in the garden by the outhouse when it happened. I knew I'd seen him before, didn't I? He was just a boy then, a teenager but I remember him clearly now.'

She was way beyond rational thought, shaking and cold. Jack said nothing but listened to her ramblings until the horror began to recede. Her delusions made a sort of logical pattern, all her guilt about Rachel had got mixed up with the gardener. Somehow she'd sensed that he was a threat, he knew about her.

Gripping his wrist in fingers of iron she asked, 'You do believe me, don't you?'

'Of course I do,' he lied, soothing. 'But there's something I've got to tell you.'

How could he phrase it, so that she'd know he was on her side? He thought about the gardener and how

256

pathetic he was, wasting away in a kind of translucence in his thinned holey clothing. Why had he taken him seriously? Losers like that didn't contact the police. Chloe must know there was no danger of it.

'Listen, Chloe. He's quite harmless. But he knows you were down by the lake with Rachel that night. He knows, and that's why you're so afraid of him. But he's just some drifter, on the wrong side of the law himself probably. He tried his luck with me and I sort of panicked, I suppose.'

Chloe was gazing at him, suddenly bright-eyed and clear. 'What d'you mean, Jack?'

'I paid him off, that's all – it wasn't much. He'd found something of yours, a *diamanté* hairclip . . . It was found on the path to the lake that night; it must've fallen out of your hair after dinner. He showed it to me,' he added, because Chloe was looking so intent and strange.

'You mean he's been blackmailing you?'

'I gave him a couple of hundred to go away – and it worked, he won't be around again. I didn't want him causing you any trouble.'

Chloe's face twisted, he recognised pain in her eyes. 'Did you pay him not to go to the police? With something he said was evidence that I was – what? Near my step-mother when she died?' Jack nodded and she went on, 'Because of what you already believed . . .?'

She laughed then, in a great bright release of sound and her chair shrieked on the kitchen tiles as she stood suddenly. 'No judge, no jury – but your loving opinion!' Her voice fell to a whisper. 'I murdered Rachel – because I'd hated her for years. I followed her out, crept up and pushed her into the water . . . It was icy cold and dark . . .' She fixed him with eyes turned blue-black, glittering. 'Then I just stood and watched her drown – you know I did.'

'Stop it,' he said sharply, pushing her face into his

shoulder to muffle the words. 'Whatever happened, it's all right. I'll protect you. No one will ever know but us.'

But Chloe was laughing helplessly in a stream of tears. 'You know what I am – I did that!'

Jack supported her to the stairs, half dragged her up. Some weariness seemed to weight her limbs. On their bed he began to undress her; she wouldn't help but struggled, shaking with silent laughter or tears. He found a nightdress to cover her up, to keep her warm but she twisted away and threw herself naked to the floor, on to her knees before him. 'Why don't you ever make love to me now,' she pleaded. 'Why not?'

With pity he stepped back from such abasement. 'You're exhausted, Chloe, just get some rest.'

But she was crawling before him, begging, 'Why don't you love me any more? I'll do anything, anything. Just tell me what to do . . .'

A kind of disgust crept into him. He grabbed her, pushed her into the nightgown. Subduing; distancing himself. Getting her into bed he went down to the kitchen and made a hot milk drink. In it he dissolved four barbiturates, the only way he could trust her safety through the night. He sat with her until she was asleep.

Downstairs, the last volume of Rachel's diary lay where he'd hidden it deep inside a drawer of old photos. From shiny posed smiles of Chloe's past he drew it out. The pages crawled with that spiky, disconnected handwriting, ended abruptly in the final entry. Jack re-read the words:

. . . the truth is that underneath that very different surface, she reminds me of him in some deep way. Some mental weakness there – inherited by his daughter.

If he hadn't died, how long before I'd have found out? Charles was so plausible, utterly convincing. It's taken years to unravel the business fraud – Beckett and

Melville are taking my assets in settlement, or how would I survive the scandal? He's made me a pauper – and the girl gets the house, and the trust fund because they couldn't touch those!

I knew about the other thing from that first week he brought me 'home' to this damn calaboose. Every one of them was young enough to be his daughter. From that first week, the little tart who calls herself Rose and stands like some hideous ghost at the gate with her bastard – trying to pass him off as Charles' son, no less. I was plagued by that crazy wretch most of all . . .

Placing the volume in the drawing-room fire Jack heaped coals over it, opening the draught below. He watched as the flames leaped growing tall and blue-green and the book turned into an ashen, book-shaped ghost of itself, into ashes that he raked over until they had no form at all but settled into the grate as if they'd never been.

Chloe's father was all that she had. She would never read those words, Rachel's only true testimony.

In the morning Jack woke to broad daylight and knew at once that something was terribly wrong.

4

The bed beside him was empty, Chloe had gone. From behind the bathroom door he heard water running.

Jumping out of bed Jack crossed the room. The door opened easily. Through clouds of steam he saw the naked figure of Chloe stepping into the bath water. Fragrant essences were carried on the rising mists – a heady mix of jasmine, rose and orange-blossom.

A broad smile of relief stretched over his face. The steam was billowing out through the draught. She turned and saw him.

'I wondered where you'd gone,' he said, grinning.

She unfurled luxuriant satin limbs in the foam. 'Come and bathe with me.' It was an invitation, innocent and sensuous, to begin again. She was unshadowed, playful.

The bath almost filled. He leaned across to turn off the hot tap, ran his hand over the foot that emerged to caress him. 'It tickles!' she laughed, floundering like a porpoise in a great tide. He was drenched. He caught hold of her ankle, pinkly warm and slippery, and hung on as she kicked out squealing like a child.

Letting go he stepped into the bath between her legs and knelt over her. His hands, immersed, ploughed furrows through the bubbles then gently soaped her shoulders and arms, her breasts. She stretched out beneath him, eyes fixed on his face. There was a kind of cunning, a knowingness in those eyes... He would've liked to take away her expression, to see her bland as a baby again and he reached out for the sponge to wipe that consciousness away. But she was stroking over the muscles of his thighs and up to his stiff cock, admiringly, light and flattering over the shape of him.

As he lowered his head to kiss her Jack saw, quite suddenly, an electric orange glow through the steam.

The flex from the electric fire was trailing down by the water, very close to it, while Chloe stirred the soap bubbles invitingly... The fire was plugged into a socket by the door and she'd switched it on. It stood perched precariously on the slippery, sloping edge of the bath...

Jack lunged forward in one fast movement. Before it could quite fall he'd hurled a bath sheet at the base and the lethal tinny sounding thing cracked backwards, down to the tiled floor while he ripped out the plug. But in his mind the fire fell in before he could quite reach and it was out of this image, in the moment of feeling them both incinerated that he screamed, 'What're you doing? What the hell are you thinking of!'

She sat up alarmed, puzzled. 'It was quite safe,' she said.

'Never, ever do that again!' he yelled, thinking: that's how her father died, by electrocution; she wanted us to die... 'It isn't even cold in here.'

'I felt cold –' she began.

He grabbed her arms and shook her hard. 'Don't you realise you nearly killed us? Jesus, Chloe – don't you know that.'

'I frightened you,' she whispered, frightened.

'Oh Chloe, Chloe...' Jack buried his face in her hair, smelling its warm human smell as it curled damp against their skins. He was still trembling with the certainty she'd meant to kill herself then him too. She'd set it up as an accident. She must have meant it.

How could he watch her every moment?

He sat holding her on the edge of the bath, rocking them both to and fro. Fear drained away and he began to feel a kind of exhilaration, a purified shining energy that almost made him laugh aloud. It was as if death was only a dream, a game. They were so alive!

She was alive, slender and slippery in his arms, her skin prickled from the cooling air. He stroked her wrist, cupped his hand to contain her hand, resting it in his. Chloe turned to him in response, pushing herself against him, seeking his mouth with her mouth and finding his tongue in a predatory kiss. She twined her arms around his taut, quickening body.

'I want you,' she said, deep against his chest. 'Let's bathe together ... Let's make love ...'

He kissed her with an aching kind of despair, responding to her need and returning it, drawn back by her into those heavily perfumed, chill waters. There she writhed sensuously, lapping him in, softly coiling and uncoiling like a snake.

Yesterday was a million years ago.

'We're back.'

Voices in the hall, the front door slamming shut. Jack stood to replace the whisky bottle on the sideboard.

They came in like a family, Tony cradling the baby asleep in his arms, Jodie pink with happiness and news. She patted the sofa and they sat on it. 'We had such a great weekend! I must put Raphael to bed in a minute.'

'This little fella's been sleeping all the way home,' Tony smiled down at her baby.

Reminding himself he'd invited Jodie's boyfriend to

supper, Jack tried to remember if there was food in the house. 'Tony, what'll you drink?'

On the way back with chilled beer for them he stumbled over nothing – it must've been exhaustion, he surely wasn't that drunk – and was aware they stopped talking, they were watching him. More than whisky he felt the effects of anxiety, of never quite knowing what Chloe might do next to harm herself. He'd given her more barbiturates, left her dozing upstairs.

Jack focussed on Jodie and Tony. 'There's some cold supper, let's eat.' He said the words carefully, why did they come out slurred? After they'd put the baby to bed, in the kitchen he concentrated on normality, conversation, things going right. 'So the trip was a success, contacts and so on?'

'It was mostly an excuse,' Tony grinned at Jodie, 'to show off my new lady to some old mates.'

'They were great,' Jodie responded, sparkling. 'And this afternoon we drove into the country. Raphael had never seen – ' She stopped suddenly.

Jack saw that Chloe was leaning against the door watching the three of them.

She looked like hell. Her skin bleached and papery, her eyes sunk in dark shadows. Strands of hair hung like hay and the old nightie had slipped off one shoulder. She seemed oblivious to the stares of Tony and Jodie. A dull, blank expression covered her face. Was she sleep-walking?

Jack went to her quickly in case she fell. 'Chloe,' he said gently. 'You need to rest.'

Her words were dredged out with a frown of concentration from somewhere deep inside, 'You're all in here ... You're with her – with Jodie.' And there was such hostility, a rigid suspicion in the way she said it.

How on earth could he explain to them? Turning to

263

Tony, registering his expression – a horrified incredulity, as if the man was witnessing something risen from the grave – Jack began falteringly, 'Chloe's been ill this weekend.'

With surprising strength she was plucking his hand away from her arm. Strength, and a dislike so obvious he cringed. 'Jodie came back,' Chloe said suddenly to him, 'with a different man this time, not Adams.'

What did she mean, what was going on in her head? Jodie looked annoyed, as she answered deliberately, 'This is Tony. You've met him before.' Then to Jack, 'What's wrong, what's happened to her?'

A sort of wild cunning swept across Chloe's face. She was quite mad. Hissing, 'Jodie is all wrong. Ask Jodie what happened, Jack – why don't you ask her?'

'Chloe, come back to bed.' And he tried to take her arm again but she shook him off.

'Don't touch me! Look at her, a Jonah, she's done so much damage to us. It was a mistake, my fault. I think she knows everything, she knows who – '

Jack tugged Chloe towards the hall. 'Come on.' She was about to tell them and he couldn't let her. He dragged at her. She fought, kicked his shins and wrenched free. Then in a rage hurled herself at the kitchen table and like a hurricane swept everything to the floor, to fragments, glass like tears flying all around. He grabbed her.

She was battering at him with her fists. 'Why won't you listen to me!' she screamed. 'Damn you – why won't you listen.'

And she began to weep in his arms, in great broken cries.

'Ssh, Chloe, it's all right.' He took in the faces of Tony and Jodie. 'I'm sorry. She's ill. Will you help me with her.'

They got her upstairs and back into bed. He heard

Tony say, 'You must see she gets help, you must call a doctor.'

'Of course I will,' he promised and Tony left. Jack lay down beside Chloe until she'd sunk back into deep sleep. She was heavily sedated but still out of her mind, and she mustn't wander around like that. The house was full of dangers. Tiredly he locked the windows, checked for hazards, took away his razor and anything else he could find that was sharp. On the landing he turned the key in the bedroom lock.

Jodie was waiting for him. 'You look terrible, Jack. What's happened to her?'

He longed to confide about Rachel's death. But he couldn't. To incriminate Chloe would mean putting her at worse risk – of prison or at best a mental hospital; and the possibility of being locked up a long time.

'Chloe seems to be having some kind of breakdown,' he said. 'I don't really know what to do, I'm terrified she might try to harm herself.' In the drawing room he poured a couple of drinks, Jodie sat beside him. 'She's been hallucinating. Full of horrors.'

'What sort of horrors?' Jodie asked.

'She's got this thing about the gardener. She thought . . . Oh, it's just that her head is full of plots, paranoia.' With a sense of disloyalty he explained. 'Chloe's always been unstable. This is an old illness back again.'

Jodie was silent for a while. Then she said, 'We must look after her. Maybe Tony was right, the doctor or a psychiatrist could help?'

Jack shook his head. He couldn't explain that no one must know the cause. 'She'd be institutionalised again, and it would be the worst possible thing that could happen. I'm sure I can help her through this.'

'Me too,' Jodie agreed quickly and she took his hand. 'I'll do everything I can.'

So they united in looking after her. But Chloe was convinced they were in league against her now. They were both afraid of the violent outbursts that punctuated each day and, in between, her deep brooding silences felt as disturbing in an unspoken, bitter accusation. It seemed she heard them talking together about her – against her – even when no one had said a word.

Exhaustion crept through Jack, numbing his mind and taking all thought, distancing him from the outside world. Then Jodie would sit with Chloe, leaving him free although he was too tired to rest. He and the girl were like fellow hostages and they grew closer over the next few days. He'd give Chloe drugged milk; when she slept he'd lock the bedroom with a sense of relief and go downstairs to recover. He was curled up on the sofa one evening, his head on Jodie's lap as they listened to music, when someone knocked at the window. Sitting up he saw a face pressed against the dark glass.

Jack opened the front door. On the step stood Justin and Anna Fairbrother. 'Well,' demanded Justin, 'are you going to ask us in – or are we interrupting something?'

They must have thought they were gazing in through the window at a love scene. Jack reddened with embarrassment and wished them to hell. For Justin of all people to sit in judgment of him now!

'We need to talk,' Anna said. 'Every time we've phoned you've put us off. So here we are . . . Where's Chloe?'

'She's got a heavy cold, she's in bed. You drove all the way through town for a talk, at this time of night? It must be important.'

'Oh Jack, don't be so obtuse,' smiled Anna. 'Anyway we were at a ghastly dinner party, you gave us an alibi. Poor Chloe – I'll pop upstairs and say hello.'

Jack stopped her. 'Chloe's asleep, don't wake her.' Jodie

was disappearing for the night, making excuses. Why didn't she stay and help him out?

Clasping a bottle, Justin searched the sideboard. 'Why d'you always hide the corkscrew ... So are you going to bring Chloe with you?'

'Where?' Vaguely Jack watched the man's fat hands at work, hating him.

'To the French locations. You are coming?'

'It would do her good,' Anna persuaded. 'Poor creature, stuck here in this ghastly old house. Must be awful for her.'

'What did you want to talk about?' He could hear the anger grating in his voice.

'Mm, good vintage,' conceded Justin approvingly. 'Cheers – here's to friendship.'

Putting down his glass of wine untasted, Jack began, 'If you've come to apologise, let's get on with it and – '

Justin spluttered, 'Me, apologise? You must be joking. After you attacked me, completely unwarranted, nearly killed me – I've still got bruises. Look!'

Jack stared at the faint yellowish bruise on Justin's chest, and at the indignation on his face. Feeling pity for Anna, exasperation and protectiveness, he couldn't confront Justin with reasons but thought: I must get rid of them, and check if Chloe's all right. 'Then what do you want?' he asked impatiently.

'You're the one who should apologise.' It was Justin who blurted out the words. 'You've made things very difficult for me.'

Anna went on, 'Yes, multi-writer scripting's normal these days. Justin took that job in good faith, but he couldn't tell you because you've been so peculiar – with us both, since last spring.'

'Peculiar? What're you talking about?' He felt dazed

267

and unreal. Why was he being attacked by these friends who'd wronged him?

'It's your bloody paranoia.' Justin poured more wine. Draining his glass Jack held it out for refilling as if this might reorientate him. 'You've always been jealous of my success. But that's no excuse for a public mashing.'

'You want me to apologise?' Jack simmered with hilarity, looking from one waiting face to the other. They were ridiculous and he began to laugh. 'After everything you've done? Justin, I do apologise for all your – deplorable vanities...' he finished as Justin interrupted triumphantly to Anna:

'I knew he'd see it, I told you he'd come round.'

Anna said, 'What's that banging upstairs?'

Something must've woken her.

As he ran up the stairs Chloe was battering at the bedroom door. He called, 'I'm here, I'll get the door open,' but the banging went on as if she hadn't heard. Fumbling in all his pockets for the key, at last finding it he struggled with the old latch.

'You've locked her in?' demanded Anna, at his heels. 'What the hell for, Jack? And what if the house had caught fire, what – '

Chloe tumbled out on to the landing between them, some vengeful thing and full of destructive power. She seared a look at him like an enemy and he stepped back. 'It's all right, I'm here,' he forced the words, 'I thought you were still asleep, Chloe.'

With a kind of calm resolution she pushed past him, not seeming to recognise Anna or Justin as he tried to reach out to her. She wouldn't let them close but stumbled across to the landing window, scrambled up to kneel on its sill and tried to open it.

The window was locked.

She struggled, pushing at the latch, then realised and

shot her fist straight through the pane. A scream – Anna's scream – and Justin darted forward to her. Chloe's hand was dripping blood. 'What are you doing?' he shouted. 'What are you doing?'

She crouched and turned a chalk-white face to them, her words came so blurred and soft they were scarcely audible. 'Jack's trying to get me to kill myself,' she said, 'because he doesn't love me now, he wants to be free.'

'That's not true!' Jack protested, explained to them, 'She's been threatening to harm herself. We just had to make sure Chloe was safe and – '

Anna was accusing him, 'But you're behaving just like some evil Victorian patriarch. What's going on, what have you done? A few weeks ago Chloe was fine! Are you trying to drive her crazy?'

'You've got it all wrong,' he insisted but felt ashamed in his chaos, seeing Chloe for a moment through their shocked eyes, glimpsing how far this nightmare had gone. 'You don't understand what she did. I've done everything to look after her, it isn't my fault she's ill.'

'She needs to see a psychiatrist,' Anna said, looking at Justin.

'You're probably right. Only I'm off to France,' he reminded her, 'so I can't very well get involved.'

Anna hesitated. 'And I've got a voice-over job starting in the morning,' she remembered. 'But when that's done, I'll be back to see Chloe . . .'

It was said almost like a warning. As if she thought that somehow he was doing harm.

Autumn had died into the thin and hollow ash of winter, a December pierced by memories of their year together, of Chloe happy and loving, filled with life and kinds of innocence. Jack couldn't understand the trap they'd fallen

269

into so deeply together; he didn't understand her illness now.

Full of self-doubt he left her more to Jodie's care. Chloe seemed to grow stronger although not well. She so distrusted the girl, was suspicious and nervous with both of them. But it was as if she'd given up some struggle, reached some acceptance of things he didn't know about. Still her violent dreams racked their nights, and she'd never tell him what troubled her. The distance between them seemed complete.

Then one day when Jodie went out, Jack thought Chloe had almost recovered. She looked better suddenly – less drawn and faded, even with some tentative aliveness in her – and she found the energy to cook a simple meal for the two of them. He watched her with a sense of hope. She wanted to know how his writing was going, sympathised with his tales of struggle. And then like a lover, tenderly, jokily she urged him to eat and speared morsels of chicken in tomato sauce to offer him. She was insistent.

Some thought had come to him as he tasted it – that there was a slight, unexplained after-taste which shouldn't be there. That she was too strangely anxious – he ought to take another mouthful, and another.

Jack made some excuse, said he wasn't hungry. And she looked at him, knowing exactly what passed through his mind.

She had no reason to wish him dead but he doubted her sanity, her reason.

Towing him out to the hall and up the stairs she said, 'Come with me, I've something to show you.' From the back of a cupboard she took out an old jacket that she used to wear. 'I found this here yesterday.' And feeling in a pocket she drew out a piece of jewellery.

It was the *diamanté* hairclip, crescent-shaped. But how could she have it here?

Chloe said, 'This is the jacket I was wearing on the night Rachel died.'

Yes, he recognised it now. But the clip . . .?

She asked him, 'Was it one like this that the gardener used to blackmail you?'

Puzzled, he examined the hairclip with its loose fastening. 'Yes.'

'I used to have two, they were a set of two,' she said, watching him. 'This is the one I wore that night. Look. Remember it had a loose clasp, how it kept sliding out? Jack, I never was with Rachel. The second clip disappeared from my bedroom here some months ago. I don't know how Adams got hold of that – I suppose he stole it. Even if you don't believe anything else, at least you must accept he lied about finding it on the path to the lake.'

He didn't know what to think. 'Maybe – could he have seen you wearing it some time earlier? And wanted me to believe . . . But I don't understand.'

'That night I was lost, Jack, and wandering for hours in the fog. Kept finding myself among trees and bushes, I must've strayed on to that long road which runs through Queen's Wood. There are no fences, and there was no light. It was frightening, and I got covered in mud and scratches . . .'

With a shock he realised that perhaps it was true, she had never been involved in Rachel's death. And if Adams had got another clip somehow, then lied about finding it on the way to the lake then maybe he – the gardener here at that time – might have had something to do with it?

Then Chloe said something that stopped all his puzzling, made all the hows and whys insignificant. She was completely lucid and resigned. 'The damage has been done to us. You never believed a thing I said, you trusted

271

anyone else more than me. You were intent on belittling me into some mad child in your head, to be drugged and locked away out of sight ... You almost took my sanity, Jack, and I can't forgive you for that – for your lack of trust in me. I'm sorry we can't stay together now. I'm so sad that it's all over for us.'

5

Stretching under the warm duvet Jodie opened her eyes. Faint winter sun lit the bedroom and she lay looking all round it, saying goodbye. She'd miss Whitting when they moved away. Raphael wriggled in the bed disturbing Tony and with a smile she watched him struggling to wake. They'd been late last night.

Soon the sheets were full of crumbs as they ate breakfast and Raphael used the bed like a trampoline. He couldn't balance for long but liked to spring up and down on all fours. 'Like a little fat frog,' Jodie laughed. 'Don't let him bounce on to the floor.' Caught by Tony her son was swung high up in the air where he crowed at being taller than them.

Footsteps were going past their door. 'Shall I tell Jack?'

'Give the poor bloke a minute,' Tony suggested. He swung Raphael to the floor and the little boy stood swaying, proud. 'You could get the train up on the twentieth.'

It was hard telling Jack, she felt like a traitor because of all they'd done for her. 'Tony's going up today,' she said. 'To sort things out. We're opening the shop in January.'

'I'm glad for you – it's a new beginning and he seems nice,' Jack said. 'Only I've got to be in France for a few days and there's no one to take care of Chloe.'

He looked worn out and there were lines on his face she'd never seen before. Jodie sat down beside him, touched his arm. 'What is it really? What's gone wrong between you two?'

'Chloe says we're finished.'

She couldn't believe it. 'But you were both so happy – '

'And she doesn't want me here,' he cut in. 'So I think she'll need to live with someone else.'

Jodie protested, 'Chloe's just been ill, I'm sure she doesn't mean that.'

'I'm afraid she does. I don't think it was ever me that Chloe wanted.' The bitterness in his voice punched at her heart. What did he mean? He got up saying, 'It's been going on for years, there's nothing I can do. And I've got to be in Normandy from tomorrow. Could you – ?'

'Of course I'll stay! But I can't believe what you've just told me.' Jack didn't answer and it seemed he wasn't going to talk about it with her any more.

Jodie told Tony and he said, 'A couple more days won't matter, I've waited two years.'

'Really? Since we first met?'

Tony smiled at her surprise. 'You only had eyes for Art. Though he was daft as a deranged dodo, you just couldn't see it.' Then his face grew tense with a question. 'Are you certain that Art's gone from here?'

'Sure he's gone, Tony. I've not seen Art for ages now.' If she felt any doubt she wasn't going to let him know. Tony had enough to worry about and soon they'd all be in Edinburgh, far away and safe.

Later that day he left in the van with most of her luggage. The next morning a location manager turned up. His assistant Martin would set up for the shoot while the first unit filmed in northern France. There was talk about access and insurance, cables and parking.

'Chloe and I will see to everything, Jack.'

They were so odd together now: distant, careful. It was Chloe's sort of breakdown still, and Jack was imagining things. He left for the airport saying, 'Look after her until I get back. These phone numbers – '

Jodie took the list. 'Go on or you'll miss the flight.'

They were alone in the house and Chloe seemed to fade, to sink back as if there was no future but only a kind of dying. She spent her days locked into silence in bed or in a chair and had to be bullied to get up. She looked a wreck. Raphael kept bringing toys to put on her lap, like offerings to a stone statue since Chloe didn't seem to notice. It was depression, Jack had said.

When the phone rang she heard Tony's voice and all of her leaped into life. He'd got the carpet down, he was putting up shelves. 'Where's my lad?' he asked. Raphael was puzzled, tried to find Tony inside the green plastic. Then they talked for an hour. She had to be with him, she could hardly wait. Wrapped in love, floating on certainty she thought: how long it took me to see him, how safe and loved I feel – maybe it was like this before I was born.

Chloe's huddled body rocked backwards and forwards in misery. Jodie put her arms round her, searched for a way into her head. 'Chloe, it's nearly Christmas. Let's buy presents for Jack.'

There was silence. Those empty eyes turned to her and Chloe said, 'I'll never see Jack again. And neither will you.'

Something sharp cracked at Jodie's happiness. She shouted, 'That's just crazy – he's coming back!'

Chloe began to cry. 'You can't see what Jack's begun, you don't know how it'll end.'

Jodie insisted, 'That's up to you. You could forgive each other.' And she hesitated. 'He thinks you've got someone else.'

Chloe laughed, suddenly lucid. 'Yes. Jack thinks so many things – and that's most of the trouble.'

They went to the High Street next day; it was crowded and bright with decoration, streams of light pierced the gloom. In Pond Square children were singing and tears flooded Jodie's face, caught in her throat: she was so completely happy. She clung to an image of Chloe and Jack, happy together, and she grew this hope like a reednest in the flowing crowds.

She cooked supper and Chloe went to bed early. Jodie packed her bag with small gifts wrapped in bright paper and left two presents for Jack and Chloe to open on Christmas Day.

Raphael slept, his face pink and satiny in the lamplight. They were going to have the kind of Christmas she'd always wanted; she'd planned for every tradition, all the trimmings. Kissing the baby goodnight she climbed into bed and lay listening a while to the sigh of the cedars outside her window.

During the night she woke because someone had come into the room and was standing, a dark presence looking down at her.

Jodie froze.

'He's gone away, hasn't he,' said Art's voice.

He was moving closer, peering down into her face. 'We're safe, the three of us, now he's gone. You are awake, Jodie? I've got to talk to you, it's very important.'

'All right, Art. We can talk.' She must stay calm and

276

humour him. He'd sat down on the bed beside her, quite close. She swallowed hard. 'What is it?'

'You've got to realise,' Art whispered softly, 'that there's a lot of treachery in the air. Not just him and you. I'm talking of greater things.'

Did he see her as a traitor? But he seemed so calm. She waited. 'Tell me. I'll understand.'

'I hope so, Jodie.' He was silent. Then he spoke again, anguish crawling in his voice, 'It was her trickery that did for me. Till then we were hand in glove, you've got to believe – I was the special one.'

'Hush . . . It's all right, I believe you.'

With a quiet horror he went on, 'I realised I'm forced to break her commands, all of them if I'm to survive. You'll ask me: What are the commandments? There were many. I was always faithful, always true.'

'I know you are.'

'You'll be surprised to learn that you were one. I was to shelter and protect you with my life, and so I did. And then the child that made one holy family. I was not to tell you anything of this – I didn't, even when I most needed to . . . But since the time of my betrayal I've seen that every law must be opposed, combatted, the circle smashed . . .'

He paused. Jodie licked her lips. 'Go on,' she said in a small voice.

'To reverse all – for his guardianship, you understand? Alone I have no power.'

'Yes,' she answered, mechanically. He was sitting very rigid and straight, she could feel the steeliness of him.

'Fate brought me to this house in the form of Rose and I was given it. Rose was blown by him, my mother destroyed into a million bits – he was cruel! I was the seed, the first-born but he denied me everything. The father. Not seeing me. She was in misery, great pain and after many years I helped her properly to do it. She had pills, every time they locked her up they gave my mother pills. I bought the brandy and sat with her . . . She'd died a thousand years before, my one all-powerful . . .

'It was right, then, that his time had come for what he'd done. I watched the man: he liked to work at things there in the outhouse. It was easy to switch over the wires in his electric chainsaw and to wet them in the plug. Easy! I watched him die, I was the tool for weeding . . . I took the watch, it bought the key to my new home. I saw the girl as I left – but I was told to leave her alone. I was fate's servant now and had no choice.'

Her world was twisting on its axis in a silence dark and vast. It spun off into space.

She made a little sound in her throat.

Art continued, 'All these years later, I had to drown the woman. But fate slipped up. The house would've been made ours, had she lived long . . . Fate was exposed – she was a bad estate agent, something wicked! How I've had to struggle and strive, you hardly know the way it's been. But I've had resources . . .' She listened, unable to form any sound to reassure him. But he was smiling into the night, his words had a cheerful shape when he went on, 'I told him his wife did it, I gave him proof, he's convinced of it. I used what you took from here, Jodie – remember them?'

She mouthed, 'I remember . . .' and salt tears slid between her lips.

'D'you understand now?'

'I understand.'

He was looking in the dark glass of the mirror opposite, he made a sign over his heart. 'How tired I am, how much better I feel,' Art said.

Jodie thought: I'm to blame. If I'd never agreed to come to this place then Rachel might still be alive, and Chloe well and Jack not alone. It was my fault ... And Art hasn't realised yet that he's going to kill me, by this code he has. He'll have to and perhaps it's right ...

She stopped trying to hold back the tears but thought of Rachel, and Chloe's and Jack's kindness. An awareness of damage swept over her like fire. She cried for a long time in racking cries, captive inside her, as if in a dream.

When she grew still Art said sleepily, 'We're here, the three of us. You don't know what I had to endure but here we are.'

Then it was quiet. Into the silence came a small sound of the baby sucking in his sleep. Jodie thought about Raphael and about Tony. She watched trains for Edinburgh leaving, empty, while she stared into the black tunnel of the long night.

Then realised, Art had fallen asleep beside her.

She almost didn't dare to move.

That afternoon Jack had stood looking round the quayside at Honfleur. Yachts lay moored against a crescent of pretty, slate-clad houses in the Vieux Bassin. They were summer creatures locked up waiting for the sun or plumply insulated like seals and whales. Some would travel tonight. Half the world would travel tonight.

'Where the hell are the drug-runners?'

'In make-up, some problem with wigs.'

'Wilhelm – is he ready? If the light changes at least we'd have him in the can.'

They were racing against darkening clouds, needing to match shots before the rain and to wrap on the French locations before dusk. Some of them were flying home tonight to join the second unit for their final shoot at Whitting House.

Shoppers crowded round to stare and the quay was cleared as if for royalty. The little knot of blue-jeaned obsessives gathered to conjure make-believe at this eventless, waiting waterside. What was the best angle for the happening, the departure under surveillance – by Alain aka Pierre – of the dope king whose most recent name was Schmidt?

The sequence was reframed against a backdrop of gin palaces reflected over water. A line of dialogue was changed. Wilhelm was found, his nose powdered, feet positioned then moved six inches. Another delay because of a cloud. Then a small procession trailed the actor to encapsulate seconds of vision and sound.

Later they wrapped and went to a nearby bar for a drink. Justin was missing; someone thought he'd left for home. A strike was causing long delays for everyone so Forbes left early for the airport with his flock. Jack stopped to watch a big white motor yacht being made ready by her crew. She was a British vessel. Lit up from within she waited, a luminescent sleek-winged bird of the night. And she stayed in his mind's eye as he walked back to the hotel.

There would be a secret crossing by sea into occupied territory.

All day he'd felt a sense of displacement as if he was living the wrong life, in the wrong body. He settled now at the table in his hotel room with five hundred virgin A4 pages and the mind of a parachutist about to jump. In the night he wrote fast and urgently, page after page scarcely pausing in unaccustomed aching handscrawl.

He never knew how long it was before some part of his mind began to filter to the outside of what he was doing. And then became aware of a bell, of alarm bells.

It was the phone ringing, on and on.

Eventually he picked it up.

'*Monsieur Maine – on vous a téléphoné d'Angleterre.*'

Then Jack heard, softly hoarse and distorted as if she was drowning underwater, or perhaps whispering, Jodie's voice.

6

He ran down the silent half-lit corridor and up a flight of carpeted stairs, his eyes sliding over numbers. Knocking sharply on Justin's door he barged in and found the light switch.

Justin, naked, jumped out of bed then saw it was only Jack. 'Bloody hell – d'you know what time it is?'

'Listen – answer two questions – where's Anna and when's your flight home?'

Then Jack noticed someone watching him from the bed.

'Oh God,' said Sarah with a wry little smile.

For a moment no one spoke. Jack looked from one to the other. 'D'you do this often?'

'Not as often as we'd like.' Justin was pulling on a bath robe. 'Come on, didn't you guess? We're all grown up – '

'But I thought – you and Chloe . . .'

'That's rather comical! I'm the one whose shoulder she cried on, all the years she was involved with Paul.'

'. . . D'you mean Paul Mann?'

'You thought it was me – and did you think it was still going on?' Justin interrogated with sudden understanding then chortled with laughter. 'I see.'

He'd been completely wrong. There was no time to think about what it meant. 'I've got to get home – now.'

'What's happened?' Justin asked.

Sarah began, 'It's Christmas, there's a strike on and the flights are packed out. You'll never – '

'Chloe's in danger. Her stepmother was murdered and Chloe – she's at risk. Jodie's taking her to your house – '

'But it's locked up, because Anna's away in Gloucestershire.'

His heart jumped with alarm. 'You mean she won't be able to get in, there's nobody there? Then he might – get to her next . . .'

'Who might?' demanded Sarah. 'Why don't you call the police?'

'And tell them what! If I can just get there . . . When are your flights home?'

'Tomorrow night, same as yours. Look, the second unit will be setting up early, won't they? All those people around – '

'You don't understand!' Jack snarled at their reasonableness, their incomprehension. He thought: she already half knew about Adams and Jodie's confirmed it; Chloe's in danger of losing her life and she must be so afraid. 'I've got to get back now.'

As they began to tell him again that it was impossible, Jack suddenly remembered. Without a word he turned and ran down the stairs and out of the hotel, through narrow silent streets towards the Vieux Bassin. The dark harbour, a few lights shimmering . . . Had she already slipped away?

Then he saw that elegant white form blazing with light, stirring, engines throbbing as a long pale gleaming rope grew stretching out from her. In a curled, trembling umbilicus.

Jack stood at the quayside and with all the power of his lungs he yelled.

The taxi was taking for ever. She'd woken Chloe, tried to

explain, got them ready to leave. She'd called Jack. Ages had passed and at any moment Art might wake and find her gone.

Raphael slept heavy in Jodie's arms. 'Come quickly,' she muttered, eyes on the door noticing behind its glass the jagged shock of dawn.

Chloe was dazed like a sleep-walker, stupidly repeating, 'Yes it was, it was him,' not seeming to understand they had to get away.

The door-bell's shriek shot through the house. She'd told the cabbie not to ring. Jodie darted in panic at the sound, grabbed Chloe's arm. 'Before Art sees. Quick!' They stumbled through the hall and she struggled with Chloe's coat, the baby, her bag with money in, got to the front door and opened it.

In the porch in the cold midwinter daybreak stood the *Kops* crew bearing clipboards and rolls of cable, tripods and packing crates.

From upstairs she heard a banging start. He was awake.

Men began to push up the steps, through the front door to crowd the hall with equipment. 'Morning,' said Martin Gann. 'We need this hallway cleared at once. Got to set up. Can you get out of the way, please. Right boys, bring everything through – this way.'

'Stop,' Jodie tried. They were trapped already among swirling coils of cable and overflowing crates, black steel-legged stands and lights. 'Stop and let us out!'

Gann stood in the door blocking the way, crackling with self-importance. 'Where are you going? Somebody's got to stay here – I've a series to shoot and a lot of valuable –'

Far away she heard the bedroom door crash. Shoving Gann aside she thrust Chloe out of the house. They stumbled through location equipment and down the steps and ran along the drive towards the gates.

Where was the taxi? Which way would it come? The bare tunnel led down to the city, the railway station and safety. Chloe was pulling back and tugging at her hand, infantile, insistent, 'I don't want to go.'

A red saloon crept up Hill Grove. Jodie clutching Raphael, grasping Chloe struggled towards it. The driver had to stop in the narrow road. He started to get out as Jodie bundled Chloe into the back. 'Quickly!' She turned and saw Art running down the drive towards them. 'Please hurry.' They were in the minicab, the door was shutting, the driver catching her urgency shot away with a shriek of tyres like a stuntman.

'What's up?' he asked with a satisfied smile as he wove a speeding swerving path around the corners of the village lanes, plunged down the long straight empty main road into town. 'House caught fire?' But he was watching the ragged desperate running of Art in the mirror, leaving him behind . . .

'Go as fast as you can towards King's Cross – then on to Putney.' She put an arm round Chloe, laughing and crying confusedly beside her.

'Do my best, lady,' the cabbie sang out. Ahead of them the lights turned red. Jodie looked back and saw the tiny figure of Art running into a petrol station.

He disappeared behind a truck and she thought: he's given up, we're safe, I'll never see Art again.

The driver saw too, he chuckled sympathetically. 'Boy-friend problems? So what's new.'

An ambulance shot out of the Whittington Hospital. It sped past, siren wailing round the corner.

She'd begun to breathe again, the driver had switched on his radio, they were in Junction Road a hundred yards from the Underground when suddenly the world exploded propelling them all into space and the driver screamed, 'Bloody maniac, fucking psycho!' as the car

285

skidded against something and Jodie hit her head on the side. When she was able to look back she saw the giant jaws of the truck careering forward to hit them again and as it bore down she screamed and the cabbie swore and swerved, shot up on to the pavement and stalled there.

She thought: he's got to kill me. Yelled to the shocked Chloe: 'You go on to Anna's – he'll come after me!' and cradling the baby unlatched the door, half fell into the street and raced for the round black hole of the Underground. It swallowed her and in its ghastly light she heard Art's feet drumming behind her down the passageway. She raced round a corner, saw a door and darted inside, pulling it shut and locking it, tunnelling through hanging coats and overalls to the furthest corner.

He didn't follow.

After a few minutes hiding there she dared to think: he's lost us now.

The yacht had slid from the French coast into a night seeming calm at first. Just a murmur in the air rushing past, a rumour of disturbance ahead. From the deck Jack watched lights shrink into tiny stars, blink out to infinity. He willed the vessel forward faster, more powerfully and felt her urgent throbbing alter as she gathered speed.

He was the fourth man on board, her only passenger. The owner and two crew were busy, expert at watch and wheel and a complex panel of instruments. They were on course between marker buoys, slicing sideways across the Channel to arrive in the early hours of morning. He tried to stop calculating when he might arrive, it was so many hours away.

Later the sea grew markerless, a huge secret hiding its signals in a hostile swell. Jack climbed up on deck again and grasped the rail, braced his body as the little boat tossed helplessly through the dark. They mustn't be delayed. He must get home quickly. He breathed a wall of salt as they tilted crazily and the wind ripped his icy clothes, stung like tears and his head filled with fragments, with useless bits of guilt and conjecture, fear.

He thought: I'm about to drown. Memories unreeled unwanted, shuttered images of Chloe and times together snapped at his brain. He thought about the last few hours. Everything she'd told him was true.

Picturing the house he imagined Chloe curled up in bed safe, sleeping. Adams had long since left. The bell was switched off on the phone. Tomorrow he'd walk back into their home to find everything as it had been before. Months ago . . .

Other imaginings flew swift and furtive into his head and he banished each image of harm before it could quite form. Each was the terrible cost of doubt.

How had he believed those things of her, how had that happened? Perhaps he'd never trusted women and if they loved him they had to be all wrong. But why?

Nothing would happen to her. Nothing bad.

Now the night was possessed. Dark limbs whirled, pressured him against the wall and rail, the slippery deck until he was hurled across the length of the boat and lay weakly, falling . . . Towards the hatch where hands grabbed and pulled at his legs . . . A man swore and laughed, a bearded face close to his. 'Bit lively, eh? Take a breather while we get on with it.'

Jack lay in a narrow cabin, obedient. It felt like the belly of the universe. And abruptly the lights went out. He clung to the sides of the bunk, pulled himself up. The boat tossed and turned in a roller coaster through chaos. The noise was deafening, pulses of the universe had swollen, furious, to a banging rushing roar. This little creature could not survive the pressure, would softly explode into dying fragments soon ... Inside him swilled a sea of salt panic, imploring it all to end in whatever way ...

He was crushed by the muscles of the night together, thrusting, encorded against continuance and in his helplessness, his face mewed into terror and despair that was silenced by the huge powerful display outside himself. He was tiny, soft, unheard by whatever lay beyond.

A band of night contracted further: his head would split, his heart would burst, his stomach turned at the hostile forced abandonment of safety, of all he'd ever known and in this wet and slippery disregard he was hurled through space towards deliverance.

Hiding in the narrow cloakroom she'd waited until the sounds grew from the odd beat of a passing traveller to the pounding drum of hurrying crowds as the rush hour started and gathered pace.

Cautiously, pushing out among the crowd she began to squeeze down the escalator past lines of people with baggage and briefcases, down to the gloomy cavern below. The platform was brimming full as she edged along, still watchful just in case he'd stayed around. The tunnel lit up and a great wind tore at the waiting passengers; a train came speeding in and people surged to get on. There were too many but she wriggled through the push of bodies and stood sandwiched in them. The baby began to cry. The train jerked into motion, the sea of occupants swayed and a roar began as they entered the dark tunnel.

Jodie thought: we've done it. Even if he's still looking he doesn't know where we're going, he doesn't know about Edinburgh.

She tried to see above and between the crush of raised arms and shoulders hunched, past someone's coat grazing her cheek and beyond the tired city faces and dust-grimed heads. There was no glimpse of Art, he hadn't got on this train. She tried to breathe calmly now. A strap-hanging wrist nearby revealed the white face of a watch and she craned to see. It was eight sixteen ... The trains to Edinburgh were engraved in her mind; there was one leaving at eight twenty-six. Surely giving her time to reach King's Cross and buy her ticket, find the platform.

They were at King's Cross, caught in conflicting swirls of baggage-laden travellers between the Underground and railway stations when she caught a glimpse, heart stopping.

The blackness of his jumper, the paleness of his hair. He was by the barrier.

Jodie wriggled through pressing crowds to the escalator, lights and music, trains waiting above. She stumbled against something fleshy, soft and vulnerable. It was the outstretched arm of a young girl begging: dirty, hungry, desperate.

Swept past she stumbled breathless between suitcases and elbows, packages and parcels, up to the bright lit concourse of shops. A tannoy blared above in Christmas muzak, lights glaring overhead tossed waves of struggling bodies. Pushing through she came to the Travel Centre, saw long queues stretch out through the doors.

She knew he was near, hidden by kaleidoscopic crowds. She felt hours had gone by while they'd struggled through this human mass. 'We'll just get on the train,' she told Raphael who clung to her, his face buried in her hair. She began to thrust through bodies, limbs and luggage towards the platform indicator.

Then she saw two things: the train to Edinburgh would leave from Platform Five, and the time was eight twenty-five ...

It was leaving in one minute.

She tore between crowds towards the platform, the waiting train – and saw the steel barrier drawn across before her eyes. Turning aside, grasping the baby tight she slid in the press of people along the metal wall. The next barrier stood open, the official turned away ... Jodie slipped through, jumped down to the empty railway track and fell against the buffers. She struggled to her feet and stumbled over the tracks, nerves crackling with danger, pierced by Art's eyes. She dragged herself up on to the next platform and ran across. The train was pulling out as she wrenched at a door and jumped up clinging to the open frame. People were shouting, someone screamed as they swayed in the doorway then hands grabbed, wrenched them inside as the train began to gather speed.

She dropped to her knees with the baby held tight in her protecting arms and saw through the glass the despairing face of Art pulled away from them by the faltering running of his feet along the platform. She heard him cry out but couldn't catch the words.

The platform fell away from the speeding train that cleared the great glass arc and Art hung suspended in the frame then fell away lost.

The train pulled out under open sky, someone asked, 'Are you all right, love?'

'Yes,' Jodie answered. 'Yes, we are.'

7

In the morning he came to Whitting and saw the location lorries grouped in the drive, under the black cedar boughs.

Chloe's car was among them.

The wrought-iron gate clanged shut and he hurried breathless, wrung out by the night. Mafia chiefs sat around, wearing sharp suits and drinking tea from plastic beakers. As he passed they called greetings, familiarly as if he was one of them. From a throbbing generator, cables and cords trailed into the house through doors and windows gaping. He followed them knowing she'd be where they led.

Jack stood listening in the hall and a deep silence closed in on him. He went quickly checking the drawing room, the dining room, study and kitchen, glancing out at the desolate garden. Emptiness, unnatural.

Then a soft footfall sounded overhead: they were filming in the bedrooms. And she'd be there watching and caught in it, not hearing or caring about messages from the outside world. Running up the stairs he paused in the gallery above the hall and yelled, 'Chloe!' so his voice echoed bouncing everywhere. No one answered. Pushing open their bedroom door he stepped into a circle of white glare.

'Cut!' called Gerry Forbes. 'All right, reset – quick as you can.'

Someone laughed and Ross said from the shadows, 'Perfect timing, Jack – enter the villain of the piece . . . Shall we try it with the boom this side – OK, Gerry?'

Jack shielded his eyes from the blinding lights. 'I'm looking for Chloe. Has anyone seen her?'

'She hasn't been here,' said somebody. It was the PA and Jack rounded on her as she added, 'Not since setting-up time – Martin said they all left. And I must say, Gerry's a bit pissed off at no one being here today – '

Jack interrupted her, 'What d'you mean, "they all left"? What time was that?'

Steve Mabe appeared. 'We had no key to the landing window for the death fall, Jack. We had to break then mend it.'

From Steve he got a picture of that dawn: Martin had told him about Jodie bundling Chloe out of the house, and the man who'd followed. None of them had been seen since. 'We've tried to keep the upheaval to a minimum, but you know how it is. They should've known what to expect.'

The PA was watching Jack's face. She reassured him, 'Your wife will be Christmas shopping today. Everyone is, unless they're working on this show.'

In the kitchen the stove was out and the kettle cold. His messages were unplayed on the answerphone. Jack called the Fairbrothers' home, he tried other friends. Chloe had simply vanished, no one had seen her.

Hovering on the edge of their magic circle he watched the film makers at work. It was Richard's last appearance and he was milking each moment, delaying his lines and ruining the pace. Gerry reshot in a simplified form so it would be easier to edit out the pauses. He was one old pro outmanoeuvring another.

Beside him Ross asked quietly, 'Well?'

Jack glanced at the young man and felt a first sympathy and a curiosity, an interest in all those changes he'd fought against. Ross had needed to push those changes, to take control – he'd been thrown into the middle of the game-board. And suddenly he was aware of himself as the obstructive, the destructive force.

'So what d'you think?' Ross's voice was still casual.

None of it mattered any more. 'It's looking fine,' Jack answered and added, 'That's entertainment.'

They wrapped at three. By twenty to four the house was deserted. At a fashionable Soho club the wrap party would erupt this evening and he must go, but he wouldn't until she'd come home. The shops stayed open late tonight and that's where Chloe might be now. He told himself that she'd escaped and was quite safe, that she'd hated the idea of the *Kops* invaders and had wanted to keep away until she could be sure they'd gone. So she might be back any minute now.

But she didn't come back.

Throughout the evening Jack searched restlessly for clues, trying to sense what might've happened and where she might be. Chloe had been so isolated, she'd gone to the edge. And in a troubled way he realised that she didn't know he was back; it was safe to come home now.

Pouring himself a whisky in the reassembled drawing room he sat down to think. There'd been other times he'd waited, wondering if he'd ever see her again. She'd always returned, it had always been all right in the end. So he made himself think about the future now. Could they forgive each other, would she forgive him? There seemed no real reason why they couldn't be happy together. They could live anywhere – even in this house. If he encouraged her to rebuild, to exorcise it as she needed ... He would write his books. Perhaps they'd have children. She was young and had time to change her mind.

By half-past nine he couldn't pretend any longer that Chloe might be shopping.

He hadn't noticed how far the world had drawn into itself or how profound was its silence until now. Tiny sounds began to crack and penetrate, so that he jumped and filled with alarm: a creaking somewhere, then a soft thud like a careless footfall; a trembling in the walls like a vibration of someone or something passing through.

A signal, a tapping . . . that was only the tip of a branch against the window pane. It was just the wind rising outside, he realised, yet instead of relief he felt a deeper dread.

There was something very wrong, he knew.

The curtains were undrawn and his eyes were held by the window's white frame and then beyond, behind his reflection, by the unknown dark garden. As if it held a secret presence, a watcher engaging with him.

And in a flash for an instant he was out there looking in and saw Jack on a bright-lit screen sitting on the sofa in a square frame. A living character cleverly composed in colour. Who moved . . .

Jack got up from the sofa, poured a second whisky and glanced at his watch. He set down the glass on a low table and straightened up. In the corner of his eye a pale figure drifted past the window outside.

It had to be her and he darted out through the back door. The garden was alive, stirring, shivering and rustling with suppressed laughter as he stumbled into branches and trod on softness underfoot. The huge pale moon filled his eyes with shadows. Soon shapes grew clear, sharp and flat as he searched all around the silver garden. She wasn't there.

But as he came back the telephone was ringing, shrill

and mocking. He tore along the path, through the house, breathlessly he raised the phone and a man's voice said, 'Sorry,' and the line went dead.

He stared at it.

Then stood still there in the hall thinking: I'm so very tired, the night's passing and I should get some rest. But instead he remained motionless, sensing. Until gradually the certainty returned: she hadn't left at all, she was close by.

A pendulous ticking filled the hall and he gazed at the clock. They'd brought it down not long ago. From the attics . . .

Climbing the staircase Jack headed across the landing and hesitated at the foot of the narrow steps. His torch made a dusty circle of light, objects leaped out disconnected so that uneasily, as he traced a way through the labyrinth of attic rooms he reached out at every doorframe to switch on lights, to drench it with ordinariness. And then remembered what he had forgotten: the tower room. At once he knew that Chloe was hiding there.

His heart dissolved into lightness. She was just hiding, afraid to come down into the house because she didn't know he was here.

He swung up steep stairs to the top and grasped the door, opened it. Going in he saw Chloe silhouetted against the moonlit window.

He said: 'It's all right, it's me,' then switched on the light.

She was naked as the first moment he'd seen her, and as beautiful. A warmth of relief then pleasure flooded him. The curves and hollows of her glowed at him and his whole being surged in response. But she was curled up on the sill with a blanket clutched in the fingers of one hand, just like a child. And she was smiling, blissful, yet didn't seem aware of him. Then her free hand went towards her mouth and she began to suck her thumb.

As gradually he allowed the knowledge to filter into him that something was wrong, he noticed how she moved around and flexed her limbs with little sounds, seeming scarcely to breathe, and then that her eyes – bright blue and round – had grown innocent of all experience. And they were unfocussing, in some way blind.

He went close and kneeling, reached out into what should have been her field of vision and tried to contact her. 'I'm home, it's me.' But she made no response.

Then he understood. She was in a secret world entirely of her own. And she was happy there, content.

She was unborn.

He felt a well of understanding rise before incredulous laughter broke from him and shook the tower round them and subsided shuddering into despair. He thought: she's completely mad. Then as swiftly: she is evil.

As she shrank before him he saw for the first time the mutations that had grown. Between those delicate fingers and toes there stretched fine webs of skin and then as she drew back her lips in a snarl of hatred, saliva beads shot silver by a gleam of tusk and with a shriek in a flash of fire she leaped at him.

Then he woke up, because somewhere outside – down in the black invisible garden – he'd heard a sound that was real, a human sound which didn't belong in any dream. It was a crying in words he couldn't make out, in Chloe's voice.

He followed it quickly through the house and out into the night garden. The sound had seemed to come from the left, from the direction of the old outhouse.

And almost silent as some creature he stumbled through the dark towards her.

8

Enjoying the sparking and tumbling on to her skin eventually, reluctantly she turned off the stream and enveloped herself in warm soft folds to dry her limbs. A glow of energy, an excitement at aliveness broke through her. Brushing steam from the mirror Chloe looked into the clear circle thinking: it's over, and I'm all right.

She dressed and wrapped her hair in a towel, walked down the thickly carpeted stairs and paused to listen. From the studio soared the silver flight of Pachelbel and she stood melting in feeling at the sound.

Looking up from her work at the big table Lily pushed back the spectacles on her nose. 'You look better. Have a good rest?'

'Slept like an angel.'

'Come and dry your hair by the fire. I'll just finish this idea.'

The room was a nest of papers, notes, sketches and rainbow watercolours. Books Lily had illustrated over the years lodged haphazard among the studio shelves, their tall stacks looked about to tumble. Stories for adults, stories for kids. Covering the table were fresh ink drawings, words scribbled. Chloe glanced through, seeing a crowd of mythological characters as from the pencil in

Lily's hand grew a woman, tall and Amazonian, striding across the universe. 'Who's that?'

'Adam's first wife, my namesake Lilith.'

'He had a first wife? I thought Eve was the original. So what happened to Lilith?'

'She left Adam. Then according to this history book she had some fantastic sex and gave multiple birth.'

Chloe laughed. 'A little-known story. I wonder why.'

'Her offspring were all she-hags, they suck out the essence of man, the seed or the strength – they're an embodiment of male paranoia.' And raking through the leaf-fall of papers, 'Here you are, some she-devils . . . But my interpretation's only personal, subjective.'

'What else is there but the subjective?' Chloe stared at the drawings, the figures. Why did they seem so familiar to her? 'They must be archetypes from the collective unconscious? I suppose you've got a deadline for this.'

'January the sixth. That's why the rush.' Lily stood up and stretched, threw a couple of logs on the fire. Then she paused to listen, her face lit up like a bulb. 'He's back. Jim, we're in my room!'

Hartsledge came stomping in, complaining, 'It's murder out there.'

Combing her long pale hair at the hearth Chloe smelled the wood-smoke, sensed age-old memories of shelter from harm, the protection of fire. She'd come to these friends but couldn't stay. Watching them together she thought how much they liked each other, how they wished each other well. An ache went through her, a sense of loss.

Jim stepped to the fireside, studied her, said to Lily, 'She's looking good, almost human again.'

Washing out a big black cloud of ink, setting the brushes to dry, Lily turned to Chloe. 'You will stay for the holiday with us? We both want you to.'

Chloe answered slowly. 'That's really kind of you, I'd

like to but I can't. Jack's due home from France tonight.'
She saw the looks on their faces. 'He'll be home for
Christmas.'

'You're not going back to him?' Lily was horrified.
'Don't do that! I met Jack once, at your party, and he
behaved like a complete thug.'

'There were misunderstandings,' Chloe started hotly.
'We should've got talking, I didn't – '

Jim weighed in, 'He's treated you like rubbish almost
since the day you married him.'

'Only because he imagined things – he's a dramatist.'

'Then he feeds off you,' Lily realised. 'And I bet Jack
was attracted by your background? That's horrible.'

'I don't mind feeding writerish dreams,' she answered.
'Although – '

'But that's no good, you're not tough enough!' Lily
came to the hearth and knelt on the rug. 'Chloe, he made
you ill again, breaking down – we've been through all
this.'

'Yes.' She remembered the nightmare weeks of madness. 'I went down again into the ashes. Everyone falls
somewhere, some time.'

They stared at her. Jim said, 'You're young and tal-
ented. Great-looking, and loaded. This is a woman who
has – or could have – everything.'

'None of what happened was Jack's fault. I know what
you think! He had no trust in me. But that can change. I
feel as if – something's changed now. Jim,' she asked, in
a voice light and heady with relief, 'can you sell Whitting
for me?'

'Are you sure? That's quite a family home and – '

'We'll put it on the market right away,' Chloe nodded.
'Time to move on. I hope – we'll travel then choose a
place together.'

Lily and Jim exchanged a glance. 'The girl's made up

her mind,' he said. 'And I'm going to set the table for lunch.'

Putting an arm around Chloe, Lily gazed into the fire. 'Can it work out? I fear for you.'

'Don't worry. I understand better now.'

'Perhaps,' Lily mused, 'we still have this damn habit of losing some parts of us when we love. And it's the strong bits that disappear, damn it.'

Chloe hugged her. She said simply, 'These last couple of days I realised, there wasn't any life for me without him.'

Her one thought was to get back before Jack arrived, to welcome him.

She stood in the hall kissing them goodbye, wishing them happiness. They'd meet again soon.

Then swinging away down the steps and out to the street, Chloe turned and waved. She laughed for no reason except the earth felt firm under her feet, she was young and life was full of possibilities. Lightly she stepped south towards the main road, a breeze touched her cheek and she crossed over into the late afternoon sun.

The roads were alive with traffic, sound rose like song and pavements ran with crowds in multicolour, bright as a toy in the eye of a child. She walked for a while, cabs passed but they were full. The sun went down, the streets turned chill. With puffing breath a tall red bus swept up to a queue and she joined the crowd straggling to board, borne away in the glaring chariot.

Pressured together in convention between the cheerful and the martyred, she thought about Jodie and Raphael. Jodie had always known more than she'd told, had put them in danger from the man she called Art . . . He flitted into, out of, Chloe's mind. There were things that could make you crazy if you thought about them too long or too hard.

Jodie ... He'd wanted to kill her, he'd kept on after ...

But she knew, she could feel it, that Jodie and Raphael were safe. There'd be a message from Scotland when she got back, or a call this evening.

There were a million things she wanted to do before Jack's return in a few hours. Small precious tasks. She'd get in supplies for the holiday, gather holly and ivy and mistletoe, decorate the rooms with candles. She would choose gifts for Jack.

She felt a warmth inside her, a longing to see him again. Soon it would be the anniversary of their first meeting, and the second most profound year of her life ... The last few weeks seemed nothing now, just some brief nightmare that had occurred, and passed on. Of course, there were things they needed to talk about ...

The bus drew up at the top of Highgate Hill. Jumping off she turned, making for the quiet avenues that wound away between the trees. It was dusk and lights were on in the houses as she passed, people coming together for the evening. How long before Jack got home? She walked quickly, purposefully.

Leaving behind the houses, their bright windows, she stepped into the descending tunnel of the lane. Winter branches touched overhead and blocked the light but she had known this way all her life; her footsteps followed the curve of crumbling brick wall to the gate. She stopped and looked through those iron circles.

Whitting loomed steep, piercing black the city's halo of red cloud. The drive was deserted and the film makers had gone, but somewhere deep inside the house a light had been left on. Her feet sank in mud as she approached and felt in her coat pocket for the keys. She didn't have them. Smiling a bit at herself, Chloe turned and felt her way along the path and through the side gate, round the house.

How dark it was now, in the shadow of the walls.

She often forgot to carry a key, always kept one hidden and found it now among the grime and cobwebs of the small back porch.

Then she saw, inside the unlit kitchen window, a pale face looking out at her. And in that first surprised instant it seemed to be herself reflected. Except, it moved close when she stood still.

The next moment she thought with a rush of gladness it was Jack, he'd come back early and ...

But the face pressing quick and sharp to the glass stared then drew back while she recognised her half-brother, that dangerous relation ... Opening the door, poised standing there while she backed stumbling down the steps driven by her heart's diving out into the black wild.

Like someone falling in dark water she fell into the pit of night. Disappearing into shadows, knowing everything that grew here, spinning out a distance from his pursuit and search. He grew silent, stalking but she could sense him near, that presence.

Then nothing. Had he gone? She dared not breathe.

She crouched hiding in the garden.

The moon rose silver, all life swam in it and a wind took up bare branches in ghost-like sighing animation. Daylight would come; even now in this false day there was nowhere to hide and she shrank into the earth's thin surface, a lake of shadow growing taller, drawn back towards an open door.

Dry, musted smells of timber, coal and oil. In the small lofted vault she reached up with trembling hands to the walls, found something there – the heavy worn wood of

302

the sickle handle – and took it down, grasped it. Armed, she would wait for morning.

She knelt in the doorway, in its shadow watching for him. The moon slid on an arc of silver, chasing clouds of mist in a starry sky; she watched the night passing. Memory slipped by. Childhood days, her father's murder. His body lying, here. A lucidity now. The moon a clear circle: no beginnings, no ending . . .

Endless night.

Small clues struck into her memory: a taunt of Rachel's many years ago, and a veil her father drew across before he died; and something in Jack's imaginings of her, too . . . Small clues.

Her father's son, the unacknowledged, come to kill her.

He was her only relation left living, and he was her enemy.

Her face was wet, awash with salt as fear melted.

Seeing herself crouched here like some little creature, waiting for death to come. She'd trapped herself. Couldn't stand to wait.

Stood, started to shout as loud as she could, to scream: *'I'm here, this is where I am, come and get me!'*

Saw his shape emerge through the bushes, solidly closer towards her hiding place. Waited. And the moon passed behind a cloud leaving perfect darkness.

But she could feel him closing in on her. She stepped out. And grasping the sickle in nerve-wired hands she raised it high, leaped at that approaching shadow and hurled the thing in a slicing sweep; saw the blade flash a silver-light circle then saw too late how he'd spread his arms to receive the blow, to welcome it. Heard him crash, the gurgle of his life flood guttering out and stumbling ran alive with terror out towards that faint house light.

Saw someone, a dark shape moving towards her through the garden.

And she stopped, suddenly not sure who it was.

<u>NOT FAIR</u>
Domini Taylor

It was not fair. Nicola Maude seemed to have everything
already: looks, intelligence, charm, prospects of a wealthy
inheritance – and the love of all who knew her. And then
she won handsome Hugh Jarvis for her fiancé. Had she
been granted too much happiness? Some vengeful destiny
seemed to think so. Some relentless Nemesis who stalked
the winding, leafy lanes of Hampshire – and struck with a
road accident which left Hugh dead and Nicola a helpless
cripple.

Only Alice, Nico's devoted mother, knew the truth of this
ever-watchful presence, but she was powerless to prove it.
Alice – to whom life most certainly had not been fair. After
her husband was tragically killed, she found herself a
widow at twenty-nine. And now she and Nico lived alone
in a cramped cottage, forever dependent upon the
generosity of her glamorous older sister Vi and Vi's rich,
elderly husband.

Alice knew the meaning of unfairness – and what it could
do to you. So when fortune smiles anew on Nico and she
becomes engaged to a long-standing admirer, Alice's fears
for her daughter's safety intensify: Nemesis would surely
strike again . . .

'Domini Taylor keeps the tension spiralling quite brilliantly
before unmasking the evil spirit'
Essentials

0 7515 0077 1

THE EYE BEHIND THE CURTAIN

Domini Taylor

Bestselling author of *Mother Love*

When Americans Dick and Mandy McCann are posted to England with Dick's job, they worry how they and their two children will fit in. However, their new neighbours in the idyllic rural village of Conyngham Smedley soon befriend these exotic newcomers to their community and make them feel at home.

Dick is suddenly seconded to Nigeria and forced to leave Mandy and the children in England. Then the burglaries begin. One after the other the wealthy houses of Conyngham Smedley are broken into, the valuable antiques and paintings they contain spirited away.

But how can it be that the thieves know immediately, every time a house is unexpectedly empty? Clearly an informer is at large in Conyngham Smedley, and tipping off a gang of professional crooks. And then the goodwill of Mandy's new English friends turns to wariness, as the whispers behind the cereal packets in the village shop start to multiply . . .

'Infuriatingly difficult to put down . . . page-turning readability'
Sunday Telegraph

0 7515 0183 2

LOST CHILDREN

Edith Pargeter
Who also writes as Ellis Peters

High on a rocky outcrop above heathland stands a
Victorian gothic mansion, built by the ancient and
aristocratic Rose family. In the lodge of the house – the rest
is owned by the National Trust – live the last two of the
fading line. Rosalba Rose, at seventeen, has always been
dutifully submissive to her ferocious eighty-year-old
great-aunt Martine, but Rosalba's life contains little
pleasure until she meets Eugene Seale, a young national
serviceman. Different as the two are, they fall in love, but is
their passion, surrounded by upheaval, doomed?

Praise for Ellis Peters

'Charm is not usual in murder mysteries, but Ellis Peters'
stories are full of it'
Mail on Sunday

'Original, civilised, sane and, as always, a compelling read'
Irish Times

0 7515 0369 X

MOST LOVING MERE FOLLY

Edith Pargeter

When Suspiria Freeland is charged with poisoning her
artist husband Theo, a scandalised country presumes her
guilty. What could one expect of a woman like that, with
her clever tongue and abrupt manners, the odd-shaped
pots she calls art and her ramshackle house – a woman
who brazenly admits her affair with a garage mechanic
fourteen years her junior?

Dissected in the full limelight of public courts and gutter
press, Dennis and Suspiria's already ill-matched liaison
seems doomed – and Suspiria's acquittal is only the start of
their real problems. Under the weight of popular sentiment
and censure, a world watching, misinterpreting and taking
possession of their every move, expecting and hoping for
disaster, how can their love survive? Worse, the question
the lovers dare not voice – if Suspiria did not kill Theo,
who did?

0 7515 0144 1

☐	Not Fair	Domini Taylor	£4.99
☐	The Eye Behind the Curtain	Domini Taylor	£4.99
☐	Lost Children	Edith Pargeter	£4.99
☐	Most Loving Mere Folly	Edith Pargeter	£4.99

Warner Books now offers an exciting range of quality titles by both established and new authors which can be ordered from the following address:

Little, Brown and Company (UK),
P.O. Box 11,
Falmouth,
Cornwall TR10 9EN.

Alternatively you may fax your order to the above address. Fax No. 0326 376423.

Payments can be made as follows: cheque, postal order (payable to Little, Brown and Company) or by credit cards, Visa/Access. Do not send cash or currency. UK customers and B.F.P.O. please allow £1.00 for postage and packing for the first book, plus 50p for the second book, plus 30p for each additional book up to a maximum charge of £3.00 (7 books plus).

Overseas customers including Ireland please allow £2.00 for the first book plus £1.00 for the second book, plus 50p for each additional book.

NAME (Block Letters) ....

....

ADDRESS ....

....

....

☐ I enclose my remittance for ....

☐ I wish to pay by Access/Visa Card

Number | | | | | | | | | | | | | | | | | |

Card Expiry Date | | | | |